"*The Highest Mountain* is a story of a young man coming of age. But beyond Bill's compelling movement from angst to a creature of light, the story teaches the reader about life even as the characters learn. Woven in a rich tapestry of detail, *The Highest Mountain* is about being born-again.

—Hal Portner, Author and Educator, 5/1999

Colored with romance, *The Highest Mountain* is a cross cultural answer to coming of age. It is a compelling story about learning intimacy and answers the age-old question: can one who is born into the modern world realize the brilliance of consciousness shared only by the world's greatest spiritual masters?

—Rev. Dr. J. Vajrayana, 5/1999

The Highest Mountain

To Bob & Helen Garland
Thankyou for your love and support

The Highest Mountain

A Love Story

John W. Worman

Writer's Showcase presented by *Writer's Digest*
San Jose New York Lincoln Shanghai

The Highest Mountain

All Rights Reserved © 2000 by John W. Worman

No part of this book may be reproduced or transmitted in any form or by any means, graphic, electronic, or mechanical, including photocopying, recording, taping, or by any information storage or retrieval system, without the permission in writing from the publisher.

Published by Writer's Showcase presented by *Writer's Digest* an imprint of iUniverse.com, Inc.

For information address:
iUniverse.com, Inc.
620 North 48th Street
Suite 201
Lincoln, NE 68504-3467
www.iuniverse.com

ISBN: 0-595-01031-8

Printed in the United States of America

For my mentors:

Charles Lorton, for teaching me to play the violin and the love of music.

George Horner, for teaching me that it's okay to be human and to never lose faith in my spirit.

Thank you.

How many times must I stumble and fall?
How many times do I blame?
What does it take for me to get it right?

One

"I dreamt about her again last night." Bill whispered returning his coffee cup slowly to the table. He turned away and looked out the diner's window. It was a typical sunlit June morning in East Los Angeles, hot, the smell of smog and heavy traffic, lots of people busying the streets. The latest Beatles hit, *I Saw Her Standing There,* played on the jukebox. The couple in the next booth sat complaining about the escalation in Vietnam.

"And?"

"We had great sex," Bill continued, looking back at his friend with a mischievous smile.

Debbie put her fork down and looked hard into Bill's dark blue eyes. After finishing a mouthful of hashbrowns she placed her hand on his forearm and said, "You think she had the same dream?"

"Actually, afraid to find out," Bill responded in a more somber tone while fidgeting his fork on a coffee stained red and white checked vinyl table cloth. He looked away once again as a cloud of sizzling bacon grease erupted from the kitchen and crawled its way across the discolored ceiling. The waitress walked hurriedly past, looking for coffee cups that might need warming.

"Why?"

"If the answer was 'no,' there'd be, like, nothing worth living for."

"Kinda melodramatic, don't ya think?"

"Deb, like, have you ever had such great sex that it left you high for days? Filling your heart with a spiritual warmth that is more satisfying than anything you could imagine?"

"In a dream? Come on, Billy! She was a summer's romance. You were fourteen!"

Bill glared at Debbie. Her words could have been right out of his mother's mouth.

"And I've got, like, an over-active imagination."

"I'll say!"

Debbie lit a cigarette and blew her breath into an already stinky room. "So, what are ya going to do about it?"

There was no easy answer. Everything seemed to be against him ever seeing Katarina again. Only in his heart was there hope. Bill glanced back at the street. He saw only a mundane world, a world he had to escape. The morning's Metro belched blue smoke as it pulled noisily from the curb.

"Somehow I gotta go to Colorado." Bill let out a huge sigh while fanning Debbie's smoke. Then he picked up his last piece of bacon and bit slowly into it. It was cold and salty, but he didn't care.

"Billy, what does someone have to do, hit you up-side the head?"

Bill sat in silence considering whether to continue the conversation or just leave. He pushed his empty coffee cup away then reached for his music case, stopping short of actually picking it up. His thoughts flashed across six years of memory: Philmont Scout Ranch in Cimmaron, New Mexico, where he and Katarina met, hundreds of letters exchanged, a few telephone conversations that he could barely afford, a ham radio conversation that broke his heart, and all the shit his mother gave him over a pen-pal love affair. But how could he explain his psychic connection? His father thought he was deranged.

"Billy, you have family here," Debbie uttered softly, pulling Bill from his reverie.

"Com' on, Deb. You always say that. You and I both know…"

"Damn you! Don't you get it? She doesn't care!"

"No! I can't believe that!" Bill retorted while staring into Debbie's solemn brown eyes.

"Can't or won't? Honestly! Sometimes you're as crazy as your mother!" Debbie crushed her cigarette into the ashtray in frustration. She saw she'd touched a nerve and turned her attention to finishing her cold scrambled eggs.

"Anyway," Debbie continued after several minutes of silence, "there's the practical side of things, your parents. They didn't let you accept that Colorado scholarship two years ago. I'm betting they haven't changed their minds a bit. Have they?"

Bill didn't answer the question. The frown on his sun-tanned face said it all.

"Why don't ya wait another year? In November you'll be twenty-one. Things'll be a whole lot easier."

"Deb, you know as well as I, if I'm going to have any chance I need to be there."

"Sounds like your mind is already made up."

"Maybe."

"Jeez, wish someone could save you from yourself!"

"That's not fair, Deb. Like, ya know I gotta do this. You've been with me the whole way."

"Yeah, Billy, I have. I've also been there when you crashed and burned. That blond bimbo has you on some sorta yo-yo."

"Deb, I gotta find love in my life!" Bill looked down at his plate then thoughtfully back up while pushing his fingers of his right hand through his thick unkempt brown hair and heaving a sigh.

"If you don't find it with her?"

"I know what's at stake."

"Do you? Do you really?" Debbie demanded.

"Yeah! My soul."

Debbie looked at Bill as if he'd just lost his mind. She pushed her empty plate noisily aside and asked the passing waitress for the check.

"Anyway," Bill extended his arms, twisting from his waist, pointing around the room. "This, mediocrity. I can't live like this."

"Damn you! That's not fair. Ya have it good, better than most, I'd say. State College, a good part time job, a great future." Debbie looked straight into Bill's eyes. "Anyway, don't take me so much for granted!"

"I do care about you, Deb. Sorry."

Debbie pressed back into her seat and crossed her arms across her chest. Her small Latin frame radiated resentment.

"Deb, I've never told this to anyone." Bill lowered his voice to a secretive whisper. "I've known Katarina from before."

"Huh?"

"Ya know, like, past life stuff. I need to…"

"Wait a minute!" Debbie pushed both hands in front of her, commanding Bill to stop. "Past what?"

"Past lives," Bill replied, the left side of his face twitching slightly.

"Whew! You've really gone over, Billy! We all have our quirks. But, this, really!"

Bill looked at Debbie's closed posture, remembering that her Catholic upbringing had well-defined limits.

"I'm sorry. Maybe I do live a fantasy," Bill apologized in hurried retreat.

"I'll say."

Several minutes passed in strained silence. Then Bill pulled a large manila envelope from his music case and opened it. He handed the contents to Debbie.

"Acceptance papers from the Music Department, University of Colorado at Boulder." Debbie looked at Bill with deadly seriousness. "Billy, last time you tried this your mom threatened to call the police the minute you crossed the State line."

Bill glared. He didn't need to be reminded of all the shit he'd received over the past several years. He was convinced that his mother couldn't possibly understand his heart. All she ever did was make him wrong.

Unexpectedly, the concern in Bill's face was exchanged for a giant grin. "What?"

"She can't do a thing. Get it, not a damn thing. I'm over eighteen. I can do, like, anything I want!"

Debbie glanced out the diner's bay window, pain sliding across her face. A small-framed gray haired woman was throwing a tantrum on the corner pay phone. Debbie felt like throwing one of her own.

Bill closed his eyes and sighed heavily.

"Billy?" Debbie asked, turning back toward Bill, speaking just above a whisper. "Does it ever occur to you that ya might be wrong?"

Two

The earth was parched by a sinister sun. Exhausted, Bill lunged toward his adversary attempting to pull him from his war-horse. But before he could get a secure grip on the warrior's leg, the stallion reared and the Red-Faced Indian screamed profanities and kicked him away. Stumbling, Bill took two arrows in the back from passing renegades and fell to the earth, writhing in agony. Then, slowly, as if he had all the time in the world, the Red-Faced Indian took an arrow from his quiver, placed it into his bow and shot Bill in the neck, near the base of his skull.

Bill awoke instantly and for what seemed an eternity he was quadriplegic. In the darkness of his motel room, he tried to remember it was only a bad dream and, like so many times before, he tried to reassure himself through several minutes of deep breathing. Though he hadn't had this nightmare in several years, once again, it was as real as always. This was the horror that caused Bill's father, Chuck, to eventually send him to a psychiatrist.

Bill pulled the blankets over his head and attempted sleep. However, the rumblings from an approaching thunderstorm kept him from it. Without warning an angry green flash and a deafening explosion disintegrated the top of a nearby telephone pole. For blocks around lights got very bright, then there was darkness. Ozone quickly irritated the night air. Reluctantly, Bill got out of bed and peered out the motel room window. He wondered if this was a sign. Many times his mother warned that God would smite him if he left home without her consent.

However, despite the gloom, Bill was fascinated by thunderstorms. This was the first he had seen in many years. As he stood watching the downpour from the safety of his open window, gradually, he began to relax. His thoughts turned to Philmont, to a summer afternoon when he and Katarina stood in awe, hand in hand, under a corrugated metal awning next to the camp trading post. Together they watched the electricity jumping cloud to cloud, cloud to ground. They saw the surrealistic panorama of dark columns of water tumbling from the sky and the bright sunlight fluorescing a rock mountain called the Tooth of Time. That awesome sky, the perfume of the rain soaked creosote bush and the magnetism in Katarina's eyes, smile and laughter created a peak experience that made certain Bill's life would never be the same.

The next morning, after devouring a homemade breakfast of dry cereal and milk, Bill drove the remaining twenty-five miles to the University of Colorado. There, he stood impatiently in registration lines and paid his fees. Then not bothering with lunch, he threw his belongings into his dorm room and fled campus in order to give Katarina the surprise of her life. She had no idea he had re-applied to the university, let alone was in the State.

The hour and a half drive between Boulder and Fort Collins seemed an eternity and as Bill drove he wrestled with his heart. He could easily accept that others didn't understand the magic he and Katarina once shared. The problem was, during her senior year of high school, she began dating other boys. And, although the recent exchange of letters indicated he still had a chance with her, a history of confusion and self-doubt now colored his certainty.

Just after four in the afternoon Bill arrived in Fort Collins and with the assistance of a friendly service station attendant he quickly found

Horse Tooth Reservoir. As he drove the dusty gravel highway in his filthy blue '57 Chevy, it didn't take long to find the road she lived on. The land was just as he imagined it, rural with lots of open space, golden fields of alfalfa awaiting harvest. This beautiful countryside was a total contrast to the blocks upon blocks of tiny look-alike houses in those post-war developments that he'd grown up with.

Spotting a tall stand of cottonwoods, a dilapidated boat dock and the burnt ruins of an old farmhouse alongside the reservoir's southwest edge, Bill pulled quietly to the side of the road and stopped. The brown fog of dust that followed him drifted slowly back toward the earth. This was where Katarina often went while horseback riding, through the years her letters had been thoroughly descriptive. Near the boat dock were several people basking in the afternoon sun looking his way, laughing and having fun. Their horses were tethered to a broken-down fence, a fence overgrown with huge weeds and dandelions. Bill strained to see if Katarina might be among the heads bobbing to and fro, but it was too far away to tell. He remembered how he often fantasize riding up to her on an afternoon such as this and sweeping her off her feet, just like in a fairy tale. Unfortunately, he hadn't been on a horse in at least three years and it was obvious there were no public stables at hand.

Slowly, hesitantly, Bill resumed the quarter mile drive toward Katarina's. The Epperson home sat alone like a blue sapphire amidst a sea of golden alfalfa. Two cottonwood shade trees and hedges of oleanders outlined a beautifully manicured front lawn. On the south side of the home and inside a chain-link fence stood a garden for food: semisweet corn, lettuce, tomatoes, a lattice of table grapes, vines of pumpkins waiting the season's ripening. On the north side of the house next to a large irrigation pond and gazebo stood a man busy splitting firewood. Bill was certain it was Katarina's father. He remembered Valdemar as intimidating, a short stocky man with massive chest and arms, standing about five foot eight, pushing two hundred pounds. He wore his dark brown hair in a Marine crew cut and spoke with few words.

"Courage," Bill mumbled to himself over and over again, a knot beginning to form in his gut. He seriously considered driving on and waiting until another day. However, he knew from years of serious stage performance, the bite wasn't half as bad as the anticipation.

Valdemar looked up from his wood splitting task, put down his maul, turned and watched Bill park and shut off his car's engine.

"Good afternoon, sir," Bill said as he exited his car. Then, apprehensively walking up the gravel driveway, he offered Valdemar his outstretched hand, trying hard to maintain the dignity his grandfather had taught him.

Valdemar, with a no-bullshit look in his eyes, slowly stoking his bushy salt and pepper mustache did not return Bill's politeness. Bill's stomach spasmed and he retreated a few feet, hopefully, to a safer distance.

"Uh, Katarina home?" Bill blurted out, his voice cracking.

"Boy, have you talked with your mother?"

"What?" Bill was caught completely off guard.

"Your mother! I've talked to her twice today. Have you?"

"Oh shit!" Bill said under his breath. His legs began turning to rubber as he struggled to maintain balance.

"Oh shit is right!" Valdemar had exceptional hearing. "What the hell is going on?"

Bill staggered to a large boulder, one of many outlining the driveway's edge. He began to sit down, then thought the better of it. He turned back toward Valdemar but spoke to the gravel driveway, something he hoped couldn't hurt him. "Well..."

"Speak up boy! What the hell is goin' on!"

"Like, I've decided to go to school here, Sir, in Colorado."

"That's not what your mother told me!"

"What?"

Valdemar continued looking hard into Bill's face.

"Guess I, I left home against my parents wishes."

"You guess?"

Bill couldn't respond.

"So, what are you doing here?"

"Hoped to see Katarina. Is she…"

"In Laramie!"

"Oh." Bill grabbed his stomach and slowly crumpled to a sitting position on the driveway. He wanted to bolt for his car, but couldn't as his peripheral vision began to cave in. The world began to spin and turn black.

"You okay?"

Bill's face was now white as a ghost and looking like he was going to puke. "Don't think so."

"You'd better come inside." Valdemar quickly picked up a shop rag and began wiping pitch and sawdust from his hands.

Bill stood, staggered a little, then he followed Valdemar quietly around to the back of the house, through a screen door and into the kitchen.

"Here's some water!" Valdemar commanded, filling a glass from the kitchen faucet after washing his hands with soap and water.

It was at that moment Bill realized that his mouth was so dry that he could hardly speak. Bill inhaled the glass of water in one huge gulp, almost choking.

Valdemar filled the glass again and handed it back to Bill. Then he filled a second glass for himself.

"Please, son, sit at the kitchen table. Try to calm down. I'm sorry I came on so strong."

As Bill sat down, he noticed Katarina's high school graduation picture sitting on top of her piano next to a dozen florist cut red roses, only ten feet away. Immediately he turned his eyes away. Another surge of panic stabbed his stomach. Who had sent her such beautiful flowers?

Unhurried, Valdemar lit the stove and started a pot of coffee. Then after lighting a cigarette, he turned and leaned against a spotless off-white tile countertop. The Epperson kitchen was immaculate, everything clean and in its place, quite a contrast to the chronic mess that Bill grew up with. Cobweb, Katarina's calico cat, jumped up on the kitchen table and tried to rub his head into Bill's folded hands. Bill loved cats. But, he was in no mood to reciprocate Cobweb's affection. Cobweb was insistent, however, and as Bill began to scratch Cobweb's tiny ears he realized that this was the trestle table that Katarina built and entered into the county fair two years previous. He remembered how impressed he was that she would even consider such an undertaking, even if her father did help.

Several minutes passed in uneasy silence while Valdemar considered options. Born and raised in rural Norway, he didn't like city people. Also, as a parent, he knew that a runaway from East Los Angeles was not to be taken lightly.

When Bill's color began to return to normal, Valdemar felt it was safe to talk and he started on Bill again. "Your mother is extremely upset, you know that."

"Hysterical!" Bill knew the game his mother played. But in his naïveté he didn't expect to hear this from Katarina's father.

"I'll say. Could hardly get a word in edgewise."

"Story of my life."

Valdemar stopped. New questions entered his mind. Intuitively, he knew Bill's flight was not entirely black and white, in spite of his mother's outrageous claims.

"All I want is to go to school, become a concert violinist."

"That all?"

Bill looked up and into Valdemar's piercing blue eyes. He knew better than to bullshit this man. "I'm, I think I'm in love with Katarina."

"Think?"

"Shit!" Bill said while shutting his eyes, wishing his nightmare would end. "Maybe I should go. I…"

"No! Let's get this out in the open."

Like a caged animal Bill wanted to scream. But, forcefully, he restrained his breath. He knew, from years of his father's reprimands, that showing emotion was an unacceptable behavior.

"Truth is, you ran away from home."

"In three months I'll be twenty-one."

"Son, it's not what you did, it's how you did it. You could be thirty, you still ran away."

Bill closed his eyes and tried to breathe deeply. He knew that he didn't leave home under the best of circumstances. Rather, he drove off while his parents and sister were vacationing in Big Sur, announcing his intentions via an emotionally written letter deposited on the kitchen table.

"You need to wake up! This is not some dream. Katarina is not the fairy princess and you're not going to live happily ever after."

Bill placed a trembling left hand over his mouth.

"Did it ever occur to you that what you had was simply a summer's romance, puppy-love?"

"That's what my mom always said," Bill answered ruefully.

"Why don't you listen?"

"My heart, what I feel. I gotta find out!"

Seeing he'd touched a nerve, Valdemar softened ever so slightly. He knew what it was like, his first love. He married her. But they had dated for several years and it was with their families' approval.

"Son, I don't have all the answers," Valdemar acknowledged while shaking his head. "But this I know: I won't have you or your parents upsetting my household. I think you should return to California and work things out, whatever that means. Maybe in a year or two."

"It's too late."

"Son, it's never too late to do the right thing."

"Classes start Monday. I'm already enrolled."

"What?"

"Sir, I'm, like, already enrolled in school."

"Your mother didn't tell me that." Valdemar's hardened look turned into a question.

"What? Like, what did my mother tell you?"

"That you ran away to elope with my daughter, that the two of you have been planning this for years."

"Sir, that's a damn lie! The only thing I've been planning is going to school where Katarina is. If I'm to have any chance." Bill glanced back at Katarina's picture, hoping it could magically give him strength. "I love her!" Bill announced, almost choking. "I don't know if she loves me, but, but I gotta find out!"

"Whew." Valdemar blew out his breath with the force of a perplexed juror. "Son, I can't judge you. But you do need to call your mother. She needs to know you're all right."

Looking like a kid ready to throw a tantrum, Bill held his breath and tightened his face.

"You can use my phone," Valdemar said while pouring himself a mug of hot coffee. He lit another cigarette, turned and walked noisily out the back door.

Hardly twitching a muscle, Bill sat in silence for almost half an hour scrutinizing the wall phone, three feet away. From time to time he glanced at Katarina's smiling picture, praying for strength. Finally, he dialed. "Hello, mom…"

Three

Professor Watley walked briskly into his classroom and placed a small worn brown book on the rostrum. The professor stood an impressive six foot four and looked as if he could hold his own as a tackle on the Los Angeles Rams. His face was well tanned and reflected nicely against his brown leisure suit. Turning to the blackboard he wrote, "Philosophy 4990, Modern Theology. M-W-F 10 to 10:50, Prof. Earl Watley." Then turning back to the rostrum, opening his book and in a moderate baritone voice, he began the semester's first lecture by telling a story:

> A young man was confounded by love and everything he did seemed wrong. He suffered a broken heart. So, after much deliberation and soul searching, he decided the best thing was to kill himself.
> I'm certain that none of you have ever felt like this.

The classroom of eight chuckled.

> But the young man didn't know how to take his own life. So he went to the village physician and asked.
> The doctor heard the youth's tale of woe and agreed. He did indeed carry a lot of pain.

"Tell you what," the physician offered. "Go to every house in this village. If you can find one person who has never experienced pain, I'll help you kill yourself, as painlessly as I know how."

Delighted, the youth set to his task. He knew his labor would be quick.

Confidently walking up to the first house, the youth asked the master if he had any pain around love. "Come in, son. Sit! Let me tell you about it," came the master's reply. "My wife hates me. My children hate me."

Again the classroom chuckled.

The next house the youth saw a woman in tears. Her spouse had been killed in the war.

The third house, he found a family burying a young child, barely six years old.

One by one, the youth searched. But he found no one, not one person who was without pain in his or her life.

Woefully, the young man returned to the physician and told him what he had discovered.

"Pain and joy!" The physician announced. "They come to us as a package."

Professor Watley stopped his lecture momentarily and looked at each of his students, one by one, as if memorizing their faces.

"Pain leads to fear. Fear leads to anxiety. It's not pain or fear that threatens one's self-affirmation, it's anxiety, the disquieting concern that fate will turn against us. That in spite of all our work and effort, life might show itself to be meaningless. That in spite of all our effort to do the right things, we may ultimately stand condemned.

"Christ knew this. The scripture is all too clear on this point. But what so many of us miss, what Christ tried to teach us, it's not about pain, fear, or anxiety where we get stuck in our lives. It's how we deal with it.

"Paul Tillich tells us, 'The courage to be' is the courage to affirm one's life despite the universal human condition: insecurity, uncertainty, and imperfection…"

Professor Watley quietly turned to the blackboard and wrote out the day's reading assignment: Paul Tillich's, *Courage to Be*, chapters one and two.

"This is goin' to be one hell-of-a class!" Bill announced to a friendly coed sitting next to him. The young woman said nothing, instead, she smiled her agreement and nodded.

Following his morning classes, Bill raced to Libby Hall, Katarina's dorm. For two days he had been trying to see her. However, each inquiry found that she had not yet checked into her room. He wasn't discouraged, however. Now, he knew she was on campus. He could feel it in his heart. All traces of previous anxiety had magically been replaced by the excitement of anticipation.

After returning to his dorm room and fixing himself a hurried sandwich, Bill walked briskly to the Macky Auditorium since his afternoon class, Form and Analysis, was to begin within the hour. As he descended the stairs toward Macky's practice rooms, the musty air announced a very old building. Wood panels and sashes were badly in need of repair and the hall lighting was dim and discolored.

Once Bill got to the basement, one by one he glanced through the little glass window in each practice room door, looking for Katarina. Also, he wondered who his competition might be. One woman was working on a Bach *Oratorio*, another on a Schumann *Art Song*. There were several pianos being put to task. A flutist. A clarinetist. Someone conducting to a tape recorder. Finally, an organ playing the slow movement from a Handel *Organ Concerto.*

Bill just stood, listening to the muffled chaos that filtered through the acoustic cracks and crevices, littering the hallway with dissonant debris. Finally he could stand it no longer and walked to the restroom.

Returning to the main hallway, Bill tried to silence his mind and touch his feelings. "Where is she?" he asked himself over and over. But two young men coming towards him talking noisily disrupted his inner dialog. Unexpectedly the door to the practice room where he'd heard the organ swung open. Then, laughing, bouncing through the doorway, saying good-bye to her professor, there she was.

"Katarina!" Bill shouted.

"Billy!"

Bill and Katarina rushed toward each other. Then they stopped and stared, inches from each other's grasp, time suspended in place.

Bill liked what he saw. This magnificent Scandinavian woman stood five foot six and weighed, perhaps, one hundred and ten pounds. Katarina had obviously grown several inches during their six years apart. Now she had breasts. Her blond hair seemed slightly darker than he remembered, but it was still waist length. Her eyes were crystal blue, bright as the morning's dawn. Gold wire rimmed glasses were delicately perched on the tip of her finely chiseled nose.

Katarina liked what she saw, too. This Irishman stood five foot eleven and weighed one hundred and thirty pounds. His hair was light brown and messy. His blue eyes were as deep as the winter's sky. He had a toothy smile that seemed to extend from ear to ear.

Bill reached out his right hand. And as if leading in a dance, Katarina took it, pulling him into a long embrace.

Evening found Bill impatiently waiting for Katarina outside Libby Hall's dining room, even though Katarina was her usual punctual self. As she walked gracefully to meet him, he couldn't help noticing her navy blue pleated skirt, her off-white Cashmere pullover sweater holding the promise of a tiny waist and nicely rounded hips. Her hair was freshly combed and held a gentle radiance. Bill wondered if she had dressed up just for him.

"You're magnificent!" Bill announced.

Katarina blushed and walked past Bill while looking at him out of the corner of her eye. Bill turned and followed.

As Bill opened the dining room door, both he and Katarina were greeted with the aroma of fresh baked bread. Bill, of course, placed more food on his tray than he could possibly eat. Then, together they found a secluded table in a far corner of the dinning room. The hour was late and the sun was near setting. Amber light magically filled the room as sunlight bounced along the oak paneling. Most of the students had already finished supper, leaving a plenitude of solitude and space.

Bill opened his music case and presented a single red rose. "I want to be your boyfriend," Bill said as he took his seat, hardly giving Katarina the chance to breathe.

Surprise immediately replaced the smile on Katarina's face. Bill sat patiently waiting for her reply.

"Billy, I'm flattered! But y'all must understand, I'm here to go to school." The look in Bill's eyes more than his words concerned Katarina. The lecture she'd received from her father about not doing anything rash was hardly a day old. "I think we should take this slow."

"I'm here to go to school, too. I also want to be your boyfriend."

Katarina's thoughts turned inside. The word "boyfriend" scared her. A disaster with a guy named Carl made her heed her father's words around being impetuous. Carl had taught her not to trust young men, no matter how wonderful they might seem.

"We'll always be friends, you know that," Katarina returned with a polite smile.

"Yeah," Bill replied, backing off. He took notice that the word "friend" was not prefaced with "boy." Discouraged, he took several bites of mealy mashed potato while remembering Debbie's advice about erring on the side of caution. He picked up the salt shaker and tried to make his potatoes more palatable.

"So, was that you I heard playing the organ this afternoon?" Bill asked, following several uneasy minutes of picking at his food, hoping he could somehow make meaningful conversation.

"Yeah."

"Didn't know you played. How long?"

"A little over two years. Fell in love with it while visiting grandma Epperson in Chicago. She plays the Cathedral organ at Saint Michaels."

"Really? You've changed your major?"

"Naw, still piano, minor is still voice. But, I'm taking all the organ classes I can get, I'll tell ya what."

Bill laughed. Katarina's mild southern accent along with her slight overbite still delighted him no end and he could hardly keep from staring at her overly expressive face. There was no question; he would be willing to throw his entire life away for just one moment in ecstasy, with her.

"You still into ballet?" Bill asked. He often dreamt of the day that he could watch Katarina dance.

"You bet!" Katarina exclaimed, grinning from Bill's laughter.

Bill took a drink of his apple juice while watching Katarina's eyes sparkle from the light of the setting sun cascading through nearby bay windows.

"Y'all? What are ya taking this semester?" Katarina asked, her face beginning to turn red.

"Well, let's see. This morning I had Modern Theology followed by Music Literature. This afternoon I had Form and Analysis. On Tuesdays and Thursdays, Woodwind Instruments and Instrumental Conducting. Tuesday evening, Orchestra and Thursday afternoon, String Quartet followed by private violin lessons."

"Whew, a full load!"

"Yeah."

"Modern Theology? That's not in the liberal studies core, is it?" Katarina asked.

"I'm taking that on my own, ya know, for the fun of it."

"Really, that's great! We should get as much out of school as we possibly can."

"You taking any classes for fun?"

Katarina wiped her mouth with a napkin, then answered, "Other than organ, not really."

"Tell me. What are you…"

"Music Theory, every day of the week. On Tuesdays and Thursdays I have Percussion Instruments, Sociology. Monday, Wednesday and Friday, Applied Voice and Folk Dance. Monday morning, Organ lessons. Tuesday morning, Piano lessons. Tuesday night, orchestra. That's about it," Katarina said apprehensively.

"You make it sound like it's not enough." Bill picked up his spoon and began eating his strawberry Jell-O, feeling threatened, intuiting there would be little time for him.

"Just wish I could do more. But my job prevents me."

"Job?"

"Yeah, I work part time at a health foods store over on Pennsylvania Avenue, fifteen hours a week."

"To help pay for school?"

"Yeah. Times are hard on my family, ya know, both my brother Erik and me in school."

"Erik here?"

"No, Johns Hopkins. Chemical Engineering."

"You still have your scholarship, I hope."

"Sure. But it only pays tuition, you know that. What about you, Billy? Did you get your scholarship back?"

"No! My parents still refuse to sign the papers."

"Oh." Katarina bit her lower lip. She couldn't understand why Bill's parents would withhold their support, especially when it was around his future success and happiness. She considered what her father had said about Bill's mother being crazy. "How y'all paying for this?"

"You remember, I worked part time as an electronic technician for the past two years."

"Oh, yeah."

"It paid well. Still, I have only enough to complete three semesters. I need to think about a job, too."

Katarina smiled, then looked at her watch.

Bill's heart twinged. "Time to go?"

"In a while. Need to polish a passage from a Schubert Sonata. My piano lesson is the first thing in the morning."

"Ya know, I've never heard you play. In fact, you've never heard me."

"We can change that really fast," Katarina said, starting to get up from her chair.

Together, Bill and Katarina walked to Bill's dorm to get his violin.

"Sorry about the mess," Bill said while opening the door, turning on the light and inviting Katarina into his room. "Haven't completely moved in yet." Bill's room was a disaster, typical male college dorm room.

Katarina tried not to look. She held some judgment.

"Not a very good likeness of me," Katarina said as she walked to Bill's desk and picked up her high school graduation picture. She noticed a healthy stack of letters bundled neatly together, almost two hundred in all. She had no idea that she'd written so many.

"I think you're beautiful," Bill said as he pulled his violin case from the shelf in his closet.

Katarina bit her lower lip and looked at Bill from the corners of her eyes while beginning to blush.

"Think we should go." Bill turned and began walking toward the door. The look in Katarina's eyes touched him. It wasn't sexual, not at all. It was more like a child, innocent, delighted, happy, filled with energy, a child who wants to run and play. It was the look he cherished from Philmont.

Warmth was gladly exchanged for the chilly night air as Bill and Katarina entered Macky Auditorium. Bill took a deep breath wondering if he was up to the task. He'd fantasized the day he would play his violin for her and his heart was pounding.

Slowly and quietly, Bill removed his beloved instrument from its case. He rosined his bow while watching Katarina open the keyboard cover on the auditorium's concert grand. Katarina was one of the fortunate students who was allowed her own key. In the bright light she looked poised and confident as she sat down on the piano bench. Smiling, she struck an A above middle C. Two maintenance men turned from their doldrums to ascertain the disturbance. Then they quickly returned to their task of repairing a broken ceiling lamp.

"Care if I warm-up a little?" Bill asked, having finished tuning.

Katarina answered Bill's question by beginning her own warm-up sequence. Bill was glad. He knew that playing cold could be disastrous.

"What's in your music case?" Katarina finally asked once her fingers were moving freely.

"*Liebesfreud*, by Fritz Kreisler," Bill answered. Then he reached for his music and handed Katarina the piano score while smiling into her eyes.

"Three, four." Bill nodded signaling the piano's entrance.

"You're an exceptional sight reader!" Bill said, almost laughing, at the *Liebesfreud's* conclusion.

"Why thank you. Y'all pretty good yourself."

"You must have a favorite?" Bill queried while placing his violin under his arm.

"Of course," Katarina returned with a warm and friendly smile on her face. She turned toward her purse and music case and pulled the music for Debussy's *Girl with the Flaxen Hair*. "Hope I can do this justice. I'm not as good as you."

The piano began to sing in Katarina's hands. Music seemed to come from everywhere. It was in Bill's ears, his head, his heart and his soul. He could only laugh out loud with his delight.

When it came Bill's turn to play again he showed off by playing Paganini's *Fourteenth Caprice* while watching Katarina's every move. But when he finished playing a round of applause shocked him, nine fellow students stood watching and listening from various parts of the auditorium. Bill's face turned flaming red.

"I'm Jack Morran." Jack, a second year graduate student, offered Bill his outstretched hand while walking across the stage.

Bill took it and shook vigorously. "Bill Colton."

Bill turned to introduce Katarina, but Jack interrupted, "I know, Katarina Epperson. I heard Bill did very well on his audition this afternoon. He might just be our new concertmaster."

"Really?"

"Ya study with Heifitz? Ya play like him."

"Not quite. I studied with…"

"Why don't you guys go have fun. I really need to practice for tomorrow's lesson." Katarina interrupted, reaching out and squeezing Bill's left forearm very firmly while smiling.

Four

Tuesday evening, as Bill strolled leisurely to the Macky Auditorium for orchestra rehearsal, he stumbled upon a large flock of sparrows pecking the lawn in the Norlin Quadrangle. For no reason, he couldn't help running at them, screaming and laughing.

"They say that if you can put salt on a bird's tail, you can catch 'em." A short green-eyed redhead carrying a violin case announced as she walked up to Bill. "Hi. I'm Peggy Furlong."

"Bill Colton." Bill returned, still laughing and slightly out-of-breath. He placed his violin case on the ground then offered his hand to Peggy. Peggy, a slender and well-built five foot three, was the type of prize that every red-blooded American male dreamt of taking home to mother.

"Whadaya play?" Bill asked.

"Violin." Peggy returned as she turned and began walking with Bill to rehearsal.

"Ya any good?"

"Yeah, Bill. I am. You any good?" Peggy asked, returning the challenge.

"Naw. They'll probably put me last stand, second violin, if they let me play at all."

"Oh." Peggy said apologetically, sorry for her arrogance. "This your first year? I haven't seen ya before."

"Yeah, just transferred." Bill answered.

"Where ya from? "

"Southern California."

"A music major?"

"You bet!"

As Bill and Peggy entered the auditorium, walking through audience seating and toward the stage, Bill became preoccupied.

"Looking for someone?" Peggy asked as she set her violin case on a front row seat.

"Something like that," Bill returned. He set his case near Peggy's, removed his violin, rosined his bow and purposely held his violin incorrectly, bending his left wrist against the violin's neck. Then he de-tuned his A and E strings, forming something slightly flat of a perfect fifth.

"Ya need help with that?" Peggy asked, genuinely concerned by Bill's seeming lack of ability.

"Naw, my teacher says I need to learn to do this by myself."

Peggy couldn't stop the grimace on her face. "Think I'll go check out the seating assignments!" Peggy, trying not to shake her head, quickly turned and walked away.

Quietly, Bill re-tuned his violin, put the instrument under his right arm then scanned the room again for Katarina. She was no where to be seen. He turned and followed Peggy to a corner of the stage where a portable black board held the semester's seating assignments.

"Second violin my ass!" Peggy gave Bill a hardened stare, as Bill approached, realizing that she'd been conned.

Bill burst into laughter. But he was relieved when he looked at the blackboard and found his name next to concertmaster. He also noticed that Peggy was assistant concertmaster. "Sorry, I always wanted to do that."

"Me, too." Peggy said, shaking her head and smiling.

Bill continued scanning the blackboard, looking for Katarina's name. She was assigned second flute and piccolo. Then, after scanning the auditorium once again for her, Bill walked to his chair and sat down. Peggy followed.

"Peg? Ya ever wondered why the percussion section is placed at the back of the orchestra?" Bill asked.

"Huh? Uh, no."

"'Cos everyone else is trying to get away from the racket!"

Peggy, as well as the Clark, the third chair first violinist, busted up with laughter. As Bill looked up, Katarina darted onto the stage and took her seat, half out of breath. She noticed Bill laughing and smiled in turn.

"Would everyone please take their seats!" Dr. Curry, the orchestra's conductor, announced.

"I'd like to introduce our new concertmaster, Bill Colton." Dr. Curry turned toward Bill, indicating that he should rise. Then he shook Bill's hand. "As a junior, this is Bill's first semester with us. He comes to us from a distinguished line of Russian violinists. We've tried for several unsuccessful years to lure him out of Los Angeles. Finally made it! Last year he was the concertmaster at Cal. State. I'm sure they're sorry to see him leave. Please join me in extending Bill our warmest welcome." Dr. Curry lead the orchestra in resounding applause while Bill's face turned red.

"This evening we'll sight read and then work on the Shostakovich *Fifth Symphony*," Dr. Curry continued. "If any of you lose your place, just play what you can. Above all, count!" Dr. Curry raised his baton, looked across his orchestra and began beating.

"Well, there it is!" Dr. Curry announced at he conclusion of the second movement. "Now ya all know what to practice this next week! Let's take a fifteen-minute break. After the break, I want to work on the third movement."

Once a violin was in Bill's hands, it was almost impossible for him to put it down. He couldn't stop himself from playing *Csárdás* by Monti. Of course, his stand partner, Peggy, joined in. Most of the other violinists in the orchestra stood in awe, listening.

"Pretty damn good, Peg!"

"Pretty damn good yourself!"

"What else do ya know? Ahhh…"

"Bill, time out, I really need to take a pit stop?"

"Ah what?"

"Like, the restroom." Peggy turned her head slightly and looked at Bill out of the corner of her eye.

"Oops, sorry."

Peggy turned away, then walked through the curtains and off stage.

Bill turned his attention to Katarina and walked to where she sat. Her eyes were dancing as she pretended to wipe her flute with a chamois.

"Didn't know you were such a show-off, Billy!"

"I confess." Bill sat down in the vacant chair next to Katarina. "Want to join me at the Student Union for some hot chocolate after rehearsal?"

"Tempting, but I've got an early morning."

"All work, no play?"

"Something like that."

"Then, can I walk you home?"

"Of course, silly."

Tap, tap, tap, Dr. Curry clicked his baton on the podium announcing the second half of the evening's rehearsal.

Bill walked to center stage and stood, waiting for the orchestra to come to silence. "For the third movement we should take an A from the harp," he announced. Then, as the harp plucked an A above middle C, the oboist tuned to it and in turn transferred the A to the orchestra.

Once the orchestra was tuned and quiet, Dr. Curry raised his baton and gave the downbeat. However, after ten measures he stopped conducting and the orchestra staggered toward silence. One cello player kept on playing, seemingly unaware.

Tap, tap, tap. Dr. Curry clicked his baton on the podium once again. "When I stop beating, damn it, I want the orchestra to stop. You can woodshed at home! We don't have time to waste!"

"Again." Dr. Curry lifted his baton and gave the downbeat. The cello entrance in the second measure sounded worse.

Dr. Curry stopped the orchestra again. "Okay, cellos by themselves." Dr. Curry gave the downbeat. Again the cellos sounded rough and ragged.

"Bill, do you have any suggestions?" Dr. Curry asked, following several unsuccessful attempts at the passage.

Bill stood. "Several years ago Arturo Toscanini was conducting the NBC Symphony in the Dvorak's *Cello Concerto*. The guest artist was a close female friend of Maestro Toscanini's. During the dress rehearsal all was going well until the cello entrance at the beginning of the second movement. Well, to put it mildly, like you guys, the cello didn't sound too good.

"Toscanini stopped the orchestra and started again. However, the cello's entrance wasn't any better. So, again Toscanini stopped and they started over a third time.

"After the fourth aborted attempt, Toscanini placed his baton on the podium, turned to his friend and said, 'Madam, do you mean to tell me, with that beautiful instrument between your legs all you can do is scratch?'"

The orchestra exploded into fits of laughter. Dr. Curry nearly fell off his podium, as he was laughing so hard. This of course made the orchestra laugh even harder.

"Okay, I give up!" Dr. Curry threw his baton on the floor in mockery.

"Cellos, begin the passage up-bow at the point," Bill resumed, once everyone had settled down. "That way you'll avoid the scratchiness of the frog and you can make the crescendo naturally. The frog is okay for a fortissimo entrance, like the beginning of the second movement. The frog is not okay for pianissimo entrances!"

"Okay, let's try it again," Dr. Curry said raising his baton, having retrieved it from the floor.

"Excellent! Let's keep playing." Dr. Curry looked at Bill, smiled and nodded his head.

"What's gotten into you? I didn't know y'all could be so funny!" Katarina exclaimed at the rehearsal's end as she walked up to Bill.

"Me neither!" Bill returned, smiling. Then he resumed wiping the rosin off his instrument, placed it carefully into its case, closed and zipped the cover.

"By any chance you playing in the string quartet?" Peggy interrupted, walking up to Bill and opening her case.

"Yeah."

"Good! Last spring our quartet talked about the Mozart *E-flat*. What do ya think?"

"Sounds like you guys've already made up your mind."

"Well, it's one of my favorites!"

"Mozart will be just fine!" Bill agreed.

"Ya want to go over to the Student Union for a bite? A bunch of us are going." Peggy asked as several of her friends approached.

Bill looked at Katarina with a question mark written on his face. "Naw, got too much to do. Still haven't gotten used to this time zone and need to get my beauty sleep." He picked up his violin case, turned towards Katarina and began walking toward the rear of the auditorium.

"You should have gone with them, Billy," Katarina complained.

"Rather be with you!" Bill replied as he opened the auditorium's front door, allowing Katarina to step through. The chilly night air caught both Bill and Katarina by surprise. Quickly, they both zipped their winter jackets. Katarina put on her gloves.

The university campus was magical in early fall. The star-studded sky was bright and clear. A quarter moon was beginning to set into the mountains to the west. The faint wisp of pine burning in the hearth wafted from a lone chimney across the street from the Macky Auditorium. Street lamps projected long shadows of trees upon the expansive lawns and surrounding buildings. A couple sat on a nearby park bench holding hands and sharing intimate whispers. Bill looked at his beloved and drank in a deep breath of air, experiencing a moment suspended in time and space.

"Billy, please don't put your life on hold because of me," Katarina said, breaking Bill's rapture.

Bill looked at Katarina strangely. "Don't know what ya mean? My life's not on hold."

Katarina opened her mouth as if to say something, but no words came out.

"Katarina, I have never felt so good in my entire life as I do this very moment!" Bill exclaimed. "Each breath is a breath of fresh air. I'm alive!"

Katarina smiled, turned her head and looked into Bill's eyes as she walked. She pushed her hair with her right hand so that it flowed evenly over her shoulders then reached into her purse for her pastel blue ski hat. "I'm glad for you Billy. You're special. You deserve a good life, better than the one you've had."

Bill smiled. "Want me to hold your things?"

"Sure." Katarina handed her flute, music case and purse to Bill so she could adjust her hat. "You'll need one of these pretty quick. It gets mighty cold here, I'll tell ya what."

"Already have one. In my room," Bill replied as he watched Katarina pull and adjust the knit hat over her ears.

"Do I look alright?" Katarina asked with flirting eyes.

"Katarina, you are magnificent!"

Katarina blushed as Bill handed her things back.

Bill looked seriously at Katarina's left hand. He considered reaching for it. But, following a moment of self-doubt, he turned and began walking again. Katarina followed.

"Maybe running away from home wasn't the best thing," Katarina offered, returning to a previous conversation.

"You really think I ran away?"

"Dunno, Billy. Our parents think so, I'll tell ya what. Personally, I think you've got guts. But, I also think we should respect our parents wishes."

"Isn't my sanity more important than their disapproval?"

Katarina looked at Bill oddly. Her overly expressive face held a question mark. "But they must love you, Billy. Otherwise they wouldn't care what you did."

"I suppose."

"My dad says that if you don't resolve this conflict you'll be sorry later in life."

Bill looked strangely at Katarina. "Is, is this, like, why you're apprehensive about us?"

Katarina looked away.

"Please tell me." Bill whined.

"Billy, what's true, we really don't know each other! Yeah, we've had sort of a pen-pal romance. And, now you stand here bigger than life." Katarina stopped talking while several students walked noisily past.

"And?"

"Billy, you bring with you a bunch of emotional baggage I can't deal with right now."

"I don't understand." Bill stopped walking.

Katarina stopped walking, too. She turned and with a touch of pain in her eyes, she looked at Bill. "Billy, I'm not ready for a relationship, with you or anyone."

Bill looked at the ground and closed his eyes. A secret tear began to form. "I don't care! I still want to be your friend. Is that okay?"

"Of course, silly."

Take it slow! Bill reminded himself in the quiet of his mind as he looked up and glanced into Katarina's eyes. Katarina turned away and resumed walking toward her dorm. Bill followed.

"Billy, y'all really don't have to escort me to my door," Katarina said as she stopped on Libby Hall's front porch, just outside the lobby's entrance. Several coeds pushed noisily through the doorway.

"If I want to?"

"Thought y'all told Peggy you needed to be in bed early? Something about beauty sleep?"

"I lied!"

"Oh." Katarina smiled while Bill opened the lobby door.

"Katarina?" Bill asked just outside her dorm room.

"Yeah?"

"Do friends give each other hugs?"

Katarina didn't answer. She turned and opened her arms to Bill. Bill held his breath. He didn't dare say his mind as he tightened his grip, patted her back and then slowly released her.

With eyes sparkling like a child at play, Katarina turned, unlocked her door. Then, after entering her room, she pulled off her ski cap and turned back toward Bill. Her long blond hair was now falling with abandon over her right shoulder and neck. Her glasses seemed to hang from the very tip of her tiny nose.

"Who are you trying to convince?" Bill asked, playfully. Then he turned and walked quickly away, not daring to look back.

Five

"Good evening. I'm Duane. I'll be your server for your evening's pleasure. Our specialty wine this evening is a California Chardonnay. But if you'd rather, any of the wines listed below are equally fine." Duane handed Katarina a wine list and menu, then likewise to Bill. "Shall I give you a few minutes?'

"Please," Bill returned.

"Y'all think he suspects we're not twenty-one?" Katarina asked, leaning towards Bill with a twinkle in her eye, the moment Duane was out of sight.

"He's just, like, being polite, I'm sure."

Bill watched Katarina read the menu. She was dressed in a white cotton blouse, a long sleeved tan sweater, brown pleated skirt just touching her knees, brown shoes and socks. Her long blond hair was tied back into a ponytail by a large brown satin ribbon. Bill found her so familiar that it was uncanny. It was the way she walked, talked, laughed, the look in her eyes when her inner child smiled through, even the way she clicked her tongue on the roof of her mouth when she was concentrating.

It was now Friday evening, the end of the first week at school. Bill and Katarina were sharing their first formal date at a local Italian restaurant. The establishment was already humming with evening guests. Oaken tables were clothed in white linen, real silverware and china, a candle, crystal wine glasses and goblets. Bill tapped on a wineglass with his right index finger to make sure.

"Sir, have you and your lady chosen a wine?"

"I think we better pass on the wine, thank you. We'll both have tea," Bill stated, trying hard to be proper. He was painfully aware that he knew nothing of etiquette.

"Very good, sir. Can I interest you in hors d'oeuvres?"

"Please. Katarina would like mushrooms stuffed with crab. For myself, oysters on the half shell."

"Very good. And for dinner?"

"We would both like the fettuccine with pesto sauce."

When the hors d'oeuvres were served, Bill made a fool of himself. He had no idea that his oysters would be raw, still attached to their shells. The sight grossed him out. Katarina, being the lady she was, simply shared her stuffed mushrooms while restraining her laughter.

"I'm planning on playing Vitali's *Ciaconna* for a November recital. I need an organist to play the figured bass accompaniment. Would you consider?" Bill asked, trying to overcome his awkwardness by making conversation.

"I'd love to. But I should have a look at the music before I commit."

"Of course."

"Your dinners are about to be served," Duane said, picking up Katarina's empty hors d'oeuvres plate. "Sir?"

Bill smiled apologetically and nodded.

Several minutes later Duane returned with artistically prepared plates and a huge basket of garlic-buttered buns. Then he freshened empty teacups and left Bill and Katarina to their indulgence.

"Oh, this smells good," Bill said, unfolding the basket of buns and offering some to Katarina.

"Yeah." Katarina closed her eyes and breathed the deep aroma before serving herself.

Bill inhaled several mouthfuls of pasta. "I can see why you recommended this place. This is great!"

Katarina nodded. She knew better than to talk with her mouth full. After taking a sip of tea and wiping her mouth with her napkin, she replied, "You can thank my piano professor. I've never been here before."

Bill stopped chewing and watched Katarina take another bite. He wished he could buy her dinner like this every night.

Katarina looked up, noticing Bill's stare. "What?"

"Just noticing how beautiful you are."

"Really?" Katarina looked down at her plate.

"You don't believe me, do you?"

"Billy, I know I'm just a country hick."

"Katarina, you're the most beautiful woman I've ever seen!"

Katarina's smile turned to concern. Bill's words scared her. She'd heard that line once before, from Carl, the night he abused her.

"So, tell me about your Modern Theology class," Katarina asked, following several minutes of forced silence. She knew she'd better change the subject. "Why're ya taking it?"

"Guess I never told you, I seem to have this passion for metaphysics."

"Really?"

"Got it from my grandfather. As a young man he went on several expeditions into Northern India, Tibet and the Gobi Desert. I still remember his stories."

"Wow, I dream of traveling like that someday. I want to see the world and have my own stories to tell!"

"I know. You've told me that many times," Bill replied.

"Yeah, guess I have." Katarina quietly took several more bites of food. "He sounds like a neat man."

"Died when I was sixteen. You remember." Bill looked away. He was at Pappy's side the moment he took his last breath. Bill remembered looking up, watching Pappy's soul dance across the ceiling.

"Sorry Billy, I do remember."

"Pappy was the only adult I could really talk to," Bill confessed. "As a child I often sat in his living room listening to his stories. Pappy would be puffing his pipe, sitting in his recliner. There'd be a fire roaring in the hearth, sometimes classical music on the radio. When I got into my teens, I told him about my life, my dreams, about you. He was the only one who never made my feelings wrong."

"Pretty special."

"Yeah. It was Pappy who got me thinking, questioning, studying ontology. After he died I began reading some of Edgar Caycey's works, but I was really interested in a five-volume set by T. Spalding, *The Life and Teachings of the Masters of the Far East*. I think because they seemed to parallel some of Pappy's experiences.

"Katarina, is it possible that enlightened masters like Jesus and Buddha really do walk today's planet in corporeal form? That people like you and I could learn to be like them? Have you ever though about that?"

Katarina sat silent, placing the fingertips of her left hand across her mouth. Bill had touched a nerve. She had thought about such things. Still, she wasn't about to discuss her beliefs, her random psychic experiences, or her lucid dreams openly with anyone. Her mother had warned her too many times. People might think she's a witch, or worse.

"Anyway," Bill continued, "College has given me the opportunity to study formally. While at L. A. State, I took all my lower division liberal studies in Philosophy and Religion, a trend I plan to continue. What about you, Katarina? Ya must have some interest?"

"Of course I'm interested, who wouldn't be? But I have to be honest, I think I'm too practical."

"Oh." Bill sat finishing his meal, thinking. Surely if Katarina had shared his psychic dreams, she'd be as excited as he was to talk and she'd pick up his lead. Alas, he thought to himself, maybe everyone is right. My dreams are pure delusion.

"Dessert?" Duane asked, startling Bill from his reverie.

"Cassata cake." Katarina responded immediately.

"Spumoni ice cream, for me," Bill quickly added.

"Very good," Duane said, bowing very slightly, then leaving.

"I'm really excited about being here. I'm hoping to swim every day. I plan on learning to ski this winter. I'm going to join the Judo club. Katarina, just think of all the fun things we can do together," Bill announced unexpectedly.

"What about school?"

"Yeah, well of course."

"Billy, school is very important to me. I'm not going to let my social life keep me from my studies. I've told you that."

"Neither am I, still…"

"Billy," Katarina's said, her voice getting considerably softer, "shouldn't we just be friends for a while?" Then she looked down at her empty tea cup while biting her lower lip. She knew she wasn't getting through.

Following dinner Bill and Katarina returned to the Macky Auditorium to enjoy a faculty recital. Towards the end of the evening, as the fourth movement of the Handel Organ Concerto began, Bill began to quake. His awareness was seized by the droning bass from the Macky pipe organ, by Katarina's soft smooth hand resting beneath his own, by the natural excitement of her effervescent personality and her Shalimar perfume, the perfume he had given her as a high school graduation present.

Katarina removed her hand from Bill's, looking at him with astonishment.

Bill tried to smile apologetically. But his body was consumed by a terrible beast and the pressure within had just turned into his worst nightmare.

"You okay?" Katarina asked as they began leaving the auditorium at the recital's close.

"Don't know. I've never felt like this." The cold wetness in Bill's pants made walking very uncomfortable. He prayed that it didn't show, that Katarina didn't look down. As he walked, instead of putting on his coat, he held it with both arms across his belly.

"Maybe we should get you to your room."

"I'll be okay," Bill lied.

"I'm worried."

"About what?"

"About the way you're acting, Billy!"

"Can we just sit and talk? I'll be okay. I just need to talk."

"Well, for a minute or two. I have to be at work early tomorrow," Katarina responded apprehensively.

Bill and Katarina sat together on a bench adjacent to one of the many expansive lawns flanking the university dormitories. Katarina made certain that there was a little distance between them. She was as quiet as the grass growing beneath her feet.

"Katarina?" Bill finally began, breaking the unearthly stillness.

Katarina didn't reply. She just held her breath.

"I'm in love with you." Bill announced with his adolescent voice.

Katarina closed her eyes while biting her lower lip.

"God! I can't stand it any more!" Bill reached toward Katarina, trying to grab her.

"No! Billy, No!"

Six

"What a stupid shit! How could I have, like, done that?" Over and over, like a needle stuck in a record's grove, Bill's internal dialog gave him no reprieve. He lay in bed motionless and helpless, staring at gray cigarette smoke stained ceiling tiles. Despite the refreshing sun light illuminating his room and the sound of laughter from a nearby volleyball game, Saturday morning found him in the worst depression ever.

Just after eleven thirty Bill showered, shaved, got dressed and put on his best slacks and only sport coat. Then he walked slowly to the health food store where Katarina worked. In addition to being accosted and scared to death by a neighborhood Weimaraner, his negative self-talk ran rampant.

Katarina had unexpectedly taken the day off. No one knew where she was. With his gut tied in a knot, Bill ran to her dorm and knocked, almost pounded, on her door. No answer. He ran to the Macky practice rooms, to the library, to the bookstore. She was nowhere to be found.

Sunday morning Bill forced himself out of bed and went to the Boulder Community Methodist Church where he knew Katarina would be playing the organ for the nine-thirty service. Once she was done with her duty, he intercepted her in the narthex.

"Morning. You play beautifully," Bill began in a rehearsed voice. His darkened eyes clearly told the lack of proper sleep.

"Thank you," Katarina returned, obviously unapproachable.

"Can you forgive me?" Bill asked, following Katarina into the parking lot, acting like a whipped puppy dog.

"You really scared me, Billy!"

"Didn't mean to. I just love you so damn much."

"Billy, wake up! We have our whole lives ahead of us!" Since Friday night, Katarina had thought a lot about what happened. Her father had warned her.

Bill looked down at the ground in shame.

"Told you I'm not ready for relationship! Look at me, Billy! I'm flesh and bones! I have needs, too! Right now, I need to go to school!"

Wilted like a pansy on a hot July afternoon, Bill looked into Katarina's familiar eyes. They were as hard as ice.

"If you think I can make you happy, you're going to get badly hurt!"

"Just being near you, like, makes me happy," Bill offered with a pained smile.

"Damn you!"

"Huh?"

"I don't think we should see each other any more!"

"What?" Bill's insides clamped a death grip around his heart. "What?"

Bill's soul seemed to leave him! And even though he went out of his way to avoid Katarina, there were brief encounters in the hallways, in and out of classrooms, practice rooms, at orchestra. Every sight of her brought its own special torture. Finally, one cold Saturday morning in late September, following a long walk across town, he called Debbie on a gas station pay phone.

"Ya know Deb, this has been the biggest mistake in my life. You were right!" Bill announced in a voice filled with tears.

"Billy, don't be so hard on yourself. I respect you for trying, even though it's been hard on me."

"I'm sorry Deb. Hurting you is, like, the last thing I ever wanted. I just thought…"

"You don't have to explain. I understand. Love is about forgiveness. Isn't that what you always said?"

"Yeah." Bill wiped away another stream of tears.

"The only thing I'm angry about is that self-righteous bimbo. Really, you deserve better!"

Bill heard Debbie's words but his pain was not diminished.

"Anyway, when you coming home? I'm thinking of moving out, getting my own place. Mmm…maybe you could move in with me, Billy."

"As much as I've hurt you, you'd still want that?"

"Of course, ya know I care about you, maybe the only one."

"I'm really touched."

"Then, is that a yes?"

Bill didn't immediately answer. The hiss along the telephone lines seemed to get louder and louder.

"Billy?"

"Whew! I have to, like, be honest. I'd better finish the semester. As much as I hurt, I can't afford to throw money away."

"You sure that's smart? Consider, what's a thousand dollars compared to the money you'll make in the years to come? It's insignificant! Anyway, Billy, I have some really good news for you."

"What?"

"Disney Studios, they're looking for musicians. They're having trouble finding strings."

"Really?"

"Remember Steve?"

"Yeah!"

"He got a job just last week, says he can help get ya in."

"Ya think they'll still have openings when I come home at Christmas?"

"Dunno, but I'm sure that someone who plays as well as you can always get a job."

Seven

"My God, Katarina, like, what did you do to your hair?" Bill stood gasping in a hallway filled with students scurrying between classes. It was late October, the Tuesday before Halloween.

Bill saw Katarina almost every day. She was courteous enough, but still unapproachable. Usually, if there was any conversation, it was reduced to a polite "hello" or, at most, school business.

"Had it cut," Katarina confessed, her face turning red.

"Why?" Bill asked in pain. He thought Katarina's hair was the most wonderful hair on earth. Sandy blond, silky smooth, waist length, at least it was.

"It'll grow back, don't worry. I do this every few years," Katarina announced, purposefully looking away from Bill.

Bill stood, staring. He didn't know what to say.

"The money I got for that hank of hair pays for a semester's room and board, I'll tell ya what."

"Sold it? To who?"

"Natural wigs. I get a premium, a hundred and fifty bucks."

"I can't believe it, for money?"

"Billy, not all of us are rich. I do what I have to. Like you, I'm trying to save so I don't have to work all the time."

Bill's frown told Katarina that he didn't approve a bit.

"I'm sorry, okay! Anyway I don't have to please you!" With a face bright red, Katarina turned and stomped off to her next class.

"Fuck me! I did it again!"

Pain quickly melted into nothingness. The only awareness left was Bill's eyesight and the metallic taste of blood. The arrow at the base of his skull made certain that he would be forever a quadriplegic. Screaming his war cry, the Red-Faced Indian dismounted his steed. He pulled his obsidian knife and ran toward Bill. However, seeing Bill utterly helpless, instead of slitting his throat, he repeatedly kicked Bill in the ribs and laughed. It was only when fresh blood began oozing from Bill's mouth and nose that his adversary stopped.

Lying flat on the desert sand under a huge acacia tree and next to her dead son, Spotted Fawn dared not move. However, her muffled sobs betrayed her. The Red-Faced Indian turned, ran and grabbed her by the right leg. Screaming with terror, she kicked and tried to escape. But he was a huge and powerful man. He pulled her from the ground and hit her on the side of her head. She fell and tumbled down a small incline, coming to rest only a few yards from Bill. Spotted Fawn panicked to get to her feet. But before she could run, the Indian hit her again and again. In agony, she reached towards Bill begging him to save her. However, he could do nothing to save his wife from the onslaught as the Red-Faced Indian raped her and slit her throat. Then, with a grotesque smile, the Indian turned, casually mounted his stallion and rode away. Bill was left to die alone, beneath a scorching sun and ruthless biting ants.

Bill awoke screaming! Would his nightmare never end?

Later, Bill closed his eyes as another round of tears began cascading down his red and irritated cheeks. The piece of notebook paper lying on the desk in front of him was totally blank. Several wads of crumpled paper lay recklessly on the floor next to the wastebasket. How could he put his pain into words? Why would anyone even care?

Bill got up from his chair, walked to the window of his dorm room and peeked through the curtains. The only thing he could see was a gray melancholy afternoon. In his mind's eye he relived the horror of Spotted Fawn's agonizing death.

Stooped over like a worn out old man, Bill shuffled to the tiny sink in the corner of his room. He pulled the razor from its safety holder and looked at it for what seemed an eternity. Several times in his life he had considered ending it all. However, somehow, he had always been able to talk himself out of it. At least when he and Katarina were pen pals there was hope in his life. He never lost faith that things would be perfect once they got together.

"Without, without her there's no reason to go on!" Bill mumbled. Then he shuffled back to his desk, still holding the razor between the thumb and forefinger of his right hand. As he sat down he glanced at Tillich's book, *Courage to Be.*

"Maybe I really don't have what it takes!" Bill told himself. "Maybe I never did. Maybe my father is right. Maybe I am crazy."

Bill looked at his left wrist and clenched his fist. His veins could easily be seen beneath the pink flesh.

"God, please forgive me."

Bill's left wrist began to sting as the razor pierced the first layers of skin. Two, three, then four large drops of blood fell to the floor. Despair cared nothing about the color of red as Bill watched the surrealistic journey began.

Knock, knock, knock, came three loud raps at the dorm room's door. Bill panicked like a kid just caught shop lifting. Involuntarily, he threw the razor across the room and forced his right hand over his wound.

Knock, knock, knock! "Bill?" A female voice called from the hallway.

Bill didn't want to answer. He ran to the sink, turned on the water and washed the blood from his wrist. He wished he had some Band-Aids.

"Bill? You in there?"

"Be with you in a minute." Bill returned as he reached for a towel and hurriedly began drying his face and forearm. He looked at his left wrist. Luckily the cut was only superficial. Quickly, he grabbed some toilet tissue and frantically wiped the blood from the floor.

"You okay in there?"

Bill cracked the door and peered into the hallway. "I'm not feeling too well," he said apologetically, relieved to see that it was only Peggy.

"You forget this afternoon's quartet rehearsal?" Peggy asked, politely keeping a little distance from Bill's door.

"Uh, guess I did," Bill answered in a monotone.

"We need you. There's still time. Can ya come?"

Bill didn't return an answer.

"Maybe I shouldn't have bothered you." Peggy felt Bill's unavailability, his gloom swallowed life like a black hole. "You're not okay, are you?"

"I'm sorry. Guess I got distracted. Actually I forgot," Bill apologized.

Peggy glanced at the cut on Bill's wrist, there were traces of fresh blood.

"Cut myself moving cardboard boxes," Bill said, looking to see how much blood was actually showing.

"Do you need a friend?"

"Whadaya mean?"

"I think you know exactly what I mean!"

"Said I cut myself moving boxes."

"I think you should get your violin and come with me. Get out of this damn room for a while."

Bill turned and walked towards his bed and sat down. Peggy followed Bill into the room. "I insist!"

Bill's gloom remained unchanged.

"Ya ever wondered why the percussion section is placed at the back of the orchestra?"

A twinge of a smile touched the corners of Bill's lips.

"See, I know it's in there!" Peggy teased. She walked to the room's windows and flung open the curtains. Then she forced Bill to stand up and gave him a long hug. "Bill, you're one of the nicest guys I know. I'll get really angry with you if you do something stupid."

Picking Bill's violin case off his desk, Peggy pushed it into Bill's arms. Then lead him by the hand to the afternoon's rehearsal.

"Anytime you need to talk," Peggy announced, "I'm here for you!"

"Thanks, Peg. But I don't need to talk. I'll be fine."

"Mister Colton, will you please remain after class," Professor Watley asked. Bill's Modern Theology class had just finished a very lively classroom discussion. However, over the past two months, Bill was contributing less and less. That worried his professor.

"Bill, everything okay?" Professor Watley asked once he and Bill were alone.

"Yeah. Uh, why do you ask?" Over the past month Bill's voice had changed. It had become almost a monotone. His handwriting had changed, too. Once nicely flowing with well-rounded loops, even and methodical, his script was gradually twisting into something stark and schizoid.

"Son, don't bullshit me."

"Whew." Slowly, Bill sat down in a nearby chair while looking at the floor.

"How can I help?"

"How? By bringing her back." Bill continued his zombie stare.

"Sometimes it helps to talk."

"Doubt that." Bill was well aware of all the lectures he'd received from his mother, all the broken promises. He was certain that talk was the one thing he didn't need.

"Maybe a friend?"

"A friend? Ha!" Bill said under his breath.

"Why not join me for lunch."

"That's okay. Don't want to be a bother."

"But I insist!"

Slowly Bill looked up and into his professor's caring eyes. Then he grabbed his books and stood, looking back at the floor. "I'll be all right." But as he said this, he could feel his jaw tremble. He knew he was not all right. But, sharing his heart, showing emotion in public, for a man, that was forbidden. His father had taught him well.

"Bill there is no shame in having feelings. Remember what we've talked about in class? We're a pendulum constantly swinging between the pits and ecstasy. That's part of being human."

Bill looked back at Professor Watley, a single tear washed from his left eye. He couldn't help himself.

"Come, share lunch with me. Let me be a friend."

As Bill and Dr. Watley walked toward the faculty cafeteria, they were mostly silent. Bill was, again, in his usual trance. He didn't notice the hour-old powder snow, the laughter of students throwing snowballs, the smell of burning pine escaping from neighborhood chimneys. He didn't even notice that he should be cold as a slight tint of blue began creeping along his bare arms.

Finally, Dr. Watley stopped and said, "Bill, look around you. Outfocus! Life is everywhere!"

"Huh?"

Dr. Watley pointed to a wedge of ducks painting its way toward the patch of blue sky over Denver. He pointed to a dozen cheerleaders practicing for Friday night's football game. He pointed to dark clouds creeping down the western slope, bringing the promise of evening snow showers. The surrealistic panorama of crystal blue sky, foreboding weather against hard rock held a poet's praise. Bill looked, but he didn't see. He didn't care.

"Some hemlock with your tea?" Dr. Watley asked as he sat down, across from Bill. The cafeteria was noisy and filled with the scent of frying fish. Several instructors sat nearby whining over their departments' new grading policy.

"Huh?" Bill asked, returning his attention to Professor Watley.

"So, who is she?"

"Oh, just a girl. Someone, someone I thought…oh, God." Bill had to stop. Embarrassed, he wiped a tear with his napkin.

"Really hurts, huh."

"Yeah."

Bill looked into Dr. Watley's caring brown eyes, then away. "I think my needs will be the death of me."

"Everything inside you is human, Bill. Sometimes love isn't easy."

"I'll say."

Dr. Watley pulled his pipe from his brief case, stuffed it with aromatic tobacco and lit it. "Why don't you tell me a little about yourself. Who is Bill Colton?"

"Well sir, I'm a music major. Hoped to be a concert violinist someday."

"Past tense?" Professor Watley asked, cocking his head, teasing Bill with his smile and dancing eyes.

Bill did not respond.

"Is that all you are?" Professor Watley asked, following several moments of thoughtful silence.

"Of course not. Was born in Bakersfield, California. My dad was in the Army. We moved to East Los Angeles when I was four." Bill took the next hour regurgitating everything, his life, his hopes and dreams, his broken heart.

When Bill finally ran out of momentum, Dr. Watley said, "Bill, you remind me of a man who stands precariously on the point of a needle. Below you in all directions is the abyss. Above you is nothing. If you jump from the needle, continuing to pursue her, you'll fall to your death. If you stay where you are, not doing anything, you'll fail. You might as well not have been born. So Bill, what are you going to do?"

Bill tossed and turned that night. The professor's riddle made his gut wrench. He thought about quitting, packing his bags and running. He thought about joining the Army, the Air Force, the French Foreign Legion, anything. He even thought about returning to his parent's home, confessing defeat. But, even suicide was better than that. It seemed, no matter what he did, he was doomed. Once again, Bill cried himself to sleep.

Thursday, reluctant and ill prepared, Bill walked into his violin lesson.

"Good afternoon, Bill," Dr. Miller said in a bright and cheery mood, purposefully trying to tease Bill out of his habitual doom and gloom.

"Good afternoon, Sir," Bill returned, emotionless, taking out his violin, reluctantly tuning it, then warming up on scales.

Once his cold fingers were loose and moving more freely, Bill took out Chausson's *Poème* and began playing. Dr. Miller watched and listened. As usual, everything went fairly well until nine measures after the Animato. There, things began falling apart. Bill stopped, almost in tears.

"Try it again," Dr. Miller requested, trying to be patient even though the last several lessons were a repeat of the same hopelessness.

Bill tried, he fumbled.

"Again."

Again Bill tried, he fumbled in identically the same way.

"Bill, don't practice mistakes!"

"Huh?"

"Relax! Play it slower." Dr. Miller picked up his violin and played the passage with exaggerated slowness.

"Forget tempo right now, that'll come. First learn to play it correctly."

Bill tried at half tempo. He fumbled.

"Slower yet!" Dr. Miller commanded.

Following several strained attempts, Bill finally got the passage right.

"Good, now learn it at this speed. You can begin to increase speed later. But remember, as soon as you blow it, start over, slower if necessary. Don't practice mistakes!"

Bill played the passage mechanically perfectly several times at less than quarter tempo.

"Excellent! Now go home and practice. Quit being so damn hard on yourself!"

Friday afternoon, Bill had a couple of hours to kill before dinner. So he went to one of Macky's practice rooms to work on the Chausson. The dark passages of Poème fit his mood. But he found it necessary to play the Animato even slower than his previous day's lesson. Several times he found himself lip-synching his professors words, "Don't practice mistakes."

Unexpectedly, like a bolt of lightening, Bill doubled over in a fit of laughter. "Don't practice mistakes! Oh, my God!"

Bill saw! He saw how he did his life, practicing one mistake after another. For the first time in his life he realized that he didn't know how to live. He didn't know how to love.

Eight

Like a door slammed shut fall became winter. Friday night, one week before Thanksgiving, Bill took his seat in the Macky Auditorium, eighth row center. Several minutes later Dr. Earl Watley and his wife pushed through the audience, finding seats next to him.

"Doctor Watley! Good evening, sir." Surprised, Bill stood and extended his right hand.

"My wife Eileen, Bill Colton." Earl returned, smiling, shaking Bill's hand and then taking his own seat.

Bill considered his professor a friend, even though he'd shared lunch and personal conversation only once. His professor challenged him to think. Bill respected that, even when it was painful.

"Do you know anything about *The Sound of Music*?" Bill asked, turning toward the Watleys.

"A little," Eileen offered. "It's a musical story about an Austrian family who fled the Nazi's at the beginning of World War Two. Got great reviews on Broadway."

"How come you're not playing in the theater orchestra?" Earl asked Bill.

"My quartet conflicted, too many critical rehearsals."

"What do you play?" Eileen questioned as she pushed the bangs of her neatly trimmed red hair to the side and away from her eyes using the two forefingers of her left hand. Her brown eyes glowed from the reflection of several stage lights.

"Violin."

"Are you playing in the symphony concert in two weeks?"

"You bet, I'm the concertmaster."

"Really! That's wonderful. I heard you guys are doing the Shostakovich *Fifth Symphony*."

"Afraid so."

"The concertmaster, afraid?"

"Yeah, it's really difficult." As Bill spoke, the Overture began and the house lights dimmed. Everyone turned his or her attention toward the stage.

Bill glanced at familiar faces in the orchestra pit, at least the ones he could see. Most were hidden by the pit railing. He wondered if Katarina was playing the flute. Someone with short blond hair was obscured by the conductor's music stand. But, it didn't matter, not any more.

It didn't take long for Bill to begin fidgeting in his seat. His attention span seemed to be getting shorter by the day. And, as his mind wandered, he wondered about his career and future. He also wondered what Debbie was doing now that she had dropped out of art school. Had she found a job? Was she even looking? What kind of guys was she hanging out with? Bill felt bad. Debbie was the one person who was always there for him. The only real disagreement they had ever had was over Katarina. But even with that, it was Debbie who had given him a going away party, inviting all his friends, the day before he left California. For a gift, she had painted him a picture of two Mallards lifting from a lotus blossom amidst a magical sunrise. How could I be so blind? He thought to himself.

Suddenly, Bill's reverie was shattered. Walking onto the stage was Katarina, as Liesl, one of the Von Trap Family children. He watched her, spellbound. Then, later, when she began singing *Sixteen going on Seventeen* and dancing with Rolfe, he began to cry. By intermission, Bill was an emotional wreck. He started to leave.

"Why don't you join Eileen and myself for pie and coffee following the show?" Earl asked, stopping Bill from his hasty retreat.

"I, I don't think so."

"Where are you going to go? What are you going to do?"

"Shit, I don't know!" Bill flopped back down into his seat, eyes now bloodshot. "Everything I do is wrong!"

"Not everything!"

"Wish I believed that."

"Bill, you're one of my brightest students. You understand things at an intuitive level that most people never get. Don't sell yourself so short."

Bill said nothing. Consciously, he didn't hear what Earl had said.

"You let your passions get in your way. Son, the only thing you lack is compassion for yourself."

Following the musical, Earl and Eileen drove Bill to their home for the promised desert.

As Bill entered the front door, he recognized that the Watleys were anything but ordinary. Their home was magnificent: hardwood floors; large Indian rugs, tastefully arranged; genuine leather furniture, soft to the touch; and quality art hanging on the walls. The dining room table was set with fine linen, china and crystal, awaiting honored guests.

Earl walked to the fireplace and lit the evening's fire while Bill studied the Watley's stereo system. An Ampex 601 stereo tape deck stood in the foreground, something Bill could only dream about owning.

"Some Mozart?" Earl asked.

"Please!" Bill replied, noticing that a large yellow-eyed black cat was scrutinizing him.

Earl pointed to several stacks of tapes stacked on a nearby bookshelf. Bill looked at each, one by one, finally selecting the *Concerto for Clarinet and Orchestra in A major*.

"Good choice," Eileen said while entering the living room with earthenware cups of fresh brewed coffee, arranged with spoons, sugar and cream on a beautiful oak platter. As she walked across the room she carried that look of elegance usually found only in modeling schools. She stood five feet ten in her stocking feet, weighed, perhaps, one hundred and thirty pounds. She was immaculately dressed in a dark green evening dress. The color was magnificent against her golden skin and red hair. Eileen's face was more round than square and perhaps a little small for her body proportion. She had hundreds of tiny little freckles high on her cheeks, just below her large warm brown eyes and across her aristocratic nose. Even though she was well into her forties, restaurants often asked to see her driver's license.

"Pywicket miss her mama?" Eileen asked as she bent over and petted the little beggar who was now happily engaged in rubbing her ankles.

Bill caught the aroma of Eileen's brew as he took a sip while watching Pywicket run and claw her cat tree. Exceptionally smooth and naturally sweet, the coffee was unlike any he'd ever known.

"Friends send this from Brazil," Eileen said, anticipating Bill's question.

Bill walked to the evening's fire, now spitting and cracking, beginning to seriously catch hold. He stared at the flames for several minutes, wondering what it was like to live in such luxury. Only once had he been in a home like this. There, for a piano recital in Altadena, California, the living room was large enough to hold two full sized grands and still comfortably seat guests. Bill remembered how he fell in love with that house, how it led him to dream and exchange house plans with Katarina. They had worked together by mail for almost a year. In his mind's eye he could still see their dream, music conservatory on the right, library on the left, five bedrooms and a sewing room up stairs. Katarina wanted children.

"Oh, crap! It's no use!" Bill finally voiced with a knot strangling his heart. "Where ever I go, no matter what I do, I think of her."

Bill walked over to the dinning room table and placed his coffee cup onto the serving tray. "I, I'd better go."

"Before you do, Eileen and I have an offer we'd like to you consider. Please, take a moment. Have a seat." Earl pointed to the leather davenport.

"Bill, years ago Eileen and I rented the room in our basement to graduate students. If you'd like, that room could be yours."

Bill was shocked. He often wished he could get out of the dorm, but knew he couldn't afford it. "H—how much?" He asked apprehensively, working his lower jaw back and forth.

"Could work it so it wouldn't cost you a thing."

"Huh?"

"Room and board in trade for some household duties."

"You mean maid service?"

"Something like that."

"What would I have to do?" Bill asked. He surprised himself by not immediately saying no.

"Help Eileen clean the house, cook dinner several times a week, a little yard work. Believe me, you'll be getting the best of the deal."

"Whew. Would I have time for school?"

"Of course! School is the most important thing for you right now, nothing should interfere with that."

"Earl, show Bill his room," Eileen said, handing Bill a freshened cup of coffee.

Together, Earl and Bill walked through the kitchen, onto the back porch, then down the stairs into a black abyss. Pywicket followed. The professor felt his way through the dark making certain not to step on a cat. He found a switch and turned on the light. Bill was greeted by a studio apartment that obviously hadn't been used in years.

"She'll need some painting. Plumbing needs some repair. But, basically she's as fit as a fiddle."

Bill walked over to the potbellied stove and touched it. It was colder than ice. Then he opened various kitchen cupboards exposing dusty pots and pans, dishes and glasses. The water in the faucets didn't come on.

"Like I said, she'll need some work. We'll get you a new bed."

Bill turned and looked back across the twelve by fifteen room. There was a small well-used desk supporting several unopened boxes of building materials sitting next to a tiny closet and bathroom. No frills. Still, the room felt good, despite the cold.

"Eoooooow!" Pywicket hollered, looking at Bill from across the room as if to say, "This is my space!"

"Don't know," Bill said, apologetically, looking back at Earl. "I'm seriously considering leaving school after this semester."

Earl looked at Bill with the compassion of a caring parent. "Well then, shall we go get warm."

"Fresh apple pie?" Eileen offered a piece to Bill as soon as he re-entered the kitchen. "We have chocolate-almond ice cream to drown your sorrows."

"Heck, why not." Bill got that Eileen and his professor were genuine and that their friendship was truly heartfelt.

The moment Eileen opened the carton of ice cream, Pywicket ran up the stairs and entered the kitchen begging.

"You know, I've dreamed of evenings such as these," Bill offered once he was seated again in the Watley's living room. "Good music, a warm fire, special friends. I can't help thinking of the song we heard this evening, *I must have had a wicked childhood.*" As Bill spoke, his body began to quake from the inside. "God, like, why do I always come back to this?"

"'Cos you're not through with it yet. Bill, these things take time. You've loved this woman for years. What makes you think you're going to get over it in a day, in a month, even a year?" Earl said, taking a seat next to Bill.

Bill said nothing, purposefully trying to breathe deeply.

"Feeling betrayed, huh?"

"Yeah, yes I do."

"What about Katarina?"

"Huh?"

"Do you think she feels betrayed?"

Bill sat, stunned. His mouth moved but no words came out.

"Here she is, hopes and dreams of her own, unrealizable, for what ever reason."

"The problem is, you're both naïve."

"Guess I need to grow up, huh. That's what my father always said."

"Naïveté has nothing to do with growing up," Earl returned. Then, after finishing a bite of pie, he continued. "Naïveté is about being too simplistic, not paying attention to what's really going on in the world around you. Anytime you feel betrayed, it's probably because you've been hanging out in naïveté."

"My love for her is because I'm naïve?" Bill experienced a twinge of anger.

"Careful, I'm not judging your love, right or wrong. I'm saying that your love could not reach fulfillment because of naïveté. Please be very clear about this."

"Whew." Bill took a bite of pie, a bite of ice cream, then he turned back to his professor. "But, but, all I wanted was a kiss. I wound up, like, scaring her half to death. I, I apologized."

"And, you knew she wasn't responding to your desires even before that fateful moment. Somehow you knew."

"Yeah." Bill looked at the floor in shame.

"I'm going to give you a clue."

Bill turned back to Earl, giving his full attention.

"In your own selfishness, in your own naïveté, you didn't hear her needs. From what you said that day we had lunch together, she told you up front that school is the most important thing for her, that she wasn't going to let her social life interfere. She also told you that she wanted to be your friend."

Bill remembered well. Katarina's words had hurt him at a core level.

"Still, headstrong, thinking you had all the answers, you didn't listen. As a result, you scared her, you betrayed her."

"Shit! Like, I never thought of it that way," Bill admitted. He leaned back in his chair, shaking his head from side to side. "Guess I really fucked it up, huh." Instantly, Bill's face turned deep red, realizing what he'd just said in front of the lady of the house.

Neither Earl nor Eileen reacted.

"After all that's happened, I'll never be able to make things right," Bill said after settling down from his embarrassment.

"Is that really true, Bill? Or is that simply your anxiety talking?"

"Every time I see her, like a terrible beast, my feelings strangle me. It's getting worse and worse."

"And, you've got to have her." Earl filled in Bill's unspoken thought.

"Most of the time I don't think I can go on." Bill closed his eyes, then asked, "What now? How can I undo the damage?"

"You already know the answer to that question. Katarina told you. Less than fifteen seconds ago, I reminded you."

Nine

"Told me what? What did she tell me? What did Professor Watley tell me?" Angry, Bill tossed and turned the night away, finally falling to sleep from sheer exhaustion.

The next morning, Saturday, the sun bright in his eyes, Bill crawled begrudgingly out of bed just after eleven. He ate a hurried brunch from scraps illegally stored in his closet, then went to one of Macky's practice rooms to try to forget. Music was now his chronic escape from thinking about her, even though he really needed to woodshed a passage in the fourth movement of Shostakovich.

"Damn it! Don't practice mistakes!" Bill yelled with frustration as he thrust his violin into the air. His rage wanted to smash everything he could put his hands on into the concrete floor. His arms began shaking violently as he forced control.

Bill tried the passage again, now adrenaline got in his way. Nothing he could do made the passage palatable.

"Like, I shouldn't be here," Bill finally admitted, trying to stare down a benign piece of manuscript. Then he shoved his violin roughly into its case and stomped back to his dorm room almost in tears.

Bill tried to study. But after reading the same paragraph from his music literature text over and over a dozen times, he figured that the day might be put to wiser use by just screwing off.

"What the fuck is wrong with me?" Bill questioned aloud as he walked from his dorm, again on the verge of tears. Talking to himself usually didn't solve problems. Frequently, it made them worse, forcing depression. But talking to himself was one thing he knew how to do really well.

Outside, Bill found the afternoon cold. Even the bright sunshine couldn't begin to melt two feet of packed snow. He put on his sunglasses, zipped his coat and secured his gloves. Then, for no reason, he headed east toward a lonely stand of pine trees since there seemed to nobody there.

"What the fuck is wrong with me?" Bill tried very hard to remember what Katarina had told him that might make it better.

"My dad is right. I am crazy!" Bill confessed under his breath as he watched some coeds laughing and building a snowman. "I don't even have friends here. At least in Los Angeles I had Debbie. Shit! Should have listened to her. But I had to try. Damn, I had to!"

Bill remembered how hard it was living with his parents, especially after his mother began babysitting a two-year-old on a regular basis. The child cried from the moment she arrived mid-morning until she was picked up late in the afternoon. The child's presence jarred the whole Colton household. It was next to impossible to study and his grades began to decline. He knew that if he hadn't come to Colorado, he would have had to move out of the house just to secure his own sanity.

"Fuck! Like, I didn't have a life!" Bill shouted. Then he looked around embarrassed, hoping that no one heard his outburst.

Bill stopped near Libby Hall, kicking his foot several times into a frozen snowdrift. He looked up at Katarina's window praying she'd look out. However, in his gut he knew she wasn't in. He wondered how it was that he could know her so well, yet every time he'd try to get close to her, somehow, he'd blow it and she'd turn away.

"Who the fuck am I?" Bill cried aloud.

"I'm a man," Bill answered, returning to his sullen disposition. "I'm the son of Virginia and Chuck Colton. I'm a student at the University of Colorado. I'm a violinist. But what else?" Bill touched an inner emptiness. Over the past several weeks, Paul Tillich's words grew more and more unsettling. "But how can I be when I don't know who I am?"

Slowly, Bill took off his gloves and looked at his hands. They looked like his grandfather's, slender with long blunt fingers, good for the violin. He looked at his flesh, considered the millions of cells that made up his body, the millions of atoms that made up his cells. "But what is this thing I call me?"

Bill remembered his grandfather's neighbor in South San Gabriel, a beekeeper. One bright sunny windless afternoon the neighbor showed Bill and some other kids something totally awesome. He opened a hive, removed the queen and placed her into flap of gauze. Then he walked about fifty feet from the hive and just stood silently, holding the queen in her gauze prison. One by one, bees flew to him and circled. Some landed on him. Some flew back to the hive. It didn't take long until the entire hive became airborne. Within the hour he was covered from head to toe with a swarm of content bees.

"Is that what I am?" Bill questioned. "Are my cells like a swarm of bees? Is the essence of me like a queen-bee who creates the propensity for life? If so, where does the essence of me exist?"

Bill thought about his center of awareness, beginning to walk once again. "It seems to be in my head. But perhaps that's an illusion. Because, other peoples in other times have considered their awareness to be in their hearts. Who's right?"

In his questioning, Bill touched an inner longing, a longing that seemed impossible to satisfy, especially since Katarina was no longer part of his equation. He realized that deep within him was the need to be loved. It wasn't a sexual thing. It was more. But he didn't know what. One thing he did know, however, just between sleep and wakefulness there was a threshold. Every so often late at night, sometimes early in the morning, he touched it. And when he did, he was filled with love so magnificent that nothing else mattered. He knew he was connected to something much more profound than just a mundane world.

"Hay! Where ya goin'?" Peggy demanded, startling Bill out of his preoccupation.

"Dunno. Just wandering, thinking, feeling sorry for myself."

"That all, join the crowd."

Bill chuckled, thankful for the interruption.

"You ice skate?"

"Yeah. Why?"

"They've dug a pond and flooded it just east of Folsom Street, making a rink. A whole bunch of people are skating over there. That's where I'm headed." Peggy held figure skates up so that Bill could see them.

"Oh, yeah. I remember reading about it in Wednesday's paper."

"Come along?"

"Sure! I'll go get my skates." Bill smiled with a little enthusiasm, realizing that he'd be better off being around others rather than alone. He turned and quickly began walking back to his dormitory as he hollered, "Be back in, like, ten or fifteen minutes!"

"Okay!" Peggy hollered back.

"How ya doin' with Shosty?" Bill asked, skating up to Peggy, sliding to a parallel stop.

"Not too well. The fourth movement is a real killer, too many accidentals, and too many high notes. I don't like playing up in the atmosphere. You?"

"I seriously considered smashing my violin this morning, I'll tell ya what." Bill stopped, catching himself. He'd never said that before. Suffixing a sentence with "I'll tell ya what" was something only Katarina did.

"You look so serious, Bill. Everything okay?"

"Sorry, lots on my mind."

"Like what?"

"My future. I don't know what to do. I think I should just go away, away from here."

"School's that bad?"

"May not be back next semester, Peg."

"Whadaya gonna do?"

"Thinking seriously about getting a job with a studio orchestra in Hollywood. A friend of mine has connections."

"Gee. I'm sorry to hear you say that, really. You're probably the best concertmaster our orchestra has had in ages."

"Thank you. I need some encouragement right now. Feels like my life's a bust."

"Still?"

"I'm, like, barely holding it together."

"Well, I certainly know how that is."

"You do?"

"Yeah, ya know my boyfriend, Fred, being at the Air Force Academy, sometimes I go for weeks without seeing him."

Bill looked at Peggy and smiled a half-assed grin of understanding.

"Got a girl friend?" Peggy asked.

Bill didn't answer. Instead he began skating backward from where Peggy stood.

"You're a man of many talents. Backwards on speed skates, I'm impressed," Peggy said, turning, following Bill's lead.

"It's not hard." Bill pivoted off the toes of his blades, coming about. "I can't dance."

"Like that girl over there?" Peggy pointed to a figure skater, perhaps thirty yards away. She was obviously a talented dancer.

"Yeah, can't do that stuff, even in my dreams."

"Let's check her out." Peggy said as she began skating across the ice, dodging people skating to and fro. Bill followed, quickly passing.

Bill stopped about twenty feet from the ballerina. "Shit!" He said under his breath.

"Why, it's Katarina Epperson! No surprise, she's exceptional at everything!" Peggy exclaimed, sliding to a stop alongside Bill.

Bill said nothing. He just watched.

"You like her, don't you?"

"Why do you say that?" Bill asked, looking back at Peggy, purposefully trying not to give himself away.

"The way you look at her. I've seen you in orchestra. It's like, when you're not playing, counting rests, you always look at the flute section, at her. Sometimes you even stare. Why on earth don't you ask her out?"

Bill was speechless. His mouth hung open. What could he say? One thing he knew for certain, he wasn't about to share his feelings.

"Race you around the pond." Peggy took off, leaving Bill in her wake.

Bill stood for a few minutes watching Katarina jump and spin a tight circle. Then the instant she stopped and looked in his direction, he took off, bulleting past Peggy.

Once, twice, three times around the rink at top speed. Bill prayed that Katarina would notice. She did, the moment he caught an edge and slid, tumbling helplessly, three quarters the distance of the rink, coming to rest in a bank of snow forty feet from where she stood. Several skaters fell, scurrying to get out of his way.

"Y'all okay?" Katarina yelled, laughing, skating nonchalantly to where Bill lay.

Bill quickly got up and brushed the snow from his jacket, pants and hair. Then he retrieved his black knit ski cap. He looked at Katarina and began laughing, too. "That's what I get for, like, trying to show off."

"You okay?" Peggy asked skating up to Bill, looking very concerned.

Katarina gave Peggy a hardened stare that lasted at least five seconds. Then, without uttering a word, she turned and skated back out on the ice toward several of her friends.

"What was that all about?" Peggy asked.

Bill looked at Peggy, then out at Katarina, then back at Peggy. He shrugged his shoulders. "Beats the hell out of me."

"I think she's jealous," Peggy announced, getting a twinkle in her eye.
"Jealous?"
"Yeah! And you know what? I think you should ask her out."
"I don't think so."
"You afraid?"
"Yeah, Peg, I am!"
"Of what?"

Bill looked at the blue-white ice beneath his feet. In a meteor's flash he debated whether or not to tell Peggy that he'd already crashed with third degree burns, deciding against it. Then, looking up and out to the rink's center, Bill watched Katarina fall from attempting a double-axle. She got up from the ice, laughing.

"Consider, if you don't ask her, you may never get another chance. Ya know, the Christmas dance is coming up. She might say 'yes.'"

Bill thought about that. He remembered what his violin teacher had once said, "The difference between success and failure is nothing more than persistence."

"Anyway, I think the two of you would make a handsome couple," Peggy added.

"What the hell!"

Bill skated five times around the rink at flank speed working up his courage. Finally he pushed toward Katarina, stopping abruptly, both blades parallel. Waves of scraped ice shot out before him, lightly spaying her polished white boots.

"Impressive! Didn't know y'all skated, Billy," Katarina said with a broad smile. Her pastel blue ski cap, fair skin and contrasting blue eyes made her look angelic. Powder blue ski jacket against navy blue stretch pants, she always knew how to dress.

"Been skating for several years now." Bill wanted to tell Katarina that he took lessons while in high school so that he might sweep her off her feet on a sunny winter's day, just like this. But he didn't.

"It shows."

"How are classes?" Bill asked.

"Great! Think I'll get straight A's again. How y'all doin'?"

"Okay." Bill lied.

"I'm glad Billy, really I am."

"I enjoyed the *Sound of Music.* You did, like, a magnificent job. Be proud!"

"Thank you. How come y'all didn't play in the orchestra? Could have used ya, I'll tell ya what."

"Other commitments. My quartet is getting ready for a major recital Wednesday after next. Hope you can come."

"Afraid I've got to work, ya know, the health food store."

"Oh." Bill's smile quickly turned to disappointment. "Katarina? Would ya, like, go to the Christmas dance with me?" Bill had to strain to say the words. He closed his eyes, afraid to look.

"Oh, I'm sorry, Billy. I can't."

"Work?"

"Yeah."

"I'm sorry, too," Bill apologized. Then, quickly, he turned and skated back to Peggy. She was beginning to untie her skates, getting ready to leave.

"Well, like, so much for that," Bill announced, another dagger in his heart.

"Bill, I'll go with you."

Ten

"I really enjoyed our quartet last Wednesday night. The Mozart *E-flat* is one of my favorites," Peggy began as soon as she and Bill entered the sidewalk outside her dorm. Her breath hung stiff in the cold night air as she spoke. The sky was crystal clean, scrubbed by cold afternoon winds rampaging down the western slopes. The smell of burning pine wafted from local neighborhoods, inviting repose before a roaring hearth.

"It did go well, huh," Bill answered, enjoying the evening fragrance.

"Yeah, an easy A for the semester!"

"Look at that moon!" Bill pointed to the eastern horizon. "It's ice brilliant!"

"Why does the moon do that, look so much bigger than life?"

"Dunno, Peg. Illusion, I guess. Someone told me that the atmosphere acts like a lens. Ya know, magnification."

Together, Bill and Peggy stood barely breathing, watching the moon inch behind a large outcropping of conifers immediately west of the football field.

"Now that the semester is over, what are your plans?" Peggy asked, breaking the mystical moment.

"Goin' to Los Angeles. I'm really surprised my parents sent me airfare. Leave tomorrow afternoon, like, after we play Handel's *Messiah*."

"The sound of your voice, you certainly don't sound excited."

"I'm not. But I gotta do something, ya know, with the dorms closing for Christmas recess."

"You must have friends here that'll put ya up?"

"I should go home. Got some serious soul-searching to do, Peg."

"Someone out there, Bill?" Peggy reached out and placed her right hand on Bill's forearm.

"Maybe. I have an old high school friend, think she wants to get married."

"Bill, can I offer you some advice?" Peggy stopped walking, turned and looked directly into Bill eyes. "Don't."

"Huh?"

"You've obviously been hurt. Give yourself some time."

"I'm that transparent?"

"A person would have to be blind not to see."

"Oh." Bill wondered if Peggy knew the details.

The Elks Club Dance Hall was dimly lit as Bill and Peggy entered and checked their heavy winter coats. The dance band had already begun their first set.

"Care if we join you?" Bill asked Stan, a casual friend from the French Horn section of the university orchestra.

"Not at all." Stan stood up after placing his cigarette in a near-by ashtray. Then, he introduced Dotty, his fiancée.

Bill ordered a pitcher of Coors from a passing waitress, after producing his driver's license as ID. "Not many people here tonight. You'd think more people would come, Christmas dance."

"It's early," Stan replied, taking a drink of his gin and tonic.

Bill looked around the room. Only four couples were on the dance floor. At several tables people were engaged in conversation. Sam and Ellen were making fools of themselves in a dark corner, as usual. Bill looked away in jealous disgust.

"Ya wanna, like, dance?" Bill finally asked after finishing a glass and a half of beer without saying a word.

"Thought you'd never ask," Peggy said, smiling. She got up from her seat and joined Bill, dance floor center.

"Band seems kinda dead," Bill apologized, trying to synchronize with the rock tune being played.

"Maybe it's you who needs to loosen up a bit. You're so tight, Bill. Don't ya like to dance?" Peggy extended her hands, taking Bill's, closing the distance between them.

"Sorry, I'm not much fun."

"You can be."

Bill looked into Peggy's big green eyes, a question in his own.

"Bill, I remember you the first week of the semester. You were so alive, bouncing off the walls, larger than life. You had the whole orchestra in stitches that night, remember?" Peggy raised Bill's arm and twirled under it.

"I remember well. Thought I could jump as high as the moon."

"The next week you changed. That when it happened, when she dumped you?"

"Kinda nosy."

"Just trying to get ya talkin', that's all, trying to be your friend. You're a nice guy and I've seen you sulking for months."

"Understand."

"Dear John letter?"

"Wish it could be so easy."

"Local gal?"

Bill didn't answer the question.

"So, ya goin' to tell me who she is, or ya going to tease me all night?"

Bill chuckled and stopped dancing. "Peg, I really don't want to go into all this."

"Bet I can find out before the evening's out."

"If it's a challenge you want, like, you won't get any help from me."

"May not, but you're not the only one in this room."

"What's that supposed to mean?"

"Means, you've got friends, must have talked to someone."

"Think I'll get another beer," Bill said, smiling as if begging Peggy to try. Then he turned, walked back and sat down at their table. Peggy followed, but remained standing.

The evening was coming alive with the arrival of more and more students. Stan and Dotty were now on the dance floor along with several dozen couples. The band responded with increased volume and heavier bass.

"Hmmm, let's see. Who knows you better than anyone?" Peggy shouted, scanning the room.

Bill watched Peggy, amused. She was dynamite in her dark green jump suit and red hair.

"Oh, there's Frank, he knows everything. See ya."

"You really are closed mouthed! Frank had no idea what I was talking about," Peggy announced upon her return. She sat down alongside Bill while he re-filled her glass, emptying the pitcher.

Bill laughed, seeing the mischief in Peggy's smile. "Let's dance."

"You know, you're a groovy guy when you loosen up. Is that what it takes, a couple of beers?"

"What the hell!" Bill grabbed Peggy's hand and threw her into a modified country swing step he learned in East LA. Peggy followed.

"Gee, Bill, I didn't know you had it in ya!" Peggy tried to shout above the music.

"Took lessons at State." Bill yelled back.

"It shows."

"Need to take a pit stop," Peggy announced following several high energy numbers.

"I'll join you. Oops, I mean…" Bill laughed. He knew Peggy understood.

Back at the table Bill and Peggy enjoyed another beer while shouting meaningless nothings to friends.

"Ya know how to waltz?" Bill shouted at Peggy, wanting to get away from Stan's cigarette smoke.

"What girl doesn't!" Peggy yelled back.

Bill drew Peggy in close as they began touring the dance floor. He liked the way her small Irish frame fit into his arms and as they danced he wondered if he should take her away from her Air Force jock. A real looker, she was always fun to be around, never any tension between them.

"Peggy?"

"Yeah?"

"If I come back next semester, ya wanna play the Bach *Double Concerto* with me?"

"Thought you'd never ask." Peggy reached up, put her right hand behind Bill's head, pulled his face down and kissed him, long and hard.

When Bill opened his eyes Katarina stood ten feet away, staring, mouth gaping. Hoping to renew her social life, she had unexpectedly taken the night off from work.

Peggy looked at Bill. Then she looked at Katarina, then back at Bill again. "Oh my Gawd!"

Bill turned and walked hastily to the men's room, almost pushing people out of the way.

"I'm sorry, Bill. That was stupid of me," Peggy apologized when Bill returned. "The last thing I want is to embarrass you."

"You sure did!"

"She's pretty special, huh."

Bill didn't answer. Instead, he stood looking intently around the room.

"Ya see where she went?" Bill demanded.

"No, I'm sorry."

"I'm going to mingle," Bill announced, leaving Peggy sitting by herself. About fifteen minutes later Bill returned. "Guess she's, like, gone."

"You okay?"

"Not really."

"I'm really sorry, Bill. I…"

"It's okay, Peg. Really it is. Every time she's around I screw things up somehow."

"But I'm the one who kissed you. She needs to know that!"

"Please, leave it alone, Peg. Think I want to leave."

Peggy got up and walked silently, ruefully, to the coat check with Bill.

"Bill? I can find my own way home."

"Wouldn't think of it. Besides, I have the right to have friends. Like, I'll be damned if I'm going to waste my life away, 'cos of her."

Bill couldn't help noticing the concern in Peggy's face as they stepped out into the cold night's air, adjusting coats and putting on gloves. "Met her when I was fourteen years old on a summer's vacation. We spent a magnificent week together, hiking, horseback riding, chasing afternoon thunderstorms. In the evenings we danced. We were enchanted. All through high school we kept our romance alive though letters. I planned on getting married."

"What went wrong?"

"Got too aggressive. In my eagerness, I scared her, scared her bad."

"Bill, can I ask you a question, I mean a personal one?"

"Might as well, you know everything else."

"Have you ever been with a woman?"

Bill stopped walking. He turned and looked at Peggy, embarrassed.

"That's what I thought."

Eleven

"Oh Billy!" Virginia ran up to Bill, throwing her arms around him as soon as the concourse at LA's International Airport yielded space enough to move.

"Hi mom."

"Good to see you, son." Chuck extended his hand, Bill shaking it in return.

Bill turned to his sister, Susan, and gave her a big hug. "Miss ya kiddo. How's life treating ya?"

"How's the weather in Denver?" Bill's father interrupted, trying to generate small talk as the Colton family turned and began walking toward baggage claim.

"It snowed, like, a foot and a half yesterday. Thought I was going to have to cancel my trip. Plows worked overtime."

"You were able to get to the airport okay?"

"A friend drove me, one of my professors actually, Doctor Watley. We seem to be kindred spirits."

"Oh?"

"Yeah, he teaches Philosophy. Took a course from him last semester, Modern Theology."

"Modern Theology? You going to become a priest, now?" Chuck ridiculed.

"Of course not, dad. Music's my gig."

"Oh, Billy, ya disappoint me so." After dinner, Virginia could contain herself no longer. Just like old times, nothing had changed, the round wobbly table in the kitchen's corner, messy, half eaten unpalatable food. Virginia, half-tipsy, lit a cigarette and poured herself another glass of cheap white wine while Chuck excused himself to go watch television football. It didn't take long until he began cursing the modulating ghosts in the picture. Now, Virginia's nightly lecture series was about to resume.

"What the hell ya mean taking off like ya did?" Virginia began.

Bill closed his eyes and took a deep breath of air. "Mom, I did what I had to do. Meant no disrespect."

"You really hurt your mama, ya took my little boy. I, I cried for days."

"Mother, I'm grown up now."

"Billy," Virginia whined as she placed her arms in a cradling position, holding an invisible infant. "I don't care if yur fifty years old. Y'all always be mama's little boy."

Bill's gut wrenched. Like flash bulb going off in a darkened room, he understood. It was classic, right out of his psychology class. His mother was playing the same bullshit psycho-sicko game she always played, trying to reduce him to his helpless state. He felt like vomiting.

"Like, I blew it with Katarina, you'll be happy to know." Bill wanted to change the subject, fast.

"Told ya years 'go she's a bitch! Mamas know these things."

"Mother, I screwed up. It's not about her. I can't control my damn emotions."

"There, there, dear," Virginia said, shaking her head, following a smile that lasted, at most, a tenth of a second. "You'll find someone else. Lots o' fish in da sea."

"Mother, like, do you think for one minute that I stand a chance of having a successful relationship? With anyone?" Bill looked deep inside himself while his mother looked at him with her usual holier than thou expression. She loved to play psychological games, one-upsmanship she called it.

"I don't even know who I am. I have all these feelings, out of control. The more I try to move forward in my life, the more I screw up. I don't know what to do, how to be. Other guys seem to do fine with girls. I've never even kissed with passion. I'm a tangle of feelings, no place to go, no one to love. In a crowd of people, I'm the one sitting in a corner, alone, like, no friends, no real social skills. I..." Bill looked away, his body began trembling from an inner core. "Jeez mom, like, why didn't ya teach me the ways of the world?"

"I did! Ya never listened!" Virginia retorted, smashing her cigarette into an over-filled ashtray. Several stale butts fell to the table, then to the dark green linoleum floor.

"No, ma! You didn't teach me, ya just made me wrong, lecture after lecture! Gawd, if I was going to blow it with her, like, it shouldn't have been because I'm an out of control kid! I'm twenty-one gawd-damn years old!"

"Go to hell!"

"Yeah, that's what it really boils down to doesn't it. Did it ever occur to you, I..." Bill looked away and clamped his jaw tightly closed. Then he looked back into his mother's eyes. They were hard, demanding, without compassion, without love.

Noisily, Bill got up from the table and walked to the kitchen sink. Then after staring out the window, at the weather beaten side of the neighbor's house for several uncomfortable minutes, he began washing dishes, the chore that was always his. He hated it. But he had to do something, anything to distance himself from her. Virginia lit another cigarette, grabbed her half-empty glass of wine and stomped out of the room.

As Bill washed, dried and put away the dishes, just like old times, he tried to escape by thinking about Katarina. He wanted to pretend, imagine a wonderful life with her. But now he couldn't. A stabbing pain entered the left side of his chest while tears flowed freely. But he wasn't about to make a sound.

"Billy, bring me more wine!" Virginia yelled from the living room.

Bill wiped his face on a clean paper napkin then picked up the nearly empty bottle, remembering what it was like not having a life, being a servant to Her Majesty the Queen. As he walked into the living room and began pouring, the L.A. Rams made another touchdown against the Oakland Forty-Niner's.

Chuck slammed his beer can down onto the rickety coffee table next to his chair. The morning's paper fell to the floor as he jumped to his feet. "Did ya see that! Did ya see that!" He hollered, his voice getting louder and louder, hurting everyone's ears.

Bill hated football.

"Where's Susan?" Bill asked after the room had returned to normal.

"Who cares!" Virginia uttered with the signs of too much to drink, not looking up from her knitting. "Only comes 'round when it's time to eat. Ya know, da little whore is probably banging da kid next door. Da thanks I get!"

"Mom, what's going on?"

"Nothin', dear, absolutely nothin'."

Bill sat down and slid back into a shredded tan love seat that the family dog had claimed as its own. Spanky, the family's shorthaired terrier opened an eye, sniffed Bill's left hand then resumed his evening nap.

Bill looked around the tiny living room in dismay. Nothing was different, the same dark dusty pictures hanging on faded walls. The same ratty furniture, the same cigarette burnt carpet, only now with more holes. Piles of old magazines and newspapers cluttered the corner next to a dilapidated piano that he once tried hard to learn to play.

"Shit!" Chuck shouted, jumping up, pounding the side of the television, making the lines in the picture worse.

Bill thought about how many times he'd fixed that television, a 1948 Hallicrafters. The problem was simple, too much cigarette tar in the tuner. Tomorrow, he'd go down the street to Papel Brother's and buy some contact cleaner. The operation would take, at most, fifteen minutes, giving the old box another month or two of life.

Bill looked at his parents, both sitting, like years past, doing the same boring things they always did, alone, each in isolated rage. Why was he here again? He quietly went to the kitchen telephone and called Debbie.

"Billy? What's it like? I mean to be away from here?" Susan asked the next morning over chocolate shakes at Newberry's soda fountain in Atlantic Square. Bill and Susan had the fountain to themselves even though the rest of the store was already busy. There was only one fountain clerk on duty, busy counting the morning's change and filling the cash register, getting ready for a bustling day ahead.

"Hard, Sis, like, life's not easy."

"Got to be better than here."

"Yeah."

"Can I come and live with you, Billy?"

Bill looked at Susan with a start. "That bad?" It never dawned on him that his sister might be living a life of horror, too.

"I hate them! Like you, all I get is lectures. They never listen to me." Susan turned back to her shake. In anger, she tried to suck the thick liquid.

Bill closed his eyes in thought. He heard what Susan had said and he understood. He also knew that Susan was very rebellious, much more so than himself. Slowly, Bill spooned several mouthfuls of his shake. The taste was disappointing, certainly not as good as he remembered.

"Gonna run away, like you."

"Please don't! Ya gotta stay in school, kiddo. Your passport to a better life is education. Besides, you know that mom and dad will never let you out of the house. After you graduate, somehow, I'll help you leave, if that's what you still want."

"Not smart like you, bro. Two more years, can't do it."

"Ya must! I'm not going to lecture you. But somehow ya must, ya gotta have that high school diploma."

Susan sucked the last of her shake, noisily pulling air through the end of the straw. Then she turned back to Bill, smacking her lips. "Mom told me what happened between you and Katarina. Said ya dropped the little whore like a hot potato."

"How could she say that? She doesn't know! She, like, must have been drunk when she told you that."

"She's always drunk! So, what happened?"

Bill looked deep into Susan's blue eyes. He was certain she wouldn't understand. "Let's just say I messed up and leave it at that, okay?"

"I can keep a secret. You always told me everything."

Bill looked away as the counter lurched suddenly beneath his elbows. The clerk had slammed the cash register drawer closed. Then without thought he turned back to Susan. "Sis, I scared Katarina, okay. All I wanted was a kiss. But I got too aggressive, of all the foolish…"

"Did she scream?" Susan asked, looking at Bill with the understanding of a sixteen-year-old.

"Not really. But she doesn't want to see me any more."

"If she loves you, it won't matter."

"What? Like, how can ya say that? I don't think you understand."

"Maybe, but I break up with Ron all the time. Then a week later we're back together like nothin' happened."

Bill smiled at Susan's innocence.

"Why don't ya just go tell her you're sorry, for Christ's sakes."

"Did that."

"She still won't talk to you?"

"She talks to me, ya know like a friend, but, not a girlfriend."

"She'll get over it!"

Bill shook his head, side to side.

Friday night, two days after Christmas, Debbie picked Bill up for an evening of skating at the Pasadena Ice Rink, just like old times. Then following their invigorating evening on the ice, they joined other friends at Bob's Big Boy for hamburgers, fries and soft drinks. Bill admitted to everyone that there was no Bill and Katarina. But he didn't offer any details. Sensing Bill's pain no one asked.

Shortly after eleven, after Bill exchanged good-byes with his comrades, Debbie invited him to see the city lights from Mount Wilson.

"Really thought it was sweet of you, helping that little boy learn to skate like you did." Debbie began as she drove her recently purchased red '59 Ford Fairlane.

"A pleasure. After all, that's how I started. Someone helped me."

"But, don't you realize, out of a rink filled with people you were the only one who took time with him."

Bill smiled.

"You're truly a nice guy." Debbie leaned over and kissed Bill on the cheek.

"So ya gonna to audition for that job with the Disney Studios?" Debbie asked as she turned onto Angeles Crest Highway from Foothill Boulevard.

"Given it a lot of thought." Bill wasn't completely sure. He didn't want to admit that, just like old times, he was confused and he feared that no matter what choices he made, life would remain painful.

"Well?"

"Guess I'm going back to Colorado for one more semester," Bill confessed, shyly.

"Shit! Should have known. Billy, you're more fickle than my senile old grandmother!"

Bill sat, staring at oncoming car lights, saying nothing.

"She that damn important?"

"It's not Katarina. I've blown that for good, you'll be happy to know. It's Professor Watley and his wife, Eileen. I feel really good about these people. They've offered me room and board in exchange for housekeeping duties."

Debbie glanced at Bill several times, trying to keep her eyes on the road, while passing a green Volkswagen Beetle.

"Professor Watley is the type of man I want to be someday. He understands so much. And, he makes me think. Eileen, well, she's a magnificent lady, kind, gentle, caring. She teaches Anthropology at the University. The Watley's live in a house that people like you and I dream about. No, they're not rich. But they know quality, even in the little things. Deb, like, let's face it, I'm a slob. Oh, yeah, I may play and love classical music. But I have no real culture. I think I can learn a lot from these people. This may be my only chance to climb out of the pits. So, I've decided to accept their offer, at least until June."

Below a barrage of radio and television antennae flashing their red beacons into the darkness of night, Debbie parked her car in a turnout overlooking the Los Angeles basin. She and Bill stepped from the car and quietly walked to the edge of a huge cliff yielding a magnificent panorama. There was a gentle breeze and the fragrance of fresh pine laid lightly in the midnight air. Below, lights sparkled like stars in a desert sky for hundreds of square miles.

"Look, ya can see the lights on Catalina!" Bill pointed excitedly.

"Wow! Don't think I've ever seen it this clear." Debbie put her arm around Bill's waist then laid her head on his shoulder, taking in the view.

"Miss ya already, you know that." Debbie whispered. A hidden tear fell from her cheek.

"Yeah."

"We've been through a lot, you and I."

"I'll say.

"Billy?"

"Yeah?"

"Want ya to know, anytime you want to come back, you have a family here. I may not be cultured, but…"

"Whadaya, like, trying to say, Deb."

"Ya know damn well what I'm trying to say!"

"Deb, I do care about you. And…"

Debbie turned before Bill could finish his sentence. She walked back to her car, got her purse, pulled out a cigarette and lit it. Bill followed.

"I'll remember our summers together for a long time, ya know. Our trips to Disneyland, Knotts Berry Farm, sunbathing at Huntington Beach, water skiing at Lake Arrowhead. I, I don't want those times to end," Debbie said, then blowing her smoke across Bill's face.

"Those days were special." Bill smiled while fanning Debbie's smoke. Even though he tolerated smoking, it was not something he liked or approved of.

"I, I love you," Debbie whispered, staring into Bill's big blue eyes. She raised up on her tiptoes and kissed him.

Bill surprised himself. He kissed Debbie in return, the kind of kiss that he hoped one day would be Katarina's.

"Oh, oh my gawd." Bill voice quivered. His breath was suddenly uneven and his body quaked.

"Make love to me." Debbie tightened her grip, pulling Bill even closer, sliding her right hand down and into his pants, making certain he was interested. Then, very quietly, she opened the back seat door of her car and crawled in.

About one o'clock, after Bill had all but exhausted himself, Debbie asked Bill to drive her home.

"Got my new place."

"Oh? Where?"

"Highland Park, in the hills."

"You actually went through with it?"

"Yup."

Debbie's place was a one-bedroom white stucco duplex removed some distance from what was obviously a larger estate, perhaps fifty years old. The dim street lamps showed that the front yard was badly in need of weeding. The picket fence looked ready to fall over from the weight of dried grapevines. As they entered the front door, a tiny orange kitten panicked for cover.

Bill couldn't help noticing that Debbie's living room was unlike anything he'd ever seen. Dimly lit, the walls were painted black. The windows were covered with tie-dyed sheets. Long strands of dark green plastic beads closed off the doorways. The furniture, at least what there was, was obviously second rate hand-me-downs, augmented with wax stained apple crates. There were many candles, some on old news print, others mounted in brass holders of far-eastern origin. On the wall, in between the two front windows, was an overpowering picture of a Hindu Yogi in meditation. Everything in the room seemed to focus on that picture.

"You've given up Catholicism?" Bill asked.

"Yeah, guess so." Debby replied as her face turned pink.

"Sounds like you're not sure, Deb." Bill chuckled. "But I think questioning one's beliefs is a good thing."

"Start a fire?" Debbie asked pointing to an earthen hearth as she walked to her stereo. She flicked the power switch and then mounted the latest Beatles album, *Hard Day's Night*. The needle noisily scratched its way into the first track. Bill thought she should show her albums a little more respect.

"Sure, but it's really late. I should get going." Bill gathered some kindling and lit it with the aid of lighter fluid. Then he threw on several scraps of pine construction material.

"Ever smoke grass before?" Debbie asked while lighting a stick of incense, then the half dozen candles sitting on an apple crate just below her Guru.

"Er, why, no. Have you?"

"Been saving this for a special occasion." Debbie opened a jewelry box sitting on a lamp stand next to the davenport. From it she pulled a plastic bag filled with pot and a pack of cigarette papers.

"But isn't that stuff dangerous?"

"Naw, that's an old wives tale."

"Sounds like ya know."

"I've smoked the stuff a few times. Believe me, it's harmless. Your parents drink, don't they."

"Yeah."

Debbie finished rolling the joint while Bill watched. He knew she must have done this more than a few times by the certainty in her fingers. Debbie lit it, then took a long continuous drag and held her breath. Then she handed the thing to Bill. Not knowing what to do, he followed her lead. The smoke burned his throat and he began to cough severely.

"I can see you've never done this before." Debbie laughed at Bill. "Inhale, slowly and gently." She demonstrated with exaggerated detail.

After Bill calmed down, Debbie handed the joint back to him and smiled. It was better this time. Again, Bill was on the verge of coughing, but didn't.

"Better?"

Bill nodded.

Together, they finished the joint in silence and sat enjoying the subtle warmth that was beginning to radiate from the hearth. For Bill, Debbie's living room quickly transformed into a gentle place. Even the music had taken on a magical aliveness.

"A little wine will help your throat," Debbie offered. Then she went to the kitchen and brought back two ordinary kitchen glasses, a corkscrew and a bottle of sweet red wine that she had chilled for this occasion.

Bill removed the cork and poured the smooth liquid into glasses. They toasted each other, then drank.

Bill looked at Debbie. She was so beautiful and sexy. Her dark Latin eyes sparkled in the fire light. Reaching over and taking her into his arms, he kissed her, passionately.

"I have another treat in store for you," Debbie said, gently pushing Bill away following several minutes of torrid embrace. Then she presented another plastic bag filled with a crushed green substance and began to roll it into a fresh cigarette paper.

"Do we need any more?"

"This isn't grass. It's Damiana, an herb that's normally made into tea. Smoking it by itself does nothing. But when you're already high, well, see for yourself." Debbie lit the huge joint, took a drag and then handed it to Bill.

Bill inhaled. "What a rush!" He choked out as he fell helplessly to the floor.

Slowly and respectfully, Debbie removed Bill's shirt and trousers. Then, with strong hands, she began massaging his shoulders. Slowly, she released the tension in every muscle. Then, deliberately, she worked her way down his back, across his buttocks, then his legs. Bill could only lay there limp as a rag. He had never had a body massage before, but it was obvious Debbie knew what she was doing. She worked her way leisurely down to his feet and then back up onto the tops of his legs, carefully and intentionally avoiding private areas. She massaged his chest, his arms and then his scalp and face. Bill kept his eyes closed and flowed with the feeling. It was like he was on top of a cloud. He loved how she made him feel.

Finally, Bill felt Debbie's warm hand touch his penis, rubbing very smoothly and deliberately. Then, without even thinking, he pulled her on top of himself. Lying there, gently moving and kissing, he prayed this feeling would never stop.

Twelve

"What color would you like your room?" Eileen asked, walking into Bill's 'fix-it-up' basement apartment. Pywicket followed and jumped up onto Bill's new bed, lay down and immediately began licking her left paw in order to wash her face.

It was now January second, five days before the start of school. Bill had just set down his last box of personal belongings. The pot bellied stove sat dull red, reflecting its warmth from dirty walls. The toilet was running again, badly in need of repair.

"Jeez, haven't thought about it. Didn't even know for sure I was coming back," Bill said, walking into the bathroom, then jiggling the toilet handle several times. "Something bright and cheery, for sure."

Bill grabbed an aerosol can of orange scent air freshener and randomly sprayed several times, trying to remove the musty odor. "Achooo."

Like a shot, Pywicket jumped from the bed, scurried through the door and charged up the stairs.

"God-bless! Some place around here I've got some paint chips." Eileen said as she walked to a white enameled kitchen cabinet and rummaged through several drawers. "Here they are."

Bill held several paint chips to the light. He noticed that the room was originally beige. "Beige is okay. But I'm really partial to blues and greens."

"May I make a suggestion?"

"Please do."

"Warm White."

Bill looked at the paint chip, comparing it against the pure white counter top. "Looks like a slight hint of pink. Like, I don't know."

"Trust me on this one, you said bright and cheery. This is your color."

Under Pywicket's casual supervision, Bill spent the next three days patching, painting, cleaning, airing out his new quarters and moving in. Then, Sunday morning he went to church where he knew Katarina would be playing the organ. He wondered if the sight of her would make him reconsider the promise he made to Debbie.

Reverend Cain stepped to the pulpit, looked out and across to his congregation, then began the morning's sermon:

> How can humanity, in the face of the modern worldview, interpret the message of Christ?
>
> We've never confirmed that political, social or economic events were performed by supernatural powers, such as gods, angels, or even demons. These events are always attributed to human wisdom or stupidity.
>
> Science is always changing. No worldview of yesterday, today or tomorrow can be definitive. Therefore, we seem to be involved in a world of becoming. Becoming what? We can only imagine.
>
> Thanks to men like Aristotle, modern peoples can only align themselves to rational order. Therefore, we cannot acknowledge miracles because they do not fit the lawful order of things.
>
> Can it only be wishful thinking that allows the Bible to be upheld?
>
> Perhaps.
>
> But, whatever you believe, the teachings of Christ present us with a challenge to be something. The message of Christ

is the methodology of opening one's heart to repentance. We don't need the modern worldview to understand it!

Love. Friendship. Faithfulness. These are not perceived by the rational, psychological or the anthropological mind. They are perceived through open readiness to personal encounters.

Bill looked at Katarina. She was sitting quietly behind the pipe organ console, listening. Her hands were folded gracefully in her lap and her eyes were closed. She wore an ankle length dress in her favorite color, pastel blue.

"God, I'd climb the highest mountain for her. Please, God, hear the ache of my soul. Like, show me what to do," Bill uttered silently to himself. "How can I overcome the weight of my past?"

Katarina looked up and glanced at Bill, then smiled. Bill reciprocated.

"Saw you in church yesterday," Katarina said walking up to Bill on the sidewalk in front of the Sibell-Wolle Fine Arts building. The afternoon was cold and overcast. But snow was not in the forecast, that would come later in the week.

"Saw you, too," Bill acknowledged, smiling, stopping, adjusting a worn-out glove, trying to keep the fingers on his left hand from freezing.

"Was hoping you'd stay after a little. I wanted to talk."

"Oh?" A twinge of fear surged through Bill.

"Our choir director is looking for some instrumental soloists. I took the liberty of giving him your name. That okay?"

"Okay? Of course it's okay!" Bill said, his smile returning.

"Going to class?" Katarina asked.

"No. Going to the library, actually."

"Can I walk with you awhile?"

"Certainly!"

Bill and Katarina turned and began walking north toward the Norlin Library. Dry snow crunched loudly beneath their advance. One could smell the dryness in the air, dryness that occurred only this time of year.

"I'm not playing in the orchestra this semester," Katarina began as she reached into her purse for a tube of lip balm.

"Oh?"

"I'm singing the mezzo-soprano solo for Verdi's *Requiem* in May!" Katarina proudly announced.

"Well, I'll be. Was hoping you'd get the part."

"You were?" Katarina asked. Then she began gently rubbing balm onto both her lips.

"Of course, you've got a beautiful voice. You deserve it!"

"Thanks," Katarina returned shyly, glancing at Bill's smile. "So, y'all taking any more philosophy this semester?"

"No. Really don't have time, only got three more semesters before graduation. So, in addition to my music, I'm taking the core requirements for the College of Education. Ya know, Public Speaking, Educational Psychology, Intro. to Ed."

"How many units? Dare I ask?"

"Twenty."

"Wow! You're lucky you don't have a job."

"Well, I do, kinda."

"Billy!" Katarina stopped walking and looked into Bill's dark blue eyes. "I can't imagine, on top of twenty units."

"It's not as bad as it sounds. I'm doing domestic duties for a family in exchange for room and board. Actually, I think it's going to work out very well."

"You've moved off campus?"

"Yeah."

Katarina blinked her eyes several times, then forced herself to look away. Bill noticed.

"So, how was your Christmas? I assume you went home?" Bill asked, turning, beginning to walk once again.

"Wonderful," Katarina returned. She was glad Bill had taken the lead as she turned and followed. "Erik was home from Johns Hopkins. He asked about you."

"What? Like, what did you tell him?"

"That," Katarina hesitated, staring at the ground as she walked, "that we're still good friends."

"Katarina said that we're still good friends!" Bill beamed while setting the dinner table, waiting for Earl to get home. "I can't believe it! I don't know what to do?"

"You're not going to do a thing, Bill. You're going to wait a time with patience," Eileen returned.

"But?"

"Didn't you already blow round one because you were too aggressive?"

"Yeah."

"Let her set the tempo, Bill. This time, hear her needs."

"I guess I don't listen very well, do I," Bill said, walking over to the stove, checking his spaghetti sauce, making certain it wasn't sticking to the bottom of the pan.

"Believe it or not, you do better than most. You're a good tracker of people. The problem is, you let your own internal shit override the obvious. When you do that, you lose contact, you lose control."

"Whadaya mean?"

"Let me put it this way. In your gut you know what's real, what others need, what they're going through. But something inside you overrides that core knowledge. When you do that, you lose touch. As an example, you haven't heard Katarina's needs. Instead, you've been trying to overwhelm her with your own. As you've seen, the result is a relationship that's unstable."

"Whew." Bill blew out his breath with considerably more force than usual.

"Bill, the wise man knows when to move forward, when to back up and when to stand still. His movements are balanced by both his needs and the needs of those around him."

Bill didn't say anything for long time. Instead, he stood leaning against the kitchen counter. He looked at the dinner table, then at Eileen, then the floor.

"This afternoon seemed, what's a good word? Precious?" Bill resumed, looking back at Eileen with moist eyes. "I don't want to, like, destroy it. I'm scared."

"There's only one thing to do. Take it from a woman. Put away your own agenda for a while. Simply make her feel warm, worthy and welcome."

Thirteen

"Ahhhh!" Bill was frightened awake by a very lucid dream. He was standing over a very large pool of water. His professor, Earl Watley, was standing to his left watching him make ripples in the water's surface with a very long wooden pole. Suddenly there was a loud commotion somewhere south of where he stood. Bill dropped his pole, running to investigate. In a large open field he found several motorcycle police officers milling about, beating on things with their nightsticks. One of the officers, a scary older black woman, saw Bill and demanded that he go back to the pool. As Bill turned and walked, she followed. Then, back at the pool, she took a drinking glass from her oversized black leather jacket and shoved it deep into the water. Removing it, she offered it to Bill and smiled a toothy grin. Enchanted, Bill found himself compelled to drink until the pool was empty. Without warning, in the center of the remaining pit, Bill saw a hairy beast staring menacingly at him.

"Here ya go!" Earl exclaimed, walking across the living room to a stack of books lying on the floor waiting to be re-shelved. He pulled one from near the bottom of the pile and held it out toward Bill.

"*Fairy Tales*, Brother's Grimm?" Bill asked, scratching his head.

"Read the story, *Iron Hans*!" Earl commanded, turning and leaving the room.

Bill sat down on the davenport. Then, finding the story, he spent the next fifteen minutes reading. Pywicket sat purring at his feet.

"I don't get it," Bill confessed as he walked toward his professor, who was getting ready to go outside to shovel snow.

"You see any parallels between the story and your life?"

Bill was taken back. "Don't think so."

"Come, help me for a while. Let's talk."

Bill went to his basement apartment, getting his coat, hat and gloves, then he followed Earl outside and into the garage to get a snow shovel. The afternoon was cold and gray. Snow was gently falling at the rate of about an inch every four or five hours. There were already three inches in the driveway from the previous night and Earl wanted to get a head start on the coming storm. It promised to be a big one.

"What do fairy tales have to do with anything?" Bill asked, sinking his shovel deep into a snow bank next to the garage, then adjusting his gloves. He barely remembered a few of the tales from his childhood. They didn't make much sense and didn't remain long in consciousness.

"They're stories about life," Earl answered, nodding his head. "Many about the inner working of the human psyche.

Bill picked up his shovel and began scraping a small section of the driveway clean. Under the fresh snow was a thick layer of frozen slush. "Damn!"

"For you, Bill, I think *Iron Hans* is particularly apropos."

"Why?" Bill asked. He stopped scraping and turned, giving Earl his undivided attention.

"Because of your dream."

"You mean, Katarina is the princess, I'm the prince?"

"I think there's more to it than that." Earl replied while attempting to chip ice from the base of a trashcan that was frozen to the driveway.

"The hairy beast at the bottom of the lake in my dream, is that the Wild Man?"

"Yup!"

"So what's it mean?"

"What do you think it means?"

Bill didn't immediately answer. While running the story through his mind, he turned and began shoveling once again. Then, following several uneasy minutes in concentration, he turned back towards Earl and replied, "It means the Wild Man is loose, and, like, I'm in a heap of trouble."

"Well, that's certainly one way of looking at it," Earl said, laughing. "It could also mean that your life will turn out grand and glorious."

"And I get the princess, right?"

"Bill, you have a one-track mind. That's for certain!"

Bill laughed. He honestly believed he could endure anything if Katarina was at the end of the tunnel.

"Fairy tales are metaphorical maps of how we do our lives," Earl continued. "Times long ago they were used as teaching tools. For instance, the Prince is a normal adolescent, somewhat rowdy, a little out of control, trying desperately to be a social being. The King and Queen represent the mother and father who feel the need to control their young son. At a selfish level, they really don't want their kid to be apart from them, to grow up or leave home. However, in reality, there is a natural child lying latent in the Prince's unconscious, a voice crying in the wilderness. Fairy tales call it a Wild Man or a Wild Woman depending on gender.

"Sometime, usually when the Prince becomes a sexual being, that Wild Man wants to be free. He doesn't want to be encumbered by social conditioning. But as fairy tales go, the parents lock him up in a cell or dungeon. The key is held by the mother, in a secret place, her bosom, under her pillow—wherever. Now, the once loving nurturing parent is seen as wicked or evil."

"Sounds a lot like my life!"

Earl chuckled, then continued. "Ultimately, according to the story, one of two things must happen. The Prince either obeys, or he disobeys. If he obeys his parents, keeping the Wild Man in prison, he can never become a King, a fully functioning human male. So the story ends. However, if he disobeys, he has the fight of his life. He has his own sexuality, his own passion, his own aliveness to contend with. If he's successful and finds balance, he earns the right to be the new King and takes the Golden Haired Princess as his bride."

"And, lives happily ever after." Bill added, shouting above the noise of an approaching snowplow.

"Well, we don't really know that," Earl shouted back, laughing. "Most fairy tales end when the Prince and Princess marry. Many end with someone getting badly punished. It's only the modern unenlightened storyteller, who adds bullshit like, 'And, they lived happily ever after.' Read *Cinderella*."

"So, what you're saying is, to get Katarina I must let the Wild Man loose?"

"In so many words, yeah," Earl returned in a more normal voice.

"But the Wild Man is what's gotten me into all this trouble!"

"Not so, Bill! Denial of the Wild Man is what's gotten you into trouble."

"Denial? I don't, like, understand."

"Bill, think of it this way. The Wild Man is your natural self, unconditioned by your parents and society. It's the magic in your life. It's the property that makes you unique. Denial of this fact is what keeps your spirit in bondage, what makes you suffer, what makes you act inappropriately."

"Now I'm, like, really confused!"

"It's not so hard to comprehend, really," Earl replied, understanding Bill's dilemma. "Look at that lot across the street. What do you see?"

Bill turned and looked. "Just an empty lot, sir. What's there to see?"

"You don't see the pine trees, the undergrowth?"

"Well, yeah. I see those. But it's just an undeveloped lot."

"Undeveloped? Shame on you!" Earl retorted. "That lot is Wildness! It's bursting with nature. It's wild because society hasn't manicured it yet. In human terms, it has no ego, no shadow, nothing to defend."

Bill stood perplexed. He wanted to understand, but knew he was missing the point.

"You don't understand because you have something to defend!" Earl announced, sharply. "Let me try to explain. You've taken psychology. You've heard of ego and shadow, I'm sure."

Bill nodded his head.

"Both ego and shadow are learned behaviors, behaviors your parents and society began pounding into your head at birth. Ego is what you've learned to present to the world, hopefully in a positive and healthy way. Bill, the good guy, the competent guy, the loving companion, the superman. Shadow, on the other hand, is all the repressed parts of your personality, the parts of yourself that you were taught to keep hidden. Bill, the insecure guy, the weak guy, the incompetent, the failure. Since both ego and shadow are learned behaviors, both are illusions, both kill your soul."

"My soul certainly seems to have gone away," Bill reflected.

"But it doesn't have to be that way."

"Really?"

"Bill, consider ego and shadow as two opposing tensions of consciousness. We know from studying physics that anytime two opposite polarities interact, a dipole is created. We also know, within the dipole field there's a null point balanced between the two tensions."

"Like the fulcrum of a teeter-totter." Bill interjected. He could easily see a childhood teeter-totter in his mind's eye, one end of the board high in the air, the opposite end resting on the ground. The fulcrum was a pipe attached to the teeter-totter's center.

"Right!" Earl returned. "One end of the teeter-totter is ego, the other is shadow. The null point, or fulcrum, is where the teeter-totter balances, not moving, even when the system is in violent motion. Using a Buddhist metaphor, the null point is the void, the uncreated, the point of infinite possibility. It is the point where neither ego nor shadow exists. It can be likened to the quietness of the newborn reaching for its first breath of air, before the roller coaster of life begins.

"Let me expand the analogy," Earl continued. "Ego and shadow can be likened to a manicured garden. Ego grows above the ground for all to see while shadow grows beneath, unobserved. Yet, as every gardener knows, there exists a wildness that remains just outside the manicuring process. We know this absolutely, because when we don't manicure wildness, it eventually grows into a forest. Wildness is unconditional! It's the magic that makes life possible. It's the essence of creativity, expanding toward infinity.

"The same is true for your soul, Bill. It's naturally wildness. And in that wildness you are the most alive, the most child-like, and the most creative. It's only social conditioning that makes you something else."

Earl walked over to Bill and placed his hand on Bill's shoulder. "We can return to wildness by letting go of either ego or shadow. Since the two form a dipole of the same wave function, when one ceases to exist, so does the other. The easiest way to do this is through self-forgiveness, meditation and non-attachment."

"Is wildness and the Wild Man the same thing? Bill asked following several moments of self-reflection.

"Yeah."

"You make it sound very simple," Bill exclaimed, thrusting his shovel back into the snow. "But, what, what if the prince fails?"

"He dies!" Earl laughed.

Bill stopped. He turned and looked at Earl, long and hard. "Fuck!"

"Here's the good news. You let the Wild Man loose the day you drove from your parents' driveway! Here's the bad news. In almost all fairy tales, the turning point is made possible only by means of magic. The Prince must learn a secret craft, sacrifices must be made, outside forces must be negotiated with."

"But there's no magic, not really."

"So certain, are you?

"Not certain about anything, least not anymore."

"Good place to be! You have less to unlearn."

Bill's facial expression turned to confusion.

"Do you think it's a coincidence that you're standing right here right now in Boulder, Colorado, shoveling snow?"

"Huh?"

"What if I told you that the Wild Man brought you."

"But." Bill stood dumbfounded. Finally he said, "I'm sorry, Sir, like, I don't know what to do with all this."

"Well, let me ask you a question. If you followed the advice of your family and friends, would you be standing in front of me right now?"

"No."

"Then, why are you here?"

"Something I have to do."

"An inner urge? The voice of the Wild Man? Magic?"

Bill looked away trying to collect his thoughts. Thoughts once polished brilliant by dreams and expectation were now in the retort of reality. "I came to Boulder because I thought I could find love in my life. I'm staying because, like, I need a good education. I think I can get it here."

"Bullshit!"

"Huh?"

"Bill, what is the reason you're here? What is your passion? What is the wildness of your soul trying to tell you? Look deep inside yourself before answering."

"I haven't the foggiest, not anymore."

"Then we both fail."

Fourteen

"Spiritual Enlightenment! That's my passion!" Bill shouted to his mentor the next afternoon, waving his arms wildly in the air, looking up from cleaning cinders out of the living room hearth. "That's what I want more than anything!"

Earl walked toward Bill with a giant grin, almost laughing at Bill's enthusiasm. Pywicket raised her small head and looked at Bill like he'd just lost his mind.

"My Pappy talked a lot about it when I was growin' up. He went to India, Tibet, the Gobi. Someday, I'm going to do that."

Earl turned and selected a pipe, one of many racked on the fireplace mantle. Slowly, with the precision of a Swiss watchmaker, he cleaned it, packed it, lit it and puffed it. A sweet aroma quickly filled the living room. Then he looked back at Bill, smacking his lips nonchalantly. "So, what's spiritual enlightenment? Why do you want it?"

"It's seeing things as they really are! Being free from all the suffering in my life!" Bill answered, his enthusiasm undaunted.

"Being able to leap tall buildings in a single bound?" Earl added, laughing.

"Why not?" Bill didn't understand his mentor's humor. He scratched his head, then looked at Earl.

"You don't have any idea of what you're asking, do you?" Earl took several more puffs on his pipe.

"Of course I know! Since I was eight years old, like, I've prayed for spiritual enlightenment."

"Do you remember anything we talked about yesterday?"

"Huh?" Bill walked over to the davenport and sat down. Pywicket immediately jumped up and claimed Bill's lap. "Sir, I don't understand what you're talking about. Enlightenment is about love, compassion, rising above the bullshit in the world. Enlightenment is about being like Christ or Buddha."

"You're naïve."

While petting Pywicket's head, Bill looked at Earl with dismay. With a sigh, he was totally lost for words.

"Bill, let's start simply. For you, enlightenment is about surrender. It's about completions. Let me explain. Think about your life for a moment. You get up in the morning, you make your breakfast. You eat your breakfast. Then, you wash and put away your dishes. Each task is started, enjoyed and carried to completion. It's a cycle that never ends. But consider, if you didn't complete each task thoroughly, eventually there would be a hell of a mess."

"I guess so." Bill chuckled. Pywicket looked into Bill's eyes, annoyed by the vibrating lap.

"So, Bill, what stops you?"

"Huh? Stops me? From what?"

"From being done with your feelings of failure, for a start."

"Oh, that! Well, think that's pretty obvious. When I'm alone in my room at night, about all I can think about is my loss. If I see her during the day, it's worse."

"Why does that devastate you so much?"

"Earl, you know. She's my dream, my reason for living!"

"Okay, let me reword what I heard you say. Without Katarina your dream cannot reach completion."

"Yeah."

"And now you have all these feelings, feelings that may never be realized. What are you doing with those feelings, Bill?"

"Nothing I can do, try to live each day, one day at a time. Let go of my expectations."

"Is it working?"

"Need to give it more time."

"Bullshit!"

"Bullshit?" Bill looked at Earl in shock. Annoyed by Bill's constant movement, Pywicket stretched, jumped to the floor and walked leisurely toward the kitchen.

"How much time do you need?"

"Dunno?"

"What if I were to tell you that, since you've never surrendered your insatiable demands on reality, since your feelings have never reached a state of completion, day by day parts of your soul are slipping away, day by day you're shoving your aliveness deep inside your shadow self. What's left of you is ashes. Bill, given the road you're walking right now, at ninety, your pain will still control you."

Bill was struck dumb. He stared at the floor in agony.

"I know you're confused. There seems to be no solution to your problem. Like the riddle I gave you some months ago, you're precariously standing on the point of a needle. Below you in all directions is the abyss. Above you is nothing. If you jump from the needle, continuing to pursue her, you'll fall to your death. If you stay where you are, not doing anything, you'll fail. You might as well not have been born."

"Then, like, I'm doomed." Bill tightened his jaw while rapidly shaking his head. His confusion was quickly turning into anger.

"Thinking like that is your mistake, yours alone."

Bill stood up as if to bolt for the door.

"Bill, stop! Breathe deeply. Calm yourself. I'm your friend! I'm not going to write you off, not like your parents did."

"Huh?"

"Let's try an experiment. Let's see if I can help you take one small step forward. I'd like you to get Katarina's pictures and all her letters, every one."

"Right now?"

"Please."

Bill left the room for several minutes. Upon his return Earl was lighting a fire in the living room hearth. Pywicket was now scent-marking Earl's ankles.

"No! Can't do that! I won't! Please don't make me burn anything!" Bill shouted. Waves of adrenaline shot through his veins as he turned to run. Pywicket panicked from the room, terrified by loud voices.

"Bill. Settle down! Burning them is no solution." Earl said quietly. "Too bad life's not that simple."

Bill had to sit down on the floor from his knees trembling.

"Bill, you once asked if you could start over with her. To start over, you must emotionally complete the cycle that's already in place. You must surrender your grief and let it go. You must forgive yourself. So, here's what I want you to do. Sit here for a while, look at her pictures, read her letters. Close your eyes and remember. Remember everything, the good times, the bad times. When you're ready to go on, I'll be back." Earl turned and walked from the room with a very stern look on his face.

Several hours later Earl returned. Without saying a word, he walked over to his stereo system and turned it on. Then he placed a recording of Puccini's *La Bohème* on the record player, adjusted the volume control and walked nonchalantly out of the room.

Bill loved this opera; he knew the love story well. And somehow, magically, as the plot began to unfold he saw himself as Rodolfo, Katarina as Mimi. But when the dissonant climax came, announcing the anguish of Rodolfo's loss in Mimi's death, spontaneously, like burying his own lover in the ground, Bill cried and cried.

Fifteen

"Noticed you've been spending some time with Katarina," Peggy began. She was smiling as Bill walked up to her outside the Norlin Library one Saturday evening in mid-February. It was cold, windless and still. Moonlight illuminated a fringe of clouds cascading down the western slopes promising snow showers by early morning. Peggy had been invited by her friend Trudy to hear a Yogi from India speak to a small group of friends. She, in turn, had invited Bill. Together they turned and began walking.

"Well, yes and no," Bill confessed. "Yeah, we're talking again, but that's all, I'm afraid."

"Still, it's a start!" Peggy reached down and took Bill's right hand into her left. "This okay?"

"Of course it's okay, Peg." Bill smiled and gave Peggy's hand a firm squeeze. Even though their hands were gloved, her closeness was fully appreciated. Bill began adjusting his coat collar with his left hand.

"I'm not coming on to you. I think you're a really neat guy and I'm glad for our friendship."

"Can't have too many of those."

"For sure," Peggy agreed. "Bill, you seem a lot happier this semester. You saw, what's her name, uh, Debbie?"

Surprised, Bill looked at Peggy curiously out of the corner of his eye.

"It's okay, you don't have to tell me. I know already."

"Know what?"

"That you made it with her, now you're having second thoughts."

"That obvious?"

"Bill, I can read you like a book, any girl with half a brain can."

Bill pulled his hand from Peggy's.

"Come, come. It's not that bad. I'm your friend, remember? Friends share things."

"Things?"

"Yeah! Ya know openness, intimacy, vulnerability."

Bill let out a big sigh. "Guess I'm confused."

"About what?"

"Peg, I can't be your boyfriend."

"Uh, don't get me wrong! Don't think words like intimacy and vulnerability means that a girl is inviting sex!"

Bill didn't know how to respond to such a remark, so he didn't.

"I'm not, ya know. Anyway, I'm glad you and Katarina are becoming friends."

"Guess I want more. Still have very strong feelings for her."

"Ya can't have what you want without the foundation of a very strong friendship."

"Thought I had that, Peg."

"Ya did, before you violated her trust."

"Huh? Like, who told you that?"

"You did, Bill. You told me that the night of the Christmas dance, remember?"

"Oh, yeah."

Peggy turned back to Bill and reached out her right hand hoping Bill would take it. "Still afraid?"

"Yeah." Bill took Peggy's right hand into his left and resumed walking.

"Admitting you're afraid is part of being vulnerable," Peggy resumed, grinning. "It's about sharing one's heart. Us girls like that in our men."

"You do?" Bill questioned.

"Of course we do. Too many guys are unfeeling duds. Who wants a relationship with someone like that?"

"Interesting you should say that. My dad always says it's unmanly to show feelings or emotions."

Peggy started laughing.

"Why're ya laughing?" Bill asked, shaking his head.

"Because my father says the same thing. He's the most insensitive clod in the world! That's the reason my mother divorced him years ago."

"Divorced? Because he didn't show his feelings?"

"Well, I don't know all the details, just what my mom tells me. I was only ten when my parents broke up. But I see him several times a year. And even though I think he's happy to see me, he's neither demonstrative nor does he ever share his feelings. I know there's a bitter unhappy man behind his mask. His life is filled with drama and he finds fault with everything. I'm sure he has no friends."

"He's never remarried?"

"Doubt he ever will. There's no one he trusts. He has never learned to open his heart and be vulnerable."

"Except for Debbie, guess I've never had any real friends."

"And why is that?"

Bill scratched his head through his blue knit ski cap. "I guess, no one I can really trust."

"Really? You don't trust me?" Peggy asked.

"Well," Bill's face began turning red. He knew he'd just put himself on the spot. "Trust is, like, such a relative thing."

"Is it, Bill? Is it really? If you got drunk and thrown in jail, would you trust me to take care of your personal effects for a few hours and bail you out?"

Bill looked at Peggy quizzically, then replied. "Of course."

"But you wouldn't trust me with secrets of your heart?"

"Like, I don't think I'd trust anyone that far."

"I know, and that's your problem." Peggy's words made Bill's gut wrench.

"Bill, I trust you."

"Why?"

"Because you know what it's like to be hurt. You understand the anguish, the despair."

"What's that got to do with anything?"

"Unless I'm wrong about you, it's taught you some empathy."

Bill stopped walking. He turned and stared at Peggy. Her smile was radiant and her green eyes sparkled from the headlights of passing cars. Tiny wisps of fresh snow were now beginning to fall from a darkening sky. Two small children stood watching from the bay window of a nearby home, awaiting the arrival of an evening guest. Peggy placed her left index finger onto Bill's lips before he could speak. "Shush! Consider, if I share my heart with you and you don't like it, that's all I have."

Bill looked at Peggy with a touch of pain in his face. "I wouldn't betray you, not purposefully, Peg."

"Nor would I, you."

Bill and Peggy stopped talking as three other people approached. Together they all stood, waiting out a busy intersection. As they paused, Peggy gazed at the wet asphalt, wondering. She'd done some inquiring about Katarina with several of her friends.

"I want to tell you something," Peggy began after she and Bill had distanced themselves from the strangers, even though she wasn't certain how much to share. "I don't think Katarina would have rejected you, had you not scared her."

"I know." Bill said ruefully.

"Ya know, rumor has it that she doesn't date."

"I'm sure of it. I've never seen her hanging out with other guys even though it's obvious others are interested," Bill returned.

"Rumor has it, she was going with some guy about a year ago and he beat the shit out of her, sent her to the hospital with a broken collar bone. Her face was black and blue for weeks."

Stunned, Bill stopped walking. He withdrew his hand from Peggy's and stared into her eyes while his face began turning red with rage. "How do you know?"

"Friendship is about trust, please don't ask."

Bill closed his eyes and shook his head repeatedly. He wanted revenge. "Who was it? Who did such a thing?"

"The past is ashes," Peggy said quietly. "If you want her love, be her friend, earn her trust. Gandhi says, 'An eye for an eye makes the whole world blind!'"

Bill and Peggy arrived at a large suburban home where their meeting was soon to begin. As they approached, they encountered small groups of people hanging out in the front yard. The smell of pot permeated the still night air, a smell that was becoming increasingly familiar around the college campus as well as many of the local neighborhoods. Once inside the white picket fence, Peggy spent some time exchanging social gossip with Trudy and a small group of mutual friends. Then, just before eight o'clock, a young man stepped onto the porch and invited everyone inside so the meeting could start.

"Who's the kid?" Bill whispered to Trudy, jutting his chin toward a teenage boy seated upon a small stage at the far end of the room. The youth was obviously meditating.

"Yogi Ghi," Trudy replied with a proud and confident look on her face.

People hurried in and took whatever position in the room they could find. Except for a davenport and two recliner chairs, there was nothing else to sit on. So most everyone either stood along the walls or sat on the hardwood floor. A young man in his early twenties walked to the center of what was obviously an altar. He lit several candles, a rather large incense burner and greeted everyone with a warm welcome. Then, without further ado, he began chanting in the traditional Hindu tongue. Many of the invited guests joined the chant while a small group of musicians at the side of the room played unfamiliar instruments. Neither Peggy nor Bill had ever seen such instruments before, but they thoroughly enjoyed the sound.

Following the half an hour of preparation and introductions, Yogi Ghi spoke. His talk droned on for a little over an hour. His English was broken, but his message was clear. The universe is one consciousness, the individual was separated from that consciousness through his own doing, and finally, the way to return to the universal consciousness was though him. Simply, he was the path to enlightenment, right here and right now. No other way could or would work. When he was through speaking, he closed his eyes and returned to a meditative state. Then, the young man whom previously lead the chanting stood and led a group recitation and prayer. Finally, the musicians began playing their instruments and the chanting resumed without further direction.

"Well, what do ya think?" Trudy demanded, turning to Bill and Peggy. She was beaming.

"Interesting," Bill replied.

"That all? Just interesting," Trudy retaliated.

Bill turned and looked at Peggy, he knew he'd just blown it.

"You don't follow the precepts of the Guru, do you?" Trudy accused.

"I have my own path," Bill returned, sharply.

"Obviously not Yogi Ghi's path."

"No."

Trudy didn't say another word. She turned and walked briskly away from where Bill and Peggy stood.

"You seem to really have a way with women, huh, Bill."

"Like, ya want me to be honest, don't you?"

"Yeah, but, maybe a little less blunt."

Bill's smile flattened to embarrassment. "Suppose you're right."

"Excuse me, some refreshments?" a young girl in full hippie regalia asked, approaching Bill and Peggy with a tray holding lemonade and carrot cake.

"Certainly," Bill responded, waiting for Peggy to help herself, then selecting his own drink and piece of cake.

"Ugh, this tastes awful!" Bill whispered to Peggy.

"Health food, it's good for you." Peggy laughed.

"If it doesn't kill me first!" Bill gulped his cake and washed it down with lemonade.

"Sir? Are you a chela of Yogi Ghi?" a young man about Bill's age asked.

"No," Bill answered, trying to clear his throat.

"We have openings and classes will begin early next month. You begin with Yogi Ghi giving you your own personal mantra. Then you will learn meditation and proper breathing techniques. This will bring inner peace and harmony resulting in health and abundance in your life, all for the fee of two hundred and fifty dollars."

"That lets me out," Bill returned, cutting the young man off.

"Why?" The young man demanded, thinking someone would have to be stupid not to jump at the chance to study under his spiritual master.

"Can't afford it," Bill returned.

"It's only money, sir. Anyway, we have an easy payment plan if you need one."

"I'm here to go to school. Like, nothing is going to interfere with that." Suddenly, in the middle of his lie, Bill's gut wrenched. Spontaneously he realized, just like his mother, he'd say anything to get off the hook.

"Sir, you're missing the chance of a lifetime."

"No!" Bill returned very matter of fact, looking directly into the young man's eyes.

"Why?"

"Because I don't believe your Yogi Ghi has the answers I'm looking for," Bill answered.

"Okay, thank you for your honesty." The young man turned and began walking toward another couple.

"This is turning into a very strange evening, Bill. You okay?" Peggy asked.

"I'm fine."

"Fine? Ya know what that means?"

"What? What are you talking about?"

"FINE! It's an acronym for Fucked-up, Immature, Neurotic and Emotional."

"That's me!" Bill howled with laughter.

Sixteen

Bill's hands were black. His face was black. His hair was black. That was the price he had to pay for cleaning the oil-fired furnace in the basement. Still, he was happy to do it. He loved the Watleys and their magnificent home. He no longer felt like a boarder. Rather, he felt like their son.

After showering, shampooing his hair and shaving, and having put on clean clothes, Bill walked upstairs and into the Watley's kitchen. There, he poured himself a glass of fresh squeezed orange juice. It was the third Saturday in February and, having finished his chores, he was content to just lie around the house for the day.

"Bill, have you ever considered the way you dress?" Eileen asked as she entered the kitchen from the living room.

"What?" Bill wasn't certain he heard Eileen's question correctly.

"Look at you. Your pants are wrinkled. They're too long. Your shirt is always baggy and hanging out. You look like you haven't bought new shoes in the past several years. Your hair is so greasy that I think you could lube my car. Do your socks match?"

Bill stood, flabbergasted.

"You look like you belong in East Los Angeles."

"I, I..."

"You want to know a secret? If you want girls chasing you, you need to dress the part."

"But..."

"Bill, I'm going to give you some motherly advice. That hurt puppy dog look doesn't work, in fact it demeans you."

"Oh."

"Did either of your parents ever take the time to teach you how to dress, how to select clothes?"

"No."

"There's an art to it, you know, styles, colors. Let you in on a little secret, Katarina knows how to dress."

"Katarina?"

"Yeah, she's taking my Anthropology 1120 class. Three times a week I see her. That lady knows."

Bill quickly inventoried his memory. Just the other day Katarina wore a blue sleeveless jump suit made from denim. It was slightly lighter than the color of her eyes. Her blouse was short sleeved and plaid. Its colors alternated in various size squares and rectangles between light blue, light purple, tan and off white. To complement her ensemble, her necklace was made from rough, natural looking beads.

"Casually smart, that's how she dresses. Colors always match, complementing her natural coloring. Not too much make-up. Little or no perfume. Her hair is always neat and combed. She walks straight with good posture.

"Bill, I'm not trying to humiliate you. Please don't mistake my intentions. But I do want to shock you a little. I want you to dress for success. Will you let me help?"

"Uh, sure." Bill wasn't quite sure.

"Do you have a couple of hours? I'd like you to go into Denver with me and buy some new clothes."

"I, I don't think I can afford it, but thanks."

"Bill, you can pay me back sometime. Go get your things and meet me back here in five minutes."

Bill stared at Eileen for several uneasy moments.

"Go! I'm not going to argue about this!"

"Eileen?" Bill began as Eileen turned her car onto U.S. Highway 36. "I'm confused."

Following several minutes of silence, Eileen turned her head and glanced at Bill. "And?"

"There, there's a big ruckus on campus right now about that Hindu boy named Yogi Ghi. Swarms of people are turning to him for spiritual guidance. I see kids meditating and reciting mantras, talking in hushed circles. It's like a huge cult is forming. Either you're in or out, no in-between. Have you heard of this guy?"

"Yes."

"What do you think about him?" Bill asked.

"Not much to think, just another fad, I'm sure."

"Really? But everyone seems so sincere!"

"And you feel left out?"

"Yeah, something like that."

"Bill, for most people, when you tell them profound truths, they quickly get bored and if they dare, they'll turn and walk away. But when you tell them absurd fables, instantly, they turn all eyes and ears."

Bill looked at Eileen quizzically, then asked, "You've heard him speak?"

"No, I haven't. But what I know is true, the material that many so-called authorities offer are simply fables, at most partial truths. Why should he be any different?"

"You're probably right," Bill agreed, nodding his head. "Some of the things he said didn't make sense."

"Like?"

"Like, he said, he was the only true Guru in the world today."

Eileen chuckled. "If you believe that, I've got a bridge in Brooklyn I know I can sell you!"

"That's what I thought," Bill chuckled..

"Does he talk about spiritual freedom?"

"Yeah, I guess. He talks about finding liberation through mantra and meditation. However, he claims that only he knows the proper spiritual forms and attitude."

"You think he's right?"

"No. I think there are many roads to town."

"Good for you! Did you know that in Proverbs it says that wisdom comes through many advisors?"

"No, I didn't."

"Good thing to remember sometimes."

"Ya mean when someone tells me they have the only possible solution to a problem."

"You got it, kiddo."

"Ya know, it's funny this should come up. My mother used to lecture me ad nauseam. She thinks her way is the only road to town. Yet…" Bill stopped talking briefly and looked out the car's side window. A small tear fell from his left eye. "Yet, now I think she's, maybe, a pathological liar. She's bullshitted her way through life so much that her reality has become rather tainted."

"The good news, Bill, you're stronger because of it."

"I am?"

"Well, I don't see you rushing to embrace the latest fad just because it's the in thing. No, you're a little skeptical. I think that's good!"

"Thank you." Bill turned and looked at Eileen, quite relieved.

"Bill, what do you think is the nature of walking a spiritual path?"

"Dunno, not really. Earl says it's about surrender, breaking my ego trance and taking Karma to completion."

"And you're not quite sure what that means."

"Not at all."

"Hmmm, maybe I can help," Eileen offered. Then, before continuing the conversation, she drove for several minutes in quiet thought.

"We are what we are based upon probabilities and outcomes. At our most basic level we are consciousness interfering with itself."

Bill turned in his seat, facing Eileen, giving his full attention.

"For an analogy," Eileen said, winking at Bill, "creating movement on the ocean's surface, the wind pushes water towards the land. The seashore, stopping the flow of water, builds pressure. This pressure pushes back out to sea creating what's called standing waves. Swells result, creating a pounding surf. Human consciousness is like this, Bill. The winds of probability push the fluid of consciousness. Truncated experience is the solid that stops the flow of consciousness, building pressure, creating standings waves of Karma. The resultant swell is a superposition of consciousness, what we are moment to moment. The more issues we have because of truncated experience the greater the number of Karmic standing waves. The more traumatic the truncated experience, the more intense our psyches, the narrower our awareness."

"What do you mean by truncated experience?" Bill asked.

"Anything that stops you."

"Anything?"

"Well," Eileen stopped talking briefly in order to safely pass another car. "Let me share a personal experience. When I was your age I was going out with a guy I was totally in love with. For the better part of a year things were wonderful. He seemed caring, considerate, intelligent, artistic, the works. Our future looked bright and I wanted to get married. But he never asked. So, I began to pressure him, you know, implications here and there. Finally a day came when I asked him, point blank. The next weekend he stood me up for an important date. I thought he was going to pick me up and drive to my parents. My family was celebrating my brother's graduation from medical school and I was planning to announce our engagement. Angry, I went to his apartment and found him in bed with some guy. He was gay! I blew up with rage and never spoke to him again. Then, thinking all men were dogs, I spent the next year wallowing in my self pity."

Bill sat, shocked into silence.

"Cat got your tongue?" Eileen finally asked.

"Yeah, guess so. You were obviously very hurt." Bill thought this a dumb thing to say, but said it anyway.

"Hurt? That's an understatement. Things like that didn't happen in my family. I felt like someone had ripped my heart out by the roots. Never again would I be able to trust a man. Never again could I love."

Bill's thoughts turned to Katarina. "Like Katarina did to me, he truncated your experience of ever loving again!"

"No, I truncated my experience," Eileen said, smiling at Bill. "It is we who do things to ourselves."

"But he was the liar."

"And, it was I who withdrew, stopping myself from having any meaningful relationships for a long time. Get it?"

"Creation of Karmic standing waves? A superposition of consciousness?"

"Yes!"

Bill sat for several minutes trying to digest Eileen's words. Finally he asked, "How did you get past it? How did you survive?"

"That's not such an easy answer, my friend," Eileen said as she slowed and stopped at a four-way intersection. Denver traffic was now slowing and becoming congested. Several drivers honked at a stalled pick-up truck. Bill considered getting out to help push the truck to the side of the road, then changed his mind. Conversation was more important. Eileen smiled, intuiting Bill's thoughts.

"I learned how to forgive myself," Eileen resumed.

"Forgive yourself?" Bill questioned.

"Yes, perhaps the hardest thing we ever do in our lives. But, it's the first step in the letting go of the past."

"Why?"

"Because it is an act of free will. It is the act of taking a burden, setting it down and walking away from it. Understand, the crack in the wall of Karma is free will, the act of doing something differently, the act of being out of character, the act of being wild."

"And this knowledge helped you survive a disastrous love affair?"

Eileen turned and gave Bill a big grin. "Yes, Bill, it did. Let me ask you a question. When you don't get what you want from Katarina, what do you do?"

"Guess I feel pretty bad about myself." Bill didn't like the question at all.

"Like it's all your fault?"

"Yeah."

"So, what would it look like if you did something differently?"

"What? What could I do differently?"

"There! That's the problem. As long as you ask that question, you're stuck. Karma has you by the throat."

Bill sat silently trying to make sense out of Eileen's words.

"One little thing differently, Bill. That's all it takes. Then, block by block you begin to tear down the nasty old wall of Karma. This is the short path to spiritual enlightenment!"

"But, Eileen? How can my romance or lack of have anything to do with spiritual enlightenment?"

"How we do our lives is how we do our lives. As we are here on earth, so we are in heaven. As we are in heaven, so we are on earth. One thing you need to understand. The soul experiences reality as a continuum. The soul does not know the difference between here and there, even life and death. These are human constructs and in them we get stuck."

"Don't know if I understand, Eileen."

"You will, trust me. There's a pie shop around the corner." Eileen announced as she pulled into an empty parking space. "I'm buying!"

"Now when we go in, pay attention. These people can teach you something," Eileen said as she pulled into the Wohlfeiler's Men's Store parking lot.

"Good morning, Doctor Watley," Mr. Wohlfeiler said, walking up to Eileen. "We haven't seen you in several months."

"Oh, you know, winter, I always hate the drive into Denver," Eileen returned as she began removing her long winter coat. "Karl, I'd like you to meet Bill Colton. Bill, this is Karl Wohlfeiler, the proprietor.

"Karl, I want you to do a Cinderella number on Bill. As you can see…"

"Say no more!"

Embarrassed, Bill glared at Eileen.

"Come, young man. What are you looking for, a suit?"

"No, Sir. Sports clothes, shirt, slacks, maybe some shoes. I want to dress," Bill turned and glanced at Eileen's approving smile, "casually smart."

"You've come to the right place." Karl scanned the back of the store, looking for his assistant. "Frank, could you help me for a few minutes."

Bill picked up a white dress shirt from a rack. It had long sleeves. He didn't like long sleeves.

"The color's wrong," Karl said, shaking his head. He picked up the shirt and held it up to Bill's face. "It makes you look washed out. Come here."

Karl took Bill to another selection of shirts. He held several up to Bill's face, each time shaking his head. "You need to get out in the sun more."

"Frank, would you take Bill's measurements while I lay out a couple of sports ensembles."

"I'd be delighted," Frank answered, pulling a measuring tape from around his neck.

"Do you want your shirts tapered?" Karl asked, stepping back, giving Frank the room he needed.

"Yes!" Eileen commanded, not giving Bill a chance to answer.

Bill turned and glanced at Eileen. He had a huge smile on his face.

"Look in the mirror, Sir, straight ahead. This'll only take a few minutes."

Two hours later, Bill hauled a dark blue sport coat, three sweaters, six sport shirts, three pairs of slacks, two pairs of shoes and eight pairs of socks out and put them into the trunk of Eileen's car.

"I don't know how I'm going to repay you," Bill worried as he and Eileen began their drive back to Boulder. "I mean…"

"Right now, I'm the rich one and you're the poor one. Someday, you'll be the rich one. I expect you to reciprocate, if not to me, to someone in need."

Bill sat staring at the slow moving afternoon traffic. He thought about what he had learned from his parents. They'd never loan anyone a dime let alone several hundred dollars. They were so selfish that they even broke their promise to pay his way through college. The truth was, he was financially on his own the day he graduated from high school.

"Besides," Eileen resumed. "Affluence or poverty is totally meaningless in the face of reality!"

Bill turned and looked at Eileen with a start.

"It's how we love that's important! Don't ever forget it!"

Seventeen

"Guess I'm screwing it up again," Bill confessed with a pained look one morning in his mentor's living room. A late winter's storm made certain everyone remained inside while a pine scented fire cracked and spit, roaring in the hearth. Pywicket was in her usual spot, warming her back from a safe distance. Bill walked across the room and planted himself on the green leather davenport. He stared at the floor with bewilderment.

"Frustrating, huh?" Earl asked, reaching for his favorite pipe. He stuffed it with some aromatic tobacco and lit it.

"Yeah, Earl. Really is." Bill sat silently for several moments, then with moist eyes, said, "Thought I was making good headway with her. It's my damn mouth, ya know. Don't know when to shut up."

"Katarina?"

"Who else!" Bill responded.

Earl sucked on his pipe, giving Bill a moment to gather himself.

"Like, the other day I had lunch with her. Everything was going really great. I was getting up my nerve to ask her to dinner and a movie. That is until I pissed her off, again." Bill looked across the room toward Earl and then out the bay window at the falling snow. "She was telling me about her piano professor's crappy chauvinistic attitude. I told her she ought to tell the asshole off, like, stand up for herself!"

"That's when she got upset?"

"Yeah, told me that I need to learn some compassion, as if I don't already have any."

"Bill?" Earl asked while shaking his head, "Did it ever occur to you that unsolicited advice is an act of violence?"

"Violence?"

"Yeah! Anytime you tell someone that their actions or feelings are wrong, denying them their own experience, it's an act of violence."

"Earl, I care about her!"

"And, what you did was to place her in an awkward position. Because, if she takes your advice, there will be a row with her professor. If she doesn't, she's got to deal with you at some level. Either way, she loses something."

Confusion immediately overtook Bill's mind. "But she loses just by sitting there and taking it!"

"So certain, are you? What about her creativity and resourcefulness in solving her own problems? Are you going to deny her the experience?"

"Huh?"

"Bill, consider. What Katarina wanted was your intimacy, not your help, certainly not your advice."

"Intimacy?"

"Of course! She wanted you to hear her heart, make contact with her innermost, her deepest, nature."

"Oh."

"Like so many of us, Bill, it's not compassion you need to learn, it's intimacy.

"Intimacy is a catalyst that allows us to become more fully human through sharing our subjective selves. It's the force that helps dissipate peer pressure, allowing individuals to contact their own potential and creativity.

"Being intimate is about listening to the story teller, not so much the story. It's about making emotional contact with another person, hearing their inner voice. It's about giving someone the permission to express themselves emotionally. Because most of us cannot even begin to solve problems rationally until our emotions have been carried to completion.

"You already know, Bill, individually and collectively, we all have our sad stories, our unfulfilled expectations, our petty tyrants. It's part of being alive. What we don't need is additional pressure from well-meaning people making us wrong, forcing us to be less than what we are."

"So you're saying, by telling her what I did, I made the problem worse?" Bill glanced out the living room's bay window. Icicles, gray sky and falling snow echoed his mood. "But, but, I had to do something, she started crying!"

"Unsettling, huh," Earl said quietly.

"Sure is." Bill pushed himself back further into the davenport and crossed his arms across his chest. Then he stared at Earl who was now leaning against the oak mantle, completely relaxed. The blaze in the hearth was beginning to die back into an amiable warmth. "Earl, when people cry I get really nervous!"

"Bill, it's okay to feel."

Spontaneously, a tear trickled down Bill's left cheek. He knew that tears were nothing to be ashamed of despite what his father had told him over the course of growing up. Still, he was embarrassed.

"If you want to be compassionate, you must first create intimacy," Earl continued. "You must be willing to listen. Hear the soul of another. Consider, people who never listen never learn how be in relationships with other human beings. Far too often they're too preoccupied with self, their own agenda getting in the way."

"So, to demonstrate compassion, next time she tells me her frustration, all I need to do is listen, that simple?"

"Perhaps a little more than that. Track her emotion, make contact with it, thereby giving her permission to go deeper into that emotion."

"How?"

"Well, let me give you an example of what I'm talking about," Earl replied, turning, then emptying the ash from his pipe into the grate. "About a year and a half ago Eileen came home from school, very upset. She'd just learned that she was passed over for tenure. I knew that she was deeply hurt.

"As Eileen shared her misfortune, by listening to the story teller rather than the story, I let her know that I heard her pain by saying a couple of simple words, 'Really hurts, huh.' She burst into tears, then went to a deeper level, touching and sharing her innermost hopes and fears. I listened, tracking and acknowledging her emotional state when appropriate, never judging her, never offering advice. The next day she went back to school and talked with her department head. Since her emotions had been dealt with, she was able to speak her mind in a professional way.

"You see, Bill, all she wanted from me was permission to express her feelings in a place of safety. She's a grown-up. She already knew what she wanted to do, long before telling me her story."

"Guess I would have given her some sort of lecture, telling her not to do this or that, not to worry, look on the bright side. I would have been so busy expounding that I would have never heard her heart. I would have stopped her, forcing her out of her experience, just like I learned from my parents." Bill understood.

"Bill, what we don't need in our world is some do-gooder telling us this or that under the guise of a compassionate slap alongside the head. That's violence! It really puts people on the defensive, creating no win situations!"

Bill stood up, then walked across the living room and began enjoying the fire's heat. Holding his hands toward the warmth, he stood silently for several minutes, thinking. Pywicket didn't stir. Finally, dropping his hands to his sides, Bill turned to Earl and offered, "Guess I've been confused. I thought compassion was enough. But, you're right, unless someone directly experiences my caring we don't go anywhere. Intimacy lets us share our hearts, lets us share our souls."

Eighteen

"Hey! Y'all come on in and shut the door." Katarina shouted, waving her right hand from inside the organ's practice room. Bill was headed home, having spent two hours practicing his violin with Peggy. Together they were working on Bach's *Double Violin Concerto*.

Bill walked in smiling, set his violin and books on the floor then closed the door behind him. "Sure it's all right? I'm not disturbing your practice?"

"Naw. I got something to show ya." Katarina turned on the organ's power switch, sat down on the console's bench and waited while the vacuum tubes warmed to operating temperature.

Except for peering through an open door, Bill had never been inside this practice room and couldn't help looking around. The room was the largest and the ugliest in Macky's basement. It easily held the old and well-used three manual dark brown Conn Organ along with two reddish-brown Leslie Speaker systems and several oaken cabinets used for music storage. Color-wise, nothing matched and the discolored acoustical tiles on both the walls and ceiling gave the room a putrid appearance.

"Go sit! No fair peeking!" Katarina commanded once the organ was ready to play. Then she turned to her music case and pulled out several pages of sheet music.

Bill walked to a small gray office stool in the corner of the room and sat down.

Katarina's face was brilliantly lit as she pulled the cathedral stops and announced, "I need a moment to warm-up." Whereupon she began several minutes of scales and arpeggios.

"Okay. Tell me what y'all think!" Katarina adjusted the volume to louder than practical for the size of the room and played Bach's *Toccata and Fugue in D minor*.

"Yes!" Bill yelled, jumping up with arms outstretched and clenched fists at the *Fugue's* conclusion.

Katarina stood and bowed. The sparkle in her eyes told that she knew she'd done good.

Bill rushed over to Katarina and took her into his arms. At the speed of light he entertained the thought of kissing her, but didn't. Now he understood, a hug did not necessarily invite anything more.

"You've obviously been practicing. That's a difficult piece of music. You should, like, feel proud," Bill stated matter-of-factly as he stepped back to a respectful distance.

"Thank you, Billy. I have put a lot of time into it," Katarina answered. Her blue eyes were filled with excitement.

"Have your parents heard you play that?" Bill asked.

"I wish. But we don't have an organ at home. They don't really come by school very often."

"Their loss."

"Maybe I'll play it for them at church when I go home at Easter." Katarina returned to the console's bench seat, pulled her pleated tan skirt to the side and sat down.

"Hope you do." Bill stood smiling into Katarina's eyes. Then, worried about overstaying his welcome, he walked back to where he'd placed his violin and books and picked them up while Katarina began replacing Bach with her assigned manuscript.

"Katarina?"

"Yeah?" Katarina looked up from the console's music rack.

"I'm going to the Peter, Paul and Mary Concert Friday night. Think you could break free?"

Katarina bit her lower lip for several seconds, then replied, "Yeah, Billy, think I can. But I want to buy my own ticket. Okay?"

"Yeah! That's just fine."

Friday evening, Bill knocked on Katarina's dorm room door about half an hour before curtain call. She didn't invite him in but was all ready to go.

"Didn't know if I was going to be able to make it," Katarina said as she and Bill began walking down the dormitory hall together. "One of the girls at the health food store called in sick and they asked me to cover for her tonight."

"Why didn't you?"

"Well, Billy, I haven't had any social outings in a long time. I need to get away from the rat race—least for one evening. I kinda like folk songs, too."

"Ya mean you don't have guys beating down your door?" Bill asked.

Katarina looked at Bill quizzically out of the corner of her eye.

"Sorry I asked! That was, like, inappropriate. I apologize."

"Naw, that's okay. After all we've been through, I can be honest. Yeah, there are a few guys. I tell them the same thing I've told you. I'm not ready for a relationship."

"And do they take it as hard as I did?" Bill asked as he opened the dormitory door for Katarina and stepping out into the cold night air. The stroboscopic effect from a flickering mercury vapor streetlight gave the surrounding buildings, rain soaked walkway and passing students an eerie quality. Bill opened his umbrella and stepped closer to Katarina.

"What's that supposed to mean, Billy? You want to know if you still have a chance with me?"

"Not at all. You made it clear months ago that you wanted nothing more than friendship. But, friends talk. They, like, share things and through sharing they become intimate. Ya know, I think you're the most magnificent woman I've ever known. I pray we're friends for the rest of our lives, that nothing ever comes between us, ever again."

Katarina was struck silent.

"So, are you willing to be my friend?" Bill asked, quite unsure of himself.

Katarina stopped walking, turned and looked directly into Bill's eyes. Then she said as a smile formed on her lips, "Of course, silly. You know that."

Following the Peter, Paul and Mary concert, Bill invited Katarina to the Student Union for pie and ice cream.

"You can eat this stuff, I mean working for a health food store?" Bill asked as he and Katarina sat down at a small table in the corner of the room. The Student Union was very busy and quite noisy for so late in the evening.

"I'm good most of the time so I can be bad once in a while!" Katarina said, laughing. Then she took a good-sized bite of her cherry-vanilla sundae. Her eyes sparkled in the evening light.

Bill looked away in order not to blush, then turned back. "Think I'm learning better habits."

"Eating?"

"Yeah, but more than that—housekeeping, hygiene, stuff like that."

"Noticed you're dressing a lot better. How come?"

"Katarina, I'm trying to be more than my upbringing. Does that, like, make any sense?"

"Yeah." Katarina smiled while nodding her head with approval. "It makes a lot of sense."

"Truth is, I come from a family of slobs and I'm trying my damnedest to get past it. Not going to be like my family!"

"That's a very interesting remark," Katarina said as she clicked her fork several times on her plate while looking at the table.

"What? What is it, Katarina? Suddenly you look so serious."

"Well, I don't know if I should say this, but your family is certainly a big concern to my dad."

"I know."

'No, you don't know." Katarina bit her lower lip for several seconds, adjusted her glasses, then continued. "My dad doesn't like your parents, Billy. Because of that, he's been against our friendship since the day we met."

"From the day we met? Ya mean like, Philmont?"

"Yeah. He says your mother is an alcoholic and your father's a wimp."

"Since Philmont?" Bill sat, dumbfounded, crossing his arms across his chest.

"I have to admit, every time I saw your mother she had a drink in her hand."

"Guess I don't remember. I only became aware of her problem during high school. Katarina?"

"Yeah?"

"Then, why did you, like, write to me all those years?"

"Because, Billy. I've always liked you! Besides, it was thrilling thinking that someday I might be able to live in the city, just like you! Y'all know I don't like being a country hick. I've always dreamt of a better life."

"So, the house plans, marriage, kids, were they for nothing?" Bill asked, almost choking.

"I truly meant them at the time, Billy."

"Now?"

"To be honest, I'm a little scared. Think I should tell ya something. Don't get upset, please. Last August, when your mother called, dad forbade me from having anything further to do with you. He told me your mother is insane."

"He may be right. But, but, what about me? Does he think I'm crazy?" Bill asked, then taking a deep breath of air.

"He's not sure about you except to say you're very immature."

"You think I'm, like, immature?" Bill's face was now flushed.

"Yeah, Billy. But I think it's…"

"Katarina?" Bill slid his chair back about a foot, ready to leave.

"Billy, don't go! Please, let me finish! Immaturity is not such a bad thing."

"It's not?"

"Not at all. People grow up. It just takes some of us longer than the rest. My aunt once told me that the higher the intelligence, the slower the maturing process."

"You believe that?"

"Guess I wouldn't have said it if I didn't believe it! Anyway, it's the only hope I have."

"You have?"

"Billy, if you hadn't noticed, I'm pretty immature, perhaps way too naïve."

"Katarina, you seem very mature to me!"

"Then I must be a good actress. Because, inside I'm a wreck, I'll tell ya what."

Bill slid his chair back to the table, then turned back to finishing his pie and ice cream. His thoughts were becoming confused with so many questions and concerns. "Katarina?"

"Yeah?"

"Does your dad hate me?"

"Hate? That's a very strong word! No, he doesn't hate you."

"But he doesn't like me."

"Dunno, since last August, you're not a topic we discuss."

Bill leaned back in his seat while covering his mouth with the fingers of his left hand.

"Anyway," Katarina continued. "Wouldn't let that concern you. I know your mother doesn't like me. That was pretty obvious at Philmont. Even my brother Erik noticed it."

"You're right," Bill said with a half-assed grin, nodding his head, dropping his hand away from his face. "She'd do anything to keep us apart."

"So, my guess would be, y'all never did resolve with your parents about coming to school here."

"I'm still an outcast," Bill laughed, looking deep into Katarina's eyes.

"Maybe that's good, Billy. I've been doing a lot of thinking. If my dad is right about your family, maybe you should say screw 'em. Maybe you were right in leaving home!"

Nineteen

"What's going on, Bill? You haven't looked so sad in months!" Earl said, watching Bill enter the back porch, ice and snow flying everywhere.

Earl had just entered the kitchen in order to freshen a pot of coffee before returning to an evening of relaxation with *Childhood's End*, by Arthur Clarke. However, the look on Bill's face demanded his immediate attention.

"Yesterday in my Educational Psychology class, Doctor Woodburn said that the basic nature of one's personality can't be changed."

"Really? I'd be concerned too, if I thought that were true," Earl replied.

"You would?"

"Yeah! 'Cos that means there's no free will in this world." Earl looked deep into Bill's sad eyes. "Well, doesn't it?"

Bill didn't answer the question. Instead, he went immediately to his concern. "Doctor Woodburn told us a story. It seems to make sense. Let me tell it to you:

> Once upon a time, there was a rattlesnake. He was getting along just fine doing what rattlesnakes always do, that is until he met a master snake one day. This master snake was very wise and told stories about the magic of a far off canyon and the riches that lay in the mountains beyond. So, eager for fame, fortune and adventure, the snake began a quest.

Fueled by enthusiasm, his days were short and it wasn't long until the snake came to the rim of the canyon he sought. His sense of direction was superb. However, once there, he was forced to stop. The canyon walls were too steep and slippery for him to continue. For weeks he looked for ways to cross the chasm, but there seemed to be none. Finally, the snake became discouraged and in his despair he doubted the magic.

One day the rattlesnake was lying out on a rock relaxing and sunning himself when an eagle set down to check out a rodent hole nearby. Spontaneously, the snake realized that if he could fly, getting to the other side would be easy. But he didn't have wings, which made him very sad. Then an outstanding idea struck.

"Excuse me. Ah, excuse me. Mister Eagle, sir, I wonder if you could help me? I need to get across this canyon very badly. I've been here for days trying. But, alas, I may have to give up my quest."

"Oh? A quest you say? What is your quest?" The eagle was always interested in matters such as these.

"A master snake told me that magic lay within this canyon, fame and fortune on the other side. But until now, I've been stuck right here. I've looked at all sorts of options. I can't get down the sides of this canyon because the walls are too steep and slippery. I can't fly. Thought I was defeated. But you, sir, you've given me hope. There is another way."

"And what, pray tell, is that?"

"Your back!" The snake hissed with excitement. "If you'd allow me, sir, to ride on your back. Why, why you could carry me across, easily."

"You've got to be kidding, really!" The eagle jumped back several feet. He wasn't about to let a rattlesnake get too close, except maybe to eat him. "Couldn't do that. No, not at all. You know what would happen?"

"Well, for one thing, I'd sure be grateful. I, I'd pay you handsomely, too, that is, when I get my fortune."

"Think not! Snakes are snakes! Can't be trusted! I'll tell you what would happen, all right. About half way across this canyon you'd be overtaken by your basic nature. You'd bite me. Then I'd fall to my death."

The snake hissed a laugh. "No, no! That doesn't make sense, not at all. If I bit you, I'd die too. I'd have no place to go, except…Hey look, I may be a snake. But, I'm not stupid."

The eagle thought. And while he didn't trust the snake, what he said made sense. So very reluctantly, the eagle agreed.

As the snake slithered up and onto the eagle's back, he knew he'd just witnessed the first act of the canyon's magic.

All was going well until about half way across. There, the snake panicked. He'd never been in the air before. The force of the wind made his eyes burn while the canyon's bottom appeared a million miles away. Finally, overcome with utter terror, he bit the eagle's neck.

Screaming with rage, hot flashes of poison shooting through his veins, the eagle folded his wings and plummeted toward his death. "You fool! You fool! Now we're both doomed!"

"Forgive me!" The snake hissed at the top of his voice, losing his grip on the eagle's back. "You were right! I can't overcome my basic nature."

As Bill finished his story, he dropped his shoulders considerably while letting out a huge sigh despite an already caved-in chest. "I'm, like, doomed!"

"Doomed? A little melodramatic, huh."

"I think Doctor Woodburn is right. There are basic things in all of us that are impossible to change," Bill finally said following an uncomfortable silence.

"Like what?"

"Like," Bill walked over to the davenport and took a seat. He didn't have to think hard. "Like with her, somehow I always seem to screw it up. I think I'm unlovable!"

"Bill, you're so full of crap I can't believe it." Earl began laughing.

Bill's posture changed to total disbelief.

"Bill! You're a very lovable guy! You've got passion for life. It shows in almost every thing you do. You've got the courage to hang in there and not give up in spite of your mistakes. The only reason you're, quote, screwing things up, unquote, is because of your preconceived expectations. You spend so much energy dreaming and planning how it's going to be that failure becomes necessary."

"Necessary?"

"Yes, Bill, necessary. One can never plan the future carefully enough to guarantee success." Earl said, sitting down in his favorite recliner, then taking a few moments to collect his thoughts.

"Like most people, you have trouble implementing new knowledge because of faulty preconceptions."

"Really?"

"Bill, you've studied some biology, haven't you?"

"Yeah."

"Do you understand photosynthesis, I mean in general terms?"

"Yeah."

"Okay. So, other than water, what are trees predominately made of?"

Bill looked at Earl strangely. "Made of? They grow from the minerals in the soil."

"Shame on you! You just told me that you understood photosynthesis," Earl announced, leaning back in his chair while interlacing the fingers of both hands and placing them behind his head with a cocky expression on his face.

"Huh?"

"Bill, photosynthesis tells us that trees are predominately made up of air! Air that's been solidified through the plant's chemistry!" Earl laughed while shaking his head side to side.

"Really?"

"Yeah, they breathe in carbon dioxide. They exhale oxygen. Like too many college students, even though you studied photosynthesis, you really didn't get it because of a preconceived notion that something invisible like air cannot become a solid."

"Like a tree."

"Yeah!"

Slowly, over the span of several minutes, a look of worried concern began creeping across Bill's face.

"So, what's going on for you right now, Bill?"

"Just thinking, seeing some other areas of my life where I have preconceptions. Realizing I came to Boulder with the idea that I'd automatically sweep Katarina off her feet and that we'd live happily ever after. I thought our love was a given. I never thought I could lose her love and respect."

"Good for you! Now you're getting somewhere. Let's go get some fresh coffee, then I tell you how to change Doctor Woodburn's, quote, basic nature, unquote.

"Two new words I want you to consider," Earl said, returning to the living room. He offered Bill a fresh cup of aromatic coffee, then sat down in his favorite recliner while taking a sip from his own cup. "Infocus and outfocus. Any ideas?"

Bill smiled. He loved the way his professor challenged him with new motifs, even though it was oftentimes painful. Bill sat silent for several minutes while gently sipping his coffee, then answered, "When I give you my full and undivided attention, I'm outfocused. When I'm totally inside my own head, I'm infocused."

"Bravo! Couldn't have said it better myself!"

Bill smiled.

"Consider, Bill, like most people, your method of problem solving is primarily to infocus. Solutions, therefore, are based solely upon preconceived ideas, too many times wrong."

"What if I were to change that? What if I, like, were to problem solve by paying more attention to the world around me, instead of my own internal crap? Outfocus, as you say."

Earl's face exploded into a giant grin. He got up from his recliner, walked to the fireplace mantle, selected a pipe, stuffed it with his favorite tobacco and lit it. The flame hissed and popped, sending a hot ember rocketing to the carpet. He chased it, stomping it with his foot, all the while laughing.

"So, with your new state of enlightenment, answer me this. What is Doctor Woodburn's basic nature?" Earl asked after recomposing himself.

"What I do when I'm infocused. Like his snake, I bite the back of the magnificent unknown."

"And what is Bill's basic nature?"

"I'm not sure, not anymore."

Twenty

Katarina's face tightened in pain as she played the final chords to Massenet's *Meditation from Thaïs* for violin and piano. Slowly, she stood up, holding her body very rigid, almost in tears. Bill put his violin down and rushed over to her, along with Charles, the choir director. The church's congregation stood, creating a crescendo of concerned chatter.

"What is it? What's wrong?" Bill demanded.

"I think…ahhhh! Need to lie down or something, quick!"

Bill put his arm around Katarina and helped her walk, almost carried her into the pastor's office. Several people rushed in from behind, offering their assistance.

As Bill lowered Katarina on to the old brown davenport, she cried out, "No! I can't sit, Billy. Please, help me lie face down."

"What is it? What's wrong?" Bill demanded, once again.

"Don't know. Stinging on my tail bone." Katarina separated her legs slightly. "Ahhhh!"

Bill looked at Charles, then back at Katarina. He felt totally helpless, a helplessness that scared him from the core of his being. He knelt on the oak floor and took Katarina's trembling left hand into the strength of his own two hands.

"Could someone put a pillow, or something under my stomach?" Katarina winced.

"Here, dear." Jessica, one of the church matrons, quickly grabbed a chair cushion and helped Katarina slide it carefully between her abdomen and the davenport.

Katarina let out a huge sigh of relief as she sank into the cushion.

"You need a doctor!" Charles ordered.

"Let me lie here for a few minutes, I'll, I'll be okay."

"Katarina, you don't look okay to me. You're, like, white as a ghost," Bill said, placing the back of his left hand against her soft cheek, then her forehead. He squeezed her left hand gently with his right.

Katarina looked into Bill's caring eyes, attempting a smile.

"What can we do?" Charles asked.

"Just let me catch my breath, please."

With the exception of Bill and Jessica, who refused to leave Katarina alone, everyone left the room in order to continue the morning service. Immediately, the congregation prayed for Katarina's healing.

"Billy, could you take me home?" Katarina asked, about twenty minutes later, her pain having eased considerably. The color in her face was now closer to normal.

"Of course."

Bill reached down and helped Katarina try to sit upright.

"Ahhhh, it's not working, still can't sit! Put me back down."

Bill eased his grip and gently let Katarina return to her face down position.

"I'll go get my car!" Bill rushed out and returned a few minutes later.

"Okay, my car is as close as I can get it," Bill announced almost out of breath.

Slowly, Bill and Jessica helped Katarina to her feet.

"You're going to be okay!" Bill insisted.

"Yeah." Katarina strained to say.

Together, Bill and Jessica helped Katarina into the back seat of Bill's car. There, Katarina lay down on her side and whimpered.

"I'm coming, too," Jessica announced. Then, before Bill could argue, she opened the passenger door and got in.

Bill began driving back to campus as if he were carrying fragile eggs. Jessica reached over the seat and held Katarina's trembling hand.

"How ya doin' back there?" Bill asked.

"Not so good. Think, maybe, you better take me to the student health center. Really hurt, I'll tell ya what."

"We're taking Katarina to the Boulder Community Hospital." The campus nurse advised Bill, almost an hour later.

"My God! What's wrong?" Bill demanded, suddenly coming to his senses.

"We're not sure. Are you her brother?"

"No." Bill almost lied.

"Boyfriend?"

"Yes." Bill didn't know if it was safe to say that or not, but given the circumstances.

"We've given her a sedative. She's out of pain right now, but something's going on at the base of her spine. She needs a work-up, something we can't do here."

"Can I see her?"

"Of course."

"Billy?" Katarina whispered.

"I'm here." Bill immediately noticed that Katarina's eyes had lost their brightness. Seeing her helpless pulled considerable anguish from the depths of his soul.

"Oh, Bee. Thank you so much." Katarina's words were slow, not like normal. Usually, she spoke slightly faster than most of the people Bill knew.

"You're going to be okay!" Bill decreed.

"Could you do me another favor?"

"Name it."

"Call my parents."

"Son, I want to thank you for helping my daughter the way you did." Valdemar extended his hand as Bill entered Katarina's semi-private room two days later. Bill shook it. Then he walked across the room to Katarina's bed, and handed her a dozen red roses.

"Gosh, Billy. You shouldn't have. I mean, really." The look on Katarina's face said she was pleased.

"Nothing is too good for you." Bill returned. Both Katarina and Bill began to blush.

"Rita and I both appreciate what you did very much," Valdemar began, trying to ease his own uneasiness.

"Glad to, sir. Just sorry I couldn't do more. What'd they find?" Bill asked, never taking his eyes off Katarina. She had regained her delicate beauty, even though she was flat on her back, in hospital garb with tubes extending from her left forearm.

"A pyelonidus cyst at the base of my spine."

Bill had no idea what that meant, but had no intention of inquiring further. "Is it gone?"

"Yeah, they did surgery yesterday morning."

"How ya feeling?"

"Thousand percent better, I'll tell ya what," Katarina answered, noticing how well Bill was dressed. He looked good.

Bill smiled. Then he looked at Rita. She had a pleasing smile on her face. He hadn't seen her since Philmont. He was startled by the close **resemblance between mother and daughter. Their hair, eyes, shape of their faces, they could have been sisters.**

"We should go, dear, leave these kids alone," Valdemar announced to his wife.

"Please, don't leave on account of me," Bill said.

"We've been here several hours already. I'm certain Katarina would enjoy someone her own age to talk to. Besides, we need to get something to eat. I can't speak for Rita, but I'm starved!"

Bill looked at Katarina's father. Presently, he seemed like a nice man. Still, at some level, Valdemar's presence scared the hell out of Bill and he was just as glad to see Valdemar leave.

"Mom, could you call a nurse on your way out?"

"Certainly." Rita leaned over and kissed her daughter on the forehead.

"'Bye, mom. 'Bye, dad. See y'all in the morning."

"How long ya gonna' be here?" Bill asked, walking to where Rita had been sitting. "May I?"

"Please. Doctor says Thursday afternoon or Friday morning, depending."

"Like, how bad is it, really?" Bill asked while sitting down.

"Dunno. Still on medication. It still hurts. They have to change the dressings several times a day."

"I was really afraid for you. It's hard to believe someone else's pain would effect me so much."

Katarina smiled. "Don't remember much of what happened. We were playing our duet. I remember that I could hardly get through it. I remember lying on the davenport in the church office. I remember the back seat of your car, you helping me to the hospital, not much else. Gosh, Billy, hope I didn't ruin it for you."

"We did just fine, even though the retinuto was a little too multo."

Katarina chuckled.

"Actually, I didn't take you to the hospital. It was the student health service, an ambulance."

"Oh. Guess I was really out of it. Did I cry?"

"A little."

Bill extended his right hand toward Katarina's left. She took it and squeezed gently.

"Everyone is asking about you."

"Great, just what I need, I'll tell ya what."
"You have a lot of friends. We're all concerned."
"Billy, could you do me a favor? Get the nurse?"
"Anything I can do?"
"Kinda a private matter."
"Oh."

Bill got up and left the room. Then coming back several minutes later, saying, as he entered the doorway, "They've got some kinda emergency down at the end of the hall. I think someone's dying. There're people running all over the place."

"Whew." Katarina looked around the room, almost in desperation. "Think I'm going to have an emergency of my own. Got to go to the bathroom bad, really bad."

"Let me help."

"You sure?"

"Of course, I'm sure."

"I don't know." Katarina bit her lower lip and looked at Bill, apprehensively. Finally she consented.

Bill helped Katarina out of bed, making certain the IV tube didn't get tangled, or worse, torn out. He all but carried her to the tiny bathroom. Respectfully, he helped her get situated then waited outside the closed door for what seemed an eternity.

"Okay!" Katarina finally announced.

Bill assisted Katarina back to her bed, tucked her in, making certain that she was comfortable, at least as comfortable as she could get.

"You're really a sweet man. I want you to know that."

"I like helping you." Bill looked into Katarina's eyes, almost blushing. Katarina got a huge smile on her face, just like old times. "Thank you."

"So, what are ya doin' this summer." Bill knew he had better change the subject before he said something inappropriate. He sat down in the chair immediately next to Katarina's bed.

"Not much. Going home to Fort Collins. I have a job at the city library. Y'all?"

"The Watleys invited me to spend the summer with them in a little town just north of Santa Fe, New Mexico."

"They the people y'all do house work for?"

"Yeah."

"Could ya hand me some tissues?"

Bill reached into the shelves behind him, pulled several tissues and handed them to Katarina. "They've invited me on a Vision Quest."

"Really!" Katarina's smile changed to concern.

"From what Eileen tells me, it's what Indians once did for initiation into manhood. Young Braves used to go into the wilderness and ask the spirits for visions about their life's purpose."

"But you already know what ya want to be when you grow up."

"Yeah, a concert violinist. But that's not all of who I am."

"Billy, many of those Braves lost their lives. I've studied this stuff, too."

"I'll be okay. I'm an Eagle Scout, just like Erik."

"Thought y'all needed a job to pay for the next school year." Katarina knew that being an Eagle Scout, though better than nothing, left one little prepared for a serious wilderness adventure.

"I did. But Earl promised that if I go with them, they'll make certain that my tuition is paid for. Sounds kinda good to me. Anyway, now that I'm twenty-one, like, I can accept that scholarship without my parents."

"Y'all really don't know what you're getting into, do ya," Katarina interrupted, trying to re-distribute her weight. Her lower back was now aching considerably.

"Maybe not," Bill replied superficially. Katarina's concern touched him. "But my grandfather ventured into some of the remotest places on this planet. He didn't die. And, he had fantastic stories to tell us kids!" Bill leaned back in his chair, smiling, placing his hands behind his head. It was now obvious that a Vision Quest was necessary.

"Anyway, Earl and Eileen are family to me and I trust them." Bill looked away, a noise catching his attention from the hallway.

"Y'all must be…"

"What can I do?" A rather tall middle-aged nurse asked, interrupting the conversation. "Sorry."

"Can I get something for my pain?" Katarina asked, shyly.

The nurse stepped to Katarina's bed and examined, then adjusted Katarina's IV ever so slightly.

Bill stood up and moved out of the way while the nurse measured and recorded Katarina's temperature, pulse and blood pressure.

"Would you like to sit up, dear?"

"No! I think that would make my back hurt worse."

"Here ya go, dear." The nurse handed Katarina a pain pill and a paper cup filled with water.

"Thanks."

"Dinner will be served in fifteen to twenty minutes," The nurse said, cleaning the tray next to Katarina's bed, then leaving the room.

"I should, like, go. I've probably tired you out," Bill said walking back to the side of Katarina's bed.

"I am exhausted. But before y'all go, how was your Junior Recital?"

"Went really well. All that hard work finally paid off."

"Chausson went okay, then? I know you were worried."

"Slowed it down a tad at the *Animato*. You would have been proud."

"Sorry I missed it."

"Me, too."

"Billy, thank you for coming. Thank you for everything. I mean that!"

Bill looked deep into Katarina's bright blue eyes. He hesitated, unsure. Then he took her left hand into both of his and smiled while bending over and kissing her respectfully on the lips. Thereupon, he turned and left the room, not daring to look back.

Twenty One

The drive from Boulder, Colorado, to Española, New Mexico, was excruciating. It seemed as though the entire state of New Mexico was experiencing road repair. After eleven long hours, tired and hungry, Earl pulled his blue Ford station wagon into a driveway leading up to a thirty-two year old whitewashed adobe home. Both Bill and Eileen looked at Earl, relieved that the trip was finally over. So was Pywicket. The poor kitty was hoarse from all the yowling.

"Gee, this place could be right out of a tourist magazine!" Bill announced as he surveyed the summer residence. On the southwest corner of several acres sat a dwelling that glistened in the afternoon sun. Attached to the villa was a picturesque verandah and beyond it several out buildings. Many varieties of cacti along with several large cottonwood trees in both the front and side yards created a plenitude of shade. The ambiance of the entire residence was typical New Mexico, complete with a bright orange Zia painted on the front of the house. Bill almost swooned with delight, remembering his own New Mexico romance seven years prior.

Earl turned off the car's engine, got out and stretched his aching muscles. Bill and Eileen followed. The afternoon was hot and dry, but calmed by a gentle breeze.

"Like, what's that sound?" Bill demanded as he looked toward a nearby cottonwood.

"Cicadas."

"Huh?"

"Insects in the trees. Look." Earl pointed to a low hanging branch about twenty-five to thirty feet from where Bill stood. On it sat a huge dark gray fly-like creature generating a piercing high frequency buzz.

"Hurts my ears!" Bill complained while walking closer to the tree and examining the pest. "They do this all the time?"

"Only during the heat of the day," Earl returned.

"Good, don't know if I could sleep with that racket."

"You think this is bad, wait until you hear the crickets, especially when they get in your room at night." Earl laughed.

"This your place?" Bill asked while walking back toward the house, watching Earl insert a key into the front door lock and give it a good hard turn.

"We own it with another couple. You'll meet them tomorrow afternoon." Earl answered, kicking the bottom of the door several times trying to get it unjambed.

Bill followed Earl into the tiny over heated living room and set down his backpack, violin and music cases. There were the usual things one would expect to find in a vacation home, stale smell, worn second-hand furniture, no frills, no television, not even a telephone.

Eileen entered the living room and placed two suitcases on the floor. Then she began opening doors and windows, allowing the hot air to escape. A mouse ran terror-stricken toward some unknown fortress as Pywicket rose to her task. Together, Bill and Earl turned and walked back out towards Earl's station wagon.

"The place looks like it hasn't been lived in for a while," Bill said as he began pulling heavy boxes filled with food and supplies from the rear of the station wagon.

"At least nine months."

"Guess there will be a lot of clean-up, huh."

Earl just grinned.

Once the food supplies had been carried into the house, Bill began to make a dinner of tuna sandwiches and a tossed green salad for everyone. Eileen was already busy cleaning the dust off the kitchen counter and appliances. Pywicket's only concern, now, was the smell of tuna as she tried to trip Bill with her back and forth begging. Bill knew the drill as he poured the tuna broth into a small bowl and led the persistent kitty to the corner of the kitchen.

"What's my job? Bill asked, as soon everyone was comfortably fed.

Earl reached for a jar of organic apple juice and poured himself a glass. Then he looked at Bill. "Let me put it this way, you're here because the Spirits have invited you."

"Spirits? Don't understand."

"It's not necessary to understand," Eileen responded, looking into Bill's eyes, causing him to jump. "What's necessary is for you to do exactly what we ask, no more, no less. Understanding will come in its own time."

Eileen placed her left hand onto the top of Bill's right. "Come." Then she led Bill down a hallway and into a small bedroom. "This is your room, Bill."

Bill walked in and looked around. The room contained a single bed, a desk, chair, dresser and a small private bathroom. It was badly in need of dusting and the hardwood floor needed mopping.

"As you know, we've asked for six weeks," Eileen continued. "We told you that you'd be going on a 'Vision Quest,' beyond that, purposefully, we've said nothing."

"Why?"

"Because Bill, you've spent most of your life planning how it's going to be, how you're going to do your life. You've learned to touch the world through your intellect, not through your heart."

Bill wanted to disagree. But before he spoke, he thought better of it. Eileen was usually right.

"We're offering you a chance to self-differentiate from your family," Earl added, entering the room. "For a time, this room is your hermitage, your sanctuary, your chance to see yourself at a core level, for spiritual enlightenment, if you will."

"Really?" Bill's mind exploded with possibilities. Like a sunburst he remembered all the stories that Pappy had told him: Northern India, Tibet, the Gobi Desert. "Really!"

"Bill, I'm not going to bullshit you. The next several weeks maybe the hardest you'll ever live," Earl continued. "There's even the possibility you might die."

Bill's smile was undaunted.

"You think this is a joke. I know. I was young once. Thought I was invincible, too. Have you ever heard the cliché, 'Scared to death?'"

Bill took a deep breath of air. His enthusiasm quickly grew serious. It wasn't often that he'd seen such sobriety in the faces of his mentors.

"Anytime you want out, just say so. Even though we've brought you here and believe you're up to this task, we're not going to force anything on you. But be warned if you do bail out, you may never have this chance again. So between now and tomorrow evening, we want you to think seriously about your commitment to your own spirituality. Because, it's the hardest, the easiest, the most fun, the most terrifying experience you'll ever have. I suggest that you get some sleep. Then in the morning, begin by cleaning your room and its adjoining bathroom." Earl turned and left the room. Eileen followed.

As Bill scrubbed his quarters the following morning, his mind wandered. "Enlightenment, eh?" He mumbled to himself. "But what's it mean? What does it really mean?"

"Pappy told me stories about enlightenment. I wonder if he ever made it? After all is said and done, did he have what it takes?"

Bill thought about Tibet's great Yogi, Lama Milarepa and wondered. He knew the story well but could never really make any sense of it. What did people like Milarepa realize that made their consciousness so brilliant? But, like so many times before, Bill saved himself from such difficult searchings. He returned to his habit of talking to an invisible Katarina.

"I don't know what to do, Katarina! We've come so far these past few months. Still, I'm afraid! Why won't you share my dream? Must I give you up to save my soul? Is that where all this is headed? Where is all this headed?"

Bill got up and walked into the bathroom, splashed water over the entire bathtub surface then sprinkled Mr. Clean and scoured.

Late afternoon found Bill's hermitage spotless. The floors were scrubbed and waxed, the windows washed, blinds dusted, even the inside of the desk drawers were now clean. Bill had replaced the bed sheets and blankets. And with the exception of several stubborn stains, the adjoining bathroom looked like it had never been used.

Bored, Bill walked into the living room and peered out a window as a sun-bleached green 1950 Buick pulled in front of the house and parked. An old leather faced Indian dressed in blue jeans, a short-sleeved khaki shirt and a dark brown cowboy hat got out and slammed the car's door. Standing five foot eleven with broad shoulders, the man was built like an Olympic athlete. His hair was shoulder length and jet black, streaked with gray. His face and eyes told of a life carved wise by seasons of wind, rain and sun.

"Worm!" Eileen screeched with the delight of seeing a lost friend. She ran into the front yard and hugged the old man. Worm reciprocated, pulling Eileen from the ground as if she were a rag doll. Bill thought it quite odd. He'd never seen an Indian show affection. But, then he didn't know any Indians.

"Worm, this is Bill Colton. Bill, Worm."

Bill walked up to Worm and offered his right hand. Worm took it and immediately threw it away, like a piece of wet garbage.

"Be a man!" Worm commanded. "You shake hand like pussy!"

Bill started backing away, trying to avoid Worm's icy stare. His mind raced toward confusion.

"Try again!" Worm thrust his right hand toward Bill, tensing every muscle in his arm.

Bill shut his eyes. He wanted to scream. He knew that Worm could take him to the mat in short order.

"What're ya gonna do, be a wimp for rest of your life? I'm a man! Now treat me like one!"

Cautiously, ready to bolt like a spooked gelding, Bill placed his hand into Worm's and gave a firm squeeze and shake.

"Yippee Ki Yi!" Worm shouted, turning toward Eileen. "This kid's gonna be okay. I don't care what ya said about 'im."

Bill glanced at Eileen, then at Earl who was now stepping off the front porch busting up with laughter. Bill surprised himself. He began laughing, too.

Just before dinner, while Bill waited patiently for his vegetarian lasagna to finish baking, there was a knock at the front door.

"Yeah?" Bill yelled, turning toward the intrusion, then walking into the living room.

"You must be Bill. I'm Bruce Kinney. My wife, Kathleen," Bruce said, opening the screen door and letting himself in before Bill had the chance. Bruce, at five foot eleven was the same height and weight as Bill. For a man of fifty-two, he was obviously in very good shape. He had short black hair, slightly graying at the temples. His face was thin holding a very large nose and smile.

Bill offered the stranger a very strong handshake. He was not about to make the same mistake twice.

"Bruce!" Earl exclaimed, entering the room. The two men laughed and immediately hugged each other.

Eileen ran from the kitchen and embraced both Bruce and Kathleen simultaneously. Bill stood watching with amusement. Was Kathleen really Bruce's wife? A short, slightly plump, blue-eyed brunette, Bill thought her much too young.

Once Bruce, Kathleen and Eileen broke their embrace Bill extended his hand to Kathleen. However, Kathleen pushed it away, stating, "Hey, we're family, here. Better get used to being hugged, especially by me!"

Bill opened and extended his arms and Kathleen did the same. Immediately, Bill patted Kathleen's back and began to move away.

"You call that a hug?" Kathleen questioned, pulling Bill back. "I don't think so!"

Bill's face began turning red.

"A hug is from your heart!" Kathleen insisted. "The last thing I want from you is a social thing."

Confused, Bill dropped his head and stared at the floor.

"I think we need to change your energy, young man," Kathleen stated as she nodded to the other people in the room. Quickly, everyone formed a circle, Bill standing in the center.

"I want you to hug everyone, one by one," Kathleen said very matter of fact.

One by one, Bill looked at everyone. Suddenly these people seemed adversarial.

"Take all the time you need," Eileen said in her usual loving voice.

Bill turned to look at Eileen. Then he reached out and gave her a hug since she seemed the most approachable of the group.

"Please, don't pat my back," Eileen asked. "Relax, just hold me, gentle and strong."

Bill did as Eileen requested. And as he did, he seemed to melt into her arms. Holding another person like this was unusual for Bill since, just like his father, he normally avoided most forms of body contact, man or woman. Finally he released his grip and backed out of Eileen's embrace, smiling.

"See, that wasn't so bad," Kathleen affirmed.

Bill, unsure, having never hugged a man before turned to Earl rather than a stranger. Earl nodded and smiled which helped considerably. Then, after a little hesitation, Bill pulled Earl into a strong hug even though he tried to end it after only a few seconds. However, Earl held Bill, saying. "Bill, don't listen to your head. You'll just hear all the social bullshit you've learned through the years. Listen to your heart!" Bill tightened his embrace, relaxed and breathed deeply.

Next to Earl stood Bruce. Bill had to admit being hugged by another man wasn't so bad even though it was certainly different than his experience with a woman.

Bill feared Worm. It was obvious. As Bill approached, Worm stood motionless with the eyes of a wild-man. Bill took a huge drink of air and extended his arms. Worm reciprocated in mockery. Then the two men broke into laughter. For Bill, Worm hugged like a giant bear. Bill was quite relieved when Worm whispered, "Thank you."

Finally Bill turned to Kathleen. "You're right, this isn't so bad. I apologize." Bill took Kathleen into his arms like he had the right. And as he did, magic happened. Bill felt an enchantment, something that he'd only experienced with one other person, Katarina.

That evening after everyone had eaten, Bill had washed and put away the dishes, Kathleen walked up to Bill, put her left hand on his right shoulder and said, "What you experienced this afternoon in my arms was not about sex. You know that."

Bill nodded, relieved.

"What you experienced was a momentary loss of ego."

Bill didn't understand, but said nothing.

"What that round of hugs did was to change your energy. You see, when a hug is truly heartfelt there's an exchange of energy, my heart to yours, yours to mine. That reciprocity cannot exist when ego is in the way. If you learn nothing else in the next several weeks, learn this!"

Several hours later, Bruce entered the living room from an outside verandah. He walked up to Bill, who was sitting on the davenport reading a magazine and said, "Bill, I'd like you to try a little experiment."

"What kind?"

"I'll show you. Lay down on the floor, on your back, face up."

Bill did as Bruce requested. As he did, Worm walked across the room and stood at his feet.

"Worm and I are going to pin you. Let's see what happens." Bruce took Bill's arms causing him to spread eagle while Worm pinned his legs in similar fashion.

Bill simply lay watching the two men while they smiled menacingly at him. He felt ridiculous and wondered what they were up to. Finally, after several boring minutes Bill tried to move by pulling his arms together, then his feet, but he couldn't.

"What the?" Bill began struggling to free himself. But he found that he was pinned to the floor by more force than he could overcome. He wiggled, he squirmed, pushed, pulled. But, he couldn't break their grip.

"Okay, I give up! You guys are stronger than me," Bill confessed. But nothing happened. No one said a thing. The men maintained their iron purchase. Bill strained to look around the room. Earl, Eileen and Kathleen were nowhere to be seen. Pywicket lay quietly snoring on the davenport.

"Damn! Let me go!" Bill pleaded, with his immature voice. Again he began to squirm, pushing and pulling against a hideous strength.

"Hey! This is not funny anymore! Let me go!" Bill yelled, struggling like trapped animal.

"Ahhhh!" Bill screamed! "Ahhhh!"

Worm and Bruce maintained their force.

"Ahhhh! FUCK YOU! Ahhhh!" Bill raged. But nothing he could do would release his bondage.

Finally, after what seemed an eternity, in a pool of sweat, arms aching, headache raging, Bill gave up.

Worm and Bruce released Bill's limbs and walked to the nearby davenport and sat down, themselves nearly exhausted. Pywicket had already escaped to another part of the house.

"What was that about?" Bill demanded, twenty minutes later, after having gone to the bathroom to regain some dignity. He was still angry, however.

"A point of reference, that's all," Bruce answered.

"A point of reference? Fuck you!" Bill stomped off into his bedroom and slammed the door.

Twenty Two

"Ugh!" Bill moaned, struggling to reach consciousness. A recurring nightmare woke him several times during the night. The vision was similar to an experience he had as a child of eight.

Bill's father, Chuck, was stationed at Fort Richardson Army Base in Anchorage, Alaska, during the Korean police action. The family lived in a tiny two-bedroom house at the tundra's edge in Steward. Bill was certain that a Red-Faced Indian lived under his bed and that it watched him with an inhuman stare. In the middle of the night he would wake up fearing for his life. Never a night passed that he didn't hide, almost suffocating, beneath blanket and pillow as he tried to go to sleep. He begged his parents to leave his bedroom door ajar or turn on a light, but they refused. What was worse, they humiliated him about his demon, openly and in public. Then, if he showed any emotion, his father slapped him on the side of the head as a bully might pick on the awkward kid in a schoolyard. And if Bill started to cry, Chuck would threaten rather loudly, "Ya better button it! Cos, if you want to cry, I'll really give you something to cry about!"

Bill got up and went to the bathroom after checking under the bed, then the closet. He knew his actions were ridiculous. But, old habits die hard.

"Where's everyone, like, gone?" Bill asked, walking into the side yard from the back porch of his summer residence.

"Everyone's gone to Santa Fe. Just us, young man," Worm replied while shooing a persistent fly. He appeared very serious and was setting up another round of firewood that needed to be split.

"Sorry I slept so late. Someone should have wakened me," Bill apologized.

"Be responsible for your own ecology!" Worm commanded. "Even animals do that. You're supposed to be human!"

"Huh? Was just trying to be polite, trying to make conversation. Have you eaten breakfast?"

"Hours ago."

"Mind if I go eat?"

"I'm not your mama!"

"Shit!" Bill said under his breath as he turned and walked away.

About twenty minutes later Worm walked through the back door and into the kitchen. He poured himself a drink from a jug of bottled water, then stood staring at Bill.

"I'm done with breakfast. What would you like me to do?" Bill asked, nervously.

"Wash your bowl and put it away."

"Young man, you come with me!" Worm demanded, hours later.

Bill got up from the living room davenport and put down a faded, well-used copy of *National Geographic*. Then he followed Worm through the kitchen and into the back yard. It was now almost four in the afternoon. Purposefully, he had been avoiding Worm like a bad dream, which yesterday's experience seemed like.

"Young man takes Sweat Lodge tonight," Worm announced matter-of-fact, pointing to a small adobe shack with a corrugated galvanized roof.

"That's a Sweat Lodge? Thought it was a storage shack!" Bill walked closer to the structure. "Like, aren't ya afraid it might fall down?" He pulled back the cloth flap and peered into a black gloom.

"You're on sacred ground, young man! Stop being an arrogant White Man! Show respect!"

Bill dropped the flap like it was poison ivy. He turned toward Worm and looked at the ground. "Sorry. I wasn't trying to be disrespectful. It, it's just that I don't know how to be around you."

Worm stepped closer to Bill and looked deep into his blue eyes. "Young man, you talk too much." Worm took hold of Bill's hands, turned them palm outward and placed them onto his own chest, just above his heart. Then he placed his own palms on Bill's chest in the same way. "Intent is from your heart, like a mother Puma protecting her young. Intention is from your head, path of logic and reasoning. This above all else, you must learn. Move through life with intent!" Worm blew lightly into Bill's hair. "Second thing you must learn is reciprocity. You are not alone. You are one with the energies and forces on our planet. The illusion of separateness leads to our greatest suffering. Separateness is social conditioning, only social conditioning." Worm blew lightly into Bill's hair once again. "Third thing young man must learn is, when ego dies, love is born." Worm blew a third time into Bill's hair.

"You are one with the Mother Earth," Worm continued. "I want you to lay your belly on the Mother Earth."

Before Bill had a chance to consider Worm's words, Worm pulled Bill's shirt up to expose his midsection. Then he pushed on Bill's shoulder, forcing him to lie face down on the bare ground. "You stay until I tell you to get up!" Worm walked to a pile of stacked wood and began carrying logs to the side of the Sweat Lodge.

"You know how make fire?" Worm asked Bill after about twenty minutes of lying on the bare earth.

Bill looked up from his prone position and nodded.

"Good! Make fire in pit!" Worm said as he walked several feet to the north and sat cross-legged on the ground. "No matches! No gasoline!"

Bill got up and brushed off his belly, then his clothes. As he did, he noticed an inner peace that he had seldom known.

Next to the Sweat Lodge stood a large makeshift steel crane. Next to the crane, an open fire pit and chute for loading the Sweat Lodge with scalding hot rocks. Bill quietly began his task. He stooped over and picked up several handfuls of dried grass, twigs and small diameter sticks along with about ten feet of small diameter hemp rope from a pile of debris near the back of the Sweat Lodge. Then he walked to the fire pit, Worm carefully watching. Bill placed his bundle on the ground and then walked to an open field looking for a palm sized granite stone. Once he found his prize, Bill took a dried cottonwood branch about four feet long a split it half way down the center with his pocket knife. At the end of the slit, he wrapped some rope and tied it off in order to prevent the slit from migrating further down the branch. Then he inserted the stone into the slit at the open end of the branch, forcing a clothespin effect. Into the slot of the clothespin, Bill put dried grass and a long piece of rope. A few dozen violent pulls on the rope followed by the force of his breath caused the dried grass to burst into flame. That flame, coaxed with more breath, jumped to the small twigs and, in turn, to the small diameter sticks. Once Bill knew the blaze was stable, he quickly built a tipi-shaped fire out of larger pieces of dried wood.

"Impressive! Even your great and mighty chiefs in Washington can't do such a simple thing!" Worm applauded.

Shortly after seven, dinner finished, dishes, pots and pans washed and put away, Kathleen escorted Bill to the Sweat Lodge. From Bill's blistering hot piñon pine fire and with the aid of a make shift crane, Worm began loading scalding hot rocks into an iron chute, sending them rolling into the lodge's bowels with a resounding thud. Sparks were popping and flying everywhere. Bill could smell the heat and was afraid that the dry grasses on the ground would catch fire.

"Take off your clothes and go in Lodge, respectfully!" Worm commanded.

Bill looked around wondering if any neighbors might be spying.

"Young man worries about being seen? Then we stop now and you go home to your mama." Worm laughed at Bill.

Bill removed his clothes and stepped into the Sweat Lodge's gloom without further ado. Then he sat down on a well-worn wooden bench seat. Several minutes later, Worm followed, then Kathleen, then Eileen, Earl and Bruce. They were also nude.

"Clear your mind of all thoughts. Relax," Bruce said in a quiet voice as Earl began throwing small buckets of water onto the glowing rocks. The water exploded into fountains of steam, filling the murk with thick burning vapors. The space became hotter and hotter until Bill's lungs began to burn. He thought he would suffocate.

Kathleen handed Bill a canteen of drinking water, then Worm began to sing unrecognizable sounds. From time to time Earl tossed several cups of water into the cauldron. Jets of light from the setting sun pierced through a myriad tiny holes that had been water-worn through the ancient adobe walls causing the thick vapor and the room to take on an ghostly quality. It didn't take long until Bill was certain he'd had enough. However, no one else appeared to feel the same way.

"Time for you to sing your song, young man." Worm announced as Earl tossed several more cups of water, creating another swell of suffocation.

Bill sat, saying nothing, singing nothing, feeling put upon. If last night seemed bad, this was worse.

"Master Earl tells me you creative man."

"I am," Bill said in his private thoughts. "But music needs form, structure. Without structure, there is only noise and chaos."

"Who makes form, structure?" Worm asked quietly.

Bill turned toward Worm, shocked. Did Worm read his mind?

"All things are formless. It is through intent that your Spirit collapses chaos into structure." Worm splattered water over the scalding hot rocks once, twice again. His eyes sparkled in the dim light. "You are Spirit. You have power."

Instantly, Bill knew that whatever he did was okay. He opened his mouth and let his song gradually flow. It wasn't Brahms, nor was it Beethoven. It was Bill Colton.

"Young man," Worm began close to midnight after everyone had sung their songs and they had reassembled in the villa's living room. "You are highly thought of by your people. Tonight I will smoke my pipe in your honor. We shall see."

Bill, turned, smiling, looking at Earl for a cue. Earl said nothing, not even returning his glance. Bill took it for a sign and remained silent.

"White Man's way to heal spirit is to throw fishing line in lake, wait for something to bite. That way is very slow. Indian way is to jump in lake, swim, catch fish with bare hands," Worm said as he pulled his long pipe from a leather case. "Come!"

"Take that blanket." Worm pointed to a beautiful Navajo blanket sitting next to the davenport. "Place on the floor, then you sit, facing North. Please, cross your legs."

Bill obeyed Worm's command.

After several minutes, Worm sat down facing Bill. He removed some tobacco from his leather pouch, stuffed his pipe, lit it and inhaled several deep breaths. Then he offered the pipe to the spirits by holding it high over his head and perpendicular to his shoulders.

"Here, take pipe and smoke!"

Bill took the pipe and tried to imitate Worm's movements. He took several short puffs followed by a long drag with his eyes closed. Then he held the pipe up and into the air and exhaled. Bill tried to hand the pipe back to Worm.

"No, to Bruce. Give the pipe to Bruce."

Bruce took several deep breaths of smoke and saluted the spirits, then passed it to Eileen. Bill realized that the four people surrounding him formed the cardinal points of a compass. Worm was North. Bruce was West. Eileen was South and Kathleen was East. Earl was sitting by himself on the davenport next to a hoop drum. Pywicket was nowhere to be seen.

"Lay down on back. Stretch out!" Worm commanded. Then he picked up a rattle and began shaking it up and down Bill's body while chanting, "Unga-wa, a-unga-wa, a-unga-wa, a-unga-wa." Over and over he chanted his words, slowly changing the pitch of his voice, higher, then lower. "Unga-wa, a-unga-wa, a-unga-wa, a-unga-wa." This went on for, perhaps, fifteen minutes. The staccato of the rattle hurt Bill's ears.

Finally, Worm stopped. He looked at Bill intently. Then he glanced at Earl who began beating the drum in a moderate tempo.

Worm rolled onto the floor like an acrobat, coming to rest next to Bill, touching him, shoulder to shoulder, hip to hip and leg to leg, both men facing the ceiling, Worm on Bill's left. Bill wanted to run from the room screaming. But he also knew this show was for him and he'd better pay attention.

"Young man, your power is Puma, Crow, Eagle and Wolf. These, your teachers," Worm announced after twenty minutes of drummed meditation.

"Puma teaches how to be own leader, overcome uncertainty, accept responsibility for one's existence."

"Wolf is pathfinder in wilderness, brings new knowledge of world."

"Eagle is light of Great Spirit. Eagle flies close to sun, doesn't get burnt. Eagle carries spirit knowledge to world of humans.

"Crow is shape shifter. When you change your thinking, you change your future. Your new name, Little Crow. Ho!"

"The South is the path of the Serpent," Eileen began. "It is about renewal, letting go of anguishes and successes, self-limiting beliefs. Bill, you must travel to the South."

"The West is about the journey to personal power," Bruce continued. "It is the Jaguar path. Let the Jaguar teach you fierceness in your life. Let yourself be reborn. You must travel West."

"North is Path of Ancestor. Dragon path. For Little Crow it holds anger, fear, blame, resentment. North you must go," Worm added.

"The East is the Eagle's path. The Eagle flies into the sun without being consumed. This is the path to enlightenment, your final journey," Kathleen concluded.

"Now you must dance one of your Power Animals!" Earl commanded as he began beating his drum again, sustaining a moderately quick tempo and accenting every fourth beat.

Bill stood and looked cautiously around the room. All eyes were upon him as stage fright began claiming his awareness. He remembered being humiliated in an Art, Music and Dance Humanities class at State College. For his final, he was to dance as a tree. He failed. Now, just like then, he didn't know what to do.

Earl smiled at Bill and nodded, not missing a beat, while saying, "The spirits will help you. You must honor them in kind with your dance. Reciprocity in all things!"

Following several more uncomfortable minutes, cautiously, Bill extended his arms like a bird of prey and began moving his feet in a manner uncoordinated. He prayed no one would burst into laughter. He remembered himself as a Boy Scout, himself poking fun at the Order of the Arrow, believing their dancing was a joke. He had no idea that someday he would be put to task. However, despite what he felt, Bill took a deep breath and began moving around the room. And as he did a subtle transformation began to take place. Slowly he began to surrender his feelings of inadequacy. Slowly, he became the dance and the energy in the room began to change.

Without warning Bill was airborne. He seemed to be somewhere very high over a vast desert, drawn toward the southwest. There were mountains, valleys, rivers, and as he looked around, everything below him began to glow, dimly at first, then brighter as he flew. Everything was connected by tiny filaments of seamless energy. In his heart and not in his head, Bill realized that there was a reciprocity of energy radiating throughout the entire planet. Life was everywhere. It was in the rocks, the Earth's backbone and skeleton. It was in the soils, the Earth's skin. It was in the water, the blood of the Earth. It was in the winds of the air as the Earth breathed. For the first time, Bill saw the Earth as the Garden of Eden, providing all manners of mammals, fishes, reptiles, insects and birds the sustenance by which to live. The creatures, in turn, gave back to the Earth the breath of awareness.

After a long time or a short time, Bill wasn't sure, there was a tree in front of him, surrealistically suspended in space. Browns, greens, blues, yellows, oranges and reds, the colors were magnificent. But the tree seemed to have no base nor top, it extended in all directions toward infinity. Bill changed the angle of his giant wings and slowly came to rest on a huge branch. But as he touched down, he was no longer an eagle. He was a blob of luminous energy, floating, without physical form. At once Bill saw another ball of conscious energy. He knew it was conscious because it was obviously aware of his presence. Glowing brilliant amber, it moved to greet him. Bill was moved to reach out and touch it. Instantly, Earl changed the beat from a rhythmic flow to four groups of seven very rapid staccato beats. Then there was silence.

Bill was wringing wet as he fell to the floor. He was seized by sporadic spasms rippling throughout his entire body. Worm quickly took Bill's right hand and extended his forefinger and forced him to tap himself repeatedly on his solar plexus. In accompaniment, Earl matched the tapping rhythm with staccato drumbeats. Little by little Bill began to relax. Slowly, he returned to normal awareness. Finally, Worm and Bruce helped Bill into the bathroom and put him into a cold tub of water.

"Like, what happened?" Bill asked as he re-entered the living room almost an hour later.

Worm began to say something but Earl put up his hand, flagging him to stop.

"How are you feeling?" Earl asked walking up to Bill and putting his arms around him.

"What the hell happened to me?"

"You went a little farther than you should have."

"Did I really fly?" Bill asked.

"Yes and no," Earl returned. "Let's just say your spirit soared like the eagle for a little while."

"My body?"

"It was right here, all the time."

"I don't understand, not at all. It was so real!"

"Understanding will come, Bill. The important thing, what do you feel right at this moment?"

Bill got a huge smile on his face, then answered. "Like I'm in love."

Twenty Three

"This evening, I'll be your guide," Kathleen announced. She escorted Bill to one of the spare bedrooms and pointed to a full-length mirror. Then she offered Bill a pillow. "Please, sit comfortably and take a good look at yourself."

"What's this about?"

"Surrender, that's what it's about."

"Surrender?" Bill looked in the mirror. He saw his same old self. "Kathleen?"

"Shush, trust the process. For now, just look." Kathleen pulled the drapes eliminating most of the light from the room. Then on her way out, she stated, "Please, relax. I'll be back when you're ready."

"Ready for what?" Bill questioned, under his breath.

At first Bill had no problem sitting and doing nothing. In fact he found the time rather enjoyable. However, slowly his legs became pain-ridden and wanted to cramp. Finally he gave in to his discomfort and moved.

"What's your experience?" Kathleen whispered from behind.

"I, I see white light. It's, like, all around," Bill lied. Kathleen had caught him off guard and he figured he should say something that sounded spiritual.

Bill momentarily straightened his legs, repositioned himself and tried to quiet his mind once again. Finally, after what seemed an eternity and his body was crying out in pain, he shifted his weight.

"What's your experience?" Kathleen queried again.

"I saw Katarina. She's laughing, sewing in the living room of her parents' home. Her cat is swatting a string dangling from her work." Bill's image was very clear and correct.

Bill cracked his eyes ever so slightly. The room was now completely dark. He knew it was night. He had been there for hours.

Slowly Bill's consciousness began drifting in and out of awareness. At first he heard voices, then he'd return to normal awareness. Soon he'd drift back and hear the voices again. This phenomenon occurred many times and he enjoyed the experience. What the voices said though, it was impossible to tell, there were too many of them. Some were laughing and some were crying. Some spoke in foreign languages while others sounded like English. None of them made any sense. Yet, they all made sense.

"What's your experience?" Kathleen queried a third time.

"I heard the voices of God."

"Please, come with me."

Bill was surprised when he opened his eyes. Now the room was filled with candlelight. Kathleen offered Bill her hand and helped him to his feet. He could barely get up as his legs tried to give out from under him.

"How long?"

"Shhh! For now, only speak when you're asked to. Come, follow me." Kathleen escorted Bill to his bedroom. The room had been changed. Now, there were several wooden benches with banks of lit candles and open trays of water. In the middle of the room was a massage table covered with linen.

"Please, remove your robe, climb onto the table and lay face down."

Bill did as Kathleen asked. Then she covered him with a linen sheet.

Several minutes later the door opened. Bruce, Eileen, Earl and Worm entered the room and took various positions around the table. For some unknown reason, Bill was glad to see Worm. Presently he felt a strange, yet, warm kinship with him.

"Tonight we are working on the balancing of your spirit," Kathleen announced as she placed her hands gently on the sides of Bill's head. "Within the muscle tissue of your body lies the stress of your past. Modern people assume that memory resides only in our heads. Tonight you will learn differently. You will understand that your entire body is mind.

"Now relax and center yourself," Kathleen continued. "Imagine a relaxing energy entering your body through the balls of your feet. Cause that energy to extend the full length of your legs, slowly and deliberately. Slowly, slowly…

"Imagine the relaxing energy entering through the palms of your hands, working its way along your arms and into your shoulders. Slowly, slowly…

"Imagine the relaxing energy entering your body through the base of your spine and traveling up your spinal chord and abdominal cavity. Good.

"Now, make it connect with the energies from your arms and legs, terminating at the very top of your head."

As Bill imagined the energy, warmth began to rise from the base of his spine, slowly ascending. Then from his spine, warmth radiated throughout his entire body.

"Good, Bill. You're a natural at this stuff!

"Now, I am going to touch you," Kathleen resumed. "I am going to touch you where there is imbalance. Your job is simple, balance yourself. I know this maybe difficult at times. This is why others are in this room with you. They will assist you with their energy when you need them. Now, breathe deeply."

Bill did as Kathleen asked.

"When I touch you, you will feel pain. The amount of pain will be proportional to the amount of imbalance between your body and your spirit. When you heal your imbalance, the pain will be gone. The way to heal is to say out loud, 'I forgive myself. The light of God flows though me.' Then visualize yourself at peace with yourself, the world and all sentient beings. When necessary I encourage you to ask for assistance from other people in this room. That assistance can take almost any form you wish. Do you understand?"

"I think so." Bill whispered.

"Ahhhh!" Bill cried out, a severe pain suddenly shooting through the back of his neck and skull.

"This is your arrogance talking. You think you're better than everyone else! Well, this is the pain those beliefs get you," Kathleen said as she pushed her left index finger into the soft tissue at the base of Bill's skull.

Bill was on the verge of crying. The pain was almost overwhelming.

"What are you going to do with it?"

Bill fumbled. He couldn't think.

"Self-importance keeps you from being a fully-functioning human being. Doesn't it?"

Bill began sobbing.

"What are you going to do with it?"

As he lay there almost helpless, Bill had no idea what to do with it. The pain began rapidly spreading across his upper back.

"Bill, repeat after me. 'I forgive myself,'" Earl whispered in Bill's left ear.

"I forgive myself." Bill choked out the words as best he could.

"The light of God flows through me."

"The light, the light of God, it flows through me." Bill could hardly remember the words, even as Earl spoke them.

"Now visualize yourself at peace with yourself, the world and all sentient beings."

Bill found the visualization impossible.

"Bill, relax, relax…relax." Eileen's spoke softly. "Repeat your mantra."

Bill struggled to remember, "I forgive myself."

"Good!"

"The light of God flows through me."

"Excellent. What else?"

Bill tried the visualization. He didn't know what it was supposed to look like.

"You're doing fine, Bill. Relax. Breathe deeply. You know what to do. You have all the tools necessary. And, you can ask for help."

"Take away my pain!" Bill blurted out.

"That's your task. But I can help you breathe." Bruce returned as he pressed his hands firmly, yet gently, on Bill's lower back, forcefully slowing down his breathing cycle. "Breathe in with tranquillity, breathe out with tranquillity," Bruce repeated, over and over again.

Slowly, as Bill began to relax, he tried to visualize the time in his life when he was the most peaceful. Gradually, he remembered. It was when he was completely filled with love. Katarina and Bill were at Philmont. They had just finished lunch and were walking across an open field near the trap range on their way to the Ranch's Trading Post, hand in hand. They were talking about their lives, their hopes and dreams. That afternoon, Bill's world was magnificent.

Suddenly, Bill's awareness was back in Española. His pain was almost gone.

"Excellent! You're doing it. Now keep doing it. What's your mantra?" Kathleen's voice was now very soothing and musical.

"I forgive myself. The light of God flows through me," Bill said softly.

"Again," Kathleen whispered.

"I forgive myself. The light of God flows through me," Bill continued with increased certainty, touching the feelings of love experienced during Philmont's special afternoon.

"Again!"

"I forgive myself. The light of God flows through me." Bill began repeating his mantra over and over as he became one with his memory of total peace and love. Finally, his pain was history and he was breathing easily on his own.

"Congratulations, Bill. Let's see if we can find some more spots," Kathleen said, like she was enjoying herself.

Suddenly, Bill's back exploded into fire. This time, however, the center was midway up his spine. "Shit!"

"Ah! Bill resents authority. Doesn't he?"

"Yes! I confess!" Bill's pain was worse than before.

"This is not confession, my dear," Kathleen said with a ring of humor in her voice. "Confession is passive. I'm afraid you're a participator in this one. What is your response?"

"I forgive myself. The light of God flows through me." Bill repeated the mantra many times trying to calm his inner landscape.

Finally Bill asked Earl to show him how to be accepting of authority. He was shocked by what happened.

Gently, so very gently, Earl helped Bill sit up on the table. Then he and Eileen took Bill into their arms and began rocking him back and forth as though they were parents nurturing a little child. Others in the room began massaging Bill's shoulders, back and scalp.

Worm spoke very quietly into Bill's left ear. "It's okay to cry. I won't push you away."

Immediately a dam broke and Bill's emotions carried him like a summer's flash flood.

After several minutes the deluge began to subside. Then Bill realized that Earl was speaking very softly into his left ear while Eileen spoke into his right. At first he didn't understand what was being said. Then he got it. They were saying, "I love you."

"I forgive myself. The light of God flows through me." Gradually Bill resumed his mantra. Over and over, perhaps a thousand times he said it while holding the visualization of Philmont and Katarina. Finally the pain dissipated completely.

"Let's take a short break. I think Bill could use some rest," Kathleen suggested.

As everyone began leaving the room, Kathleen offered Bill a glass of water.

"God, I can't believe how thirsty I am." Bill gulped the cool liquid down.

"So many questions," Bill said softly after wiping his mouth with the back of his hand. Why did Kathleen's touch create such affliction? Why did a simple mantra and the visualization of love remove it? He didn't understand how he could feel both relaxed and tense at the same time.

"You're doing just fine," Kathleen said, smiling. "You'll understand in due time. For now, relax and enjoy your experience."

Kathleen turned, walked from the room, quietly shutting the door behind her.

Bill glanced around the room as best he could from his reclining position. It was the same drab room he'd just spent many hours cleaning up. Yet, in the candlelight it held a quality of magic. Somehow, he knew that he'd remember this special room for the rest of his life. He shut his eyes and slowed his internal dialog.

About half an hour later, to Bill's surprise, Kathleen, Earl, Worm, Bruce and Eileen returned to the room and took their respective places. It seemed only minutes since they left.

"Ready to go on?" Kathleen looked at Bill in a way he thought a mother might look at her precious child.

"Yeah, think so."

"Roll back on your stomach, please."

Bill did as Kathleen asked.

"Let's see if we can find some resentment! Ah, there it is."

Bill's back lit up like the Fourth of July. "I forgive myself! The light of God flows through me!"

"Resentment destroys your soul. It comes from aged anger. It comes from feeling powerless. It comes from playing the role of victim. Bill, for you its about feeling unwelcome on this planet."

Bill heard what Kathleen said. He continued his mantra of self-forgiveness.

"Bill, you have the right to be here!" Worm's words were crystal clear.

Inside Bill a little voice said, "No! Not true!" Again Bill began to sob. The conflict inside his body began tying him in knots.

"Help me to be born again," Bill asked.

Very quietly but quickly Bill found himself covered with a mass of people. It became hard to move. Their bodies removed all the light, or maybe someone turned out the room lights. He wasn't sure. Bill felt suffocated and wanted free. But they held him in and amongst them. Unexpectedly, Bill heard a soft slow beating drum. He realized that, somehow, it was synchronous to his own heartbeat. Slowly, so very slowly, Bill found peace within himself.

Once Bill was calm, people began moving. He felt like he was in a cosmic womb being pushed through time and space. First his head was free then his upper body, pelvis, legs. Finally his friends were holding him as if he were an infant. The electric light in the room was turned off so that the only light came from seven lit candles.

Eileen spoke softly, "Welcome, welcome to the world, my child."

Spontaneously Bill burst into tears. This time, however, his tears only lasted a minute or two. He was surprised at how fast they came and went. Because he knew he held so much resentment that he could go into depression for days.

Shortly, Bill turned back and lay face down on the table asking Kathleen to go on.

"Ah, here's a big one for you. Confusion."

This time Bill's pain was different. It was like someone opened his spine with a dull axe.

"Confusion comes from your unwillingness to sort information. It's your unwillingness to take responsibility for your own clarity. You use confusion to protect yourself by not getting too close to your issues in life. But it's a smoke screen. The only one who can't see it is you."

Again Bill said his mantra. He visualized himself at peace with the world. But the pain remained.

"I think I need help with this one, too. I don't know what, though. Maybe you all could just be with me."

"Take all the time you need." Eileen began repeating over and over again into Bill's right ear.

"I love myself." Bruce began repeating in Bill's left ear.

Then Bill heard the others in the room begin to chant with him. "I forgive myself. The light of God flows through me." Quickly, Bill was able to focus and let the pain go. When they began chanting, it was like someone turned on a dynamo. The room became electric.

"Our mind traps keep us from being fully human. Because they keep us out of the present. Worry and hope are creative. Yet they buy us nothing but anxiety," Kathleen said as she began massaging Bill's back and neck.

Finally there were no more spots. They were through. As Bill lay there so very quietly, he realized the world was now a gentler place. He was truly thankful.

"Now for the icing on the cake," Kathleen announced as she pulled the sheet from Bill's naked body.

Respectfully, five pairs of hands began to massage Bill's physical presence.

"Remember this always: the price you pay for clinging to your mind traps is the loss of intimacy. Loss of intimacy with yourself, your family, the entire world. Bill, where you place your life's energy is a matter of choice. Continue with your mantra."

"I forgive myself. The light of God flows through me." Bill whispered over and over as those wonderful hands removed any remaining tension from his body.

"Go look at yourself in the mirror," Kathleen finally whispered.

Bruce helped Bill off the table. Then he walked back into the room that he had started from. With the exception of one lone candle in the northeast corner, the room was without artificial light. Yet the room was filled with a light that became brighter as Bill walked further in. Suddenly, he realized the light's source.

"Oh, my God!" Bill stood in front of the mirror, dazed. "The light is me." He could see very plainly. Standing in front of the mirror was a magical being bathed in brilliant violet light. His heart radiated all the colors of the rainbow. His spine was a shaft of pure gold. The top of his head was a deeper violet while the outer fringes of his aura radiated gold. "I am that magical being."

"Of course you are." Bruce said, standing at the room's entrance and watching Bill. "You always have been. You just forgot. That's your only problem!"

Twenty Four

"Bill, for the next several weeks you will not speak, and except for Earl and me, you will not contact other people," Eileen began, the next morning just before breakfast, before Bill had the chance to shower and shave. "You will not leave this room. You will sleep eight hours a day, eat your meals at the allotted time. You will meditate the remaining period. To awaken you each day, one of us will rap three groups of seven on your door. At food time we will rap on your door three times, at which time you will turn away and not watch us in your room. At bedtime one of us will rap once. If at any time we find you doing something inappropriate you will be rapped on the head with a stick. Do you understand?"

"I don't, like, understand anything."

"Suffice it to say, you haven't even begun your quest, Bill," Earl added. "I know you feel on top of the world right now. Your heart is filled with beauty and love. You think if you get much higher, you'll explode. But your experience is a result of our assistance and if you stop now, in a few days or weeks your awareness will return to what it was. At some point in time you must learn to stand on your own!"

"What must I do?"

"Trust the process! For now silence is very important. So, until one of us tells you otherwise, merely nod your head. You are no longer allowed to speak. From now on, speaking is inappropriate," Eileen continued.

Bill nodded. Then he looked back at Earl whose face seemed strangely foreboding.

"Of course, you may go to the bathroom anytime. It is essential that you take care of yourself. However, you may not shower, shave or otherwise wash your body. We will provide you with a fresh change of clothing every day. At the end of seven days, you will be escorted to another room and asked to bathe. But you still may not speak. Do you understand?"

Bill nodded once again.

"Please, begin your meditations now."

Both Earl and Eileen turned and left Bill's room, closing the door quietly behind them. Bill sat on his bed, confused. Whatever his expectations were for the summer, it wasn't this. Besides, he didn't know how to meditate, even though he had attended a university lecture and read about it in a book.

"How did it go? Empty your mind of all thoughts? Hold your posture erect? Place your hands across your belly, palms up, right on top of left, thumbs touching just below your navel?" Bill tried to imagine a meditating Buddha and propped himself on his pillow using the wall at the head of the bed to support his back. He closed his eyes and immediately began thinking about Katarina.

"What's she doing right now?" Bill's internal dialog began. In his mind's eye he could imagine Katarina stacking books in the library. He fantasized walking between the shelves, putting his hands over her eyes and saying, "Guess who?" And, of course, she'd know. She'd turn and, together, they would blush. It would be like old times, like the times they experienced with each other at Philmont. Only now since they were adults, he'd take her into his arms and kiss her. Time would become eternal and, together, they would merge into one, just like in his dreams.

Suddenly the door opened, Earl walked in and rapped Bill lightly on top of the head with a three-foot long stick. Then he turned and left the room.

"Empty your mind of all thoughts?" Bill spoke in his throat, not moving his jaw. "But how?"

Once again Bill closed his eyes. It didn't take long until he began thinking about the music he would play at his senior recital. "Let's see, Bach, *Partita Number 2 in D minor*, *The Devil's Trill*, a movement for a violin concerto, probably Beethoven. Shit! I'm doing it again. Empty your mind!" Bill commanded himself.

As Bill sat, having little or no success stopping his internal dialog, he remembered that saying something over and over again while mentally watching ones breath was a meditative technique he'd read about.

"Let's see, I breathe in with tranquillity," Bill said, as he filled his lungs with air.

"I breathe out with tranquillity," Bill said, exhaling.

"Oh yeah, slowly, rhythmically.

"I breathe in with tranquillity, five, six, seven.

"Hold, two, three, four.

"I breathe out with tranquillity, five, six, seven.

"Hold, two, three, four." Bill began repeating his breathing cycle over and over again. After about a half an hour, for several seconds, he was able to maintain a moment of quietness within his mind. And in that quietness, he became acutely aware of his entire body. Suddenly, he knew the Red-Faced Indian was staring at him.

Startled, Bill jumped up and surveyed the room with dispatch. Nothing. He threw open the curtains and pulled the blinds on the room's window. Nothing. He ran to the bathroom. Nothing. He even looked under the bed. Nothing.

Bill started to call out to see if Earl or Eileen was pulling some prank. Then he remembered his agreement around silence, several weeks!

Slowly, cautiously, Bill tried to resume his meditation. But now he was unnerved. Following several hours with no success, in despair, he picked up a pencil and paper and wrote a poem:

Puberty love
  The strongest of all.
Knows no bounds
  Neither wisdom nor fall.

That was the day
  I came alive.
Filled with such passion
  I could hardly survive.

Together we shared
  As souls understand.
Transfixed and aloof
  To social demand.

Like rings in a pool
  From stones thrown untamed.
Heaven and Earth touched
  I know it ordained.

I prayed God
  The moment not end.
Came the reply
  My heart would descend.

Lingers my touch
  Such beautiful eyes.
My parent's distrust
  Completes my despise.

The days grew long
  As I went into battle.
But parents won out
  I lost to their prattle.

Not to look back
  My master's reply.
Being human
  Is not to deny.

Heart's ache
  Now lingers my days.
The tomb of my beloved
  Is still touched by my blaze.

Earl walked into the room and rapped Bill several times on the head with his stick.

Twenty Five

Tap, tap, tap, came the promised three groups of seven raps on the second morning of Bill's spiritual sojourn.

"Ugh!" Bill moaned. Slowly he got up and took care of his morning toilet.

Following breakfast, Bill began his promised meditations. But it was difficult as memories permeated his awareness…

It was Tuesday afternoon, July Sixteenth, 1957. The Colton family was on vacation at Philmont Scout Ranch in Cimarron, New Mexico, so that Bill's father could attend a District Commissioner's training conference.

"There's a ranch tour we should go on," Chuck announced as soon as the Coltons were unpacked and settled into their assigned tents.

Walking toward the ranch house where the posted tour was to begin, Bill saw hundreds of tents forming a virtual city.

"It says here that there are over thirteen-hundred people here this week," Chuck explained to his wife and children, paraphrasing a camp brochure. "This is only one of many training conferences going on. There are programs for adults and youths alike. They offer training for every phase of Scouting and people come from all over the United…"

All of a sudden, Bill lost the ability to hear what his father was saying. Sitting on a low brick wall in the ranch house verandah were two girls about his own age engaged in conversation. One girl especially caught his eye. Dressed in a white cotton sundress and a dark blue barrette in her long blond hair, she was magnificent. Directly, she caught Bill's stare. She smiled and waved shyly. Involuntarily, Bill began to walk towards her.

"C'mon let's go." Out of nowhere, Virginia yanked Bill's arm, digging her fingernails into his wrist, breaking the skin. It stung as he recoiled against his mother's pull and he let out an agonizing yelp. "Don't stare, damn you! Ya know that's impolite as hell," she reprimanded.

"I wonder if that was an omen?" Bill asked himself, returning to normal awareness. "Even the first time I saw Katarina, it was painful."

Bill closed his eyes and took a huge drink of air, then let it slowly back out.

"Philmont was the most wonderful experience in my life." Bill reminded himself, remembering many wonderful days where he and Katarina romped through the camp trading post together, enjoying evening square dancing, hiking in the desert, fantastic desert thunderstorms, horseback riding…

"Y'all want to go with me to the riding stables?" Katarina asked, walking up to Bill the afternoon of the second day.

"You bet," Bill replied, glancing at Katarina's slacks. They were light khaki and fitted her very well. She stood about five foot one, was slender and extremely attractive, even for a thirteen-year-old.

"These are riding slacks." Katarina noticed Bill looking at her in a different way and started turning red. "That's why they look strange." Pointing to her hips, "These side panels allow more comfort and freedom of movement when I'm riding, see."

As Bill looked into Katarina's eyes, he began to blush. "What do you do besides ride?" He asked, trying to change the subject.

"Well?" Katarina scratched her head. "I dance. I..."

"What kind?" Bill interrupted.

"Ballet."

"Wow! I'm impressed. What else?"

"I like music."

"Really! You play?" Bill asked excitedly.

"Yeah!"

"What instrument?"

"Piano and flute. Y'all?"

"Violin! I take lessons from Mister Babashoff. He plays in the Los Angeles Philharmonic."

"Gee! That's great! My parents really can't afford for us kids to study privately. Luckily the teacher at school is very good. Is that what y'all want to be when you grow up? I mean, a violinist?"

"You bet. You?"

"A school teacher. Mom says I should have a career, ya know just in case."

"In case of what?" Bill asked.

"Well, in case something happens."

"Huh? What would happen?"

"Well, ya see it's like this. My Aunt Margaret lost her first husband in the war. If it wasn't for her college degree, she probably wouldn't have made it. My Mom and she are big on education. I think they're right, well what they say makes sense. Mom believes that you've got to plan for the future. Before you know it we'll be all grown up and living the lives we dream about. So you've got to have the right dreams, I mean ones that are practical and make sense."

"My dad is afraid of dreams." Bill felt his voice quiver. He couldn't help thinking about his own hopes and dreams. The ideas Katarina had seemed different from those held by his own family.

"Why?"

"He says, 'Living one's life with dreams is immature and a complete waste of time.' He says, 'When you spend all your time dreaming, and all is said and done, what have you got to show for it? Nothin'.'" Bill had to pause in thought, then he went on. "But I do have lots of dreams and hopes for the future."

"Me too! I'm going to have a wonderful life, just know it!" Katarina smiled like she had a secret.

Bill looked deep into Katarina's crystal blue eyes. He had secrets, too. "I dream a lot at night, ya know, when I'm asleep. Many dreams seem real. Sometimes, they come true. Like, I know things are going to happen before they do."

"Really? ESP?"

"Guess ya could call it that."

"I have those. Please, tell me."

"Well, about six months ago I had a dream about a bridge that was being demolished near Huntington Beach. A week later, I saw that bridge being demolished, for real."

"Gee!"

"I, I dreamt about you."

Katarina stopped cold in her tracks. Then she looked straight into Bill's face while biting her lower lip.

"I dreamt about a sandy blond haired girl who played the piano." Without warning, Bill's stomach spasmed. He stopped talking and looked away. He remembered that being too open with this kind of talk had turned peers against him.

"That's all?"

"No, of course not. In my dream we lived in separate cities and wrote lots of letters."

"Y'all holding things back. There is somethin'."

"Oh no! Just a crazy dream."

Bill sensed that Katarina was getting scared, too. Luckily, Katarina spotted an Appaloosa and they could easily change the subject.

Circling the corral fence quietly, dodging puddles of muddy water and several angry anthills, Bill fell in behind Katarina's lead. He was obviously the observer while she was on her home turf. Picking up a couple of pieces of broken hay flake from the ground, Katarina moved slowly toward the gelding.

"Tsk, tsk, tsk." Katarina clicked her tongue on the roof of her mouth while holding her teeth closed and lips pushed forward. Her face was lit with excitement.

The horse raised its ears. Then he walked nonchalantly towards Katarina as she coaxed him with the hay in her outstretched hand. When he began nibbling, she closed in, blowing very gently into his nostrils. She had obviously made a friend.

"But, somehow, I always messed up," Bill reminded himself with a tear in his eye, returning from the bathroom, remembering the final evening of the encampment...

Bill and Katarina were sitting together in an award ceremony. Bill received an honorable mention for a model car he had carved out of pine and entered into the slot car race. Katarina received first place in her age group for a hand-embroidered towel.

"I have a secret." Toward the end of the evening Bill leaned over and whispered into Katarina's ear.

"What?" Katarina asked, turning towards Bill, her expressive eyes smiling brightly at him.

Bill hesitated, then resumed. "Don't know if I should say."

"Come on, silly." Katarina nudged Bill's left knee with her right.

"Time to get a marriage license."

"I, I…" Turning red as a beet, Katarina jumped up and ran from the auditorium.

Bill ran after her, apologizing, begging her to wait. But she disappeared in the dark shadows between the tents. He looked and looked. But, damn, it was all useless. He hated himself! What an idiot!

Twenty Six

"I breathe in with tranquillity," Bill began again, following lunch.
"I breathe out with tranquillity." Bill exhaled.
"I breathe in with tranquillity, five, six, seven.
"Hold, two, three, four…"

Slowly, Bill's mind cleared. He found himself reliving an afternoon in early February during his senior year in high school. He was walking into the kitchen of his parents' house and sitting down at the dining table. His mother was fixing stew, his least favorite meal…

"How's Debbie, dear? You haven't mentioned her in quite awhile." Bill knew that his mother was looking for ways to distract his attention from Katarina. But he didn't want to play her game.

"I can't believe it! I finally got a letter, after a whole month."

"I didn't know you two were writing."

"Oh, Mom. From Katarina, like, ya know that."

"I think you should see more of Debbie. She's such a sweet girl.

"Debbie and me…"

"And I," Virginia corrected.

"We're good friends, nothing more."

"Billy, how many times must I tell you? Katarina is…"

As his mother began to ramble, once again Bill tuned her out, his thoughts turning toward school. String music class was actually an open study period to do anything one wanted. Though practicing was encouraged, his teacher was more interested in band and usually spent the time preparing for parades or football games. Almost every day Bill and Debbie would go into one of the practice rooms together. She would simply listen while he practiced. He always started with scales in three octaves beginning with open G, then ascended in half steps. First long bows, then the flying spiccato, four bounces to a note, then three, two and finally one. Single bounce spiccato was difficult because the fingers traveled so fast. But Bill knew almost anything could be mastered if one was willing to practice. He was learning the Bach *Unaccompanied Violin Sonatas*. However, Debbie really liked the Beethoven's *Violin Concerto in D* best.

"Billy! Come back! Don't daydream on me!" Virginia shouted.

"Ah, sorry, mom." Bill jumped. "Was thinking about school today. Debbie said one of the Bach sonatas I played sounded like laughter."

"You must learn to control your daydreaming. Your father doesn't like it a bit! Why don't you take Debbie to a school dance or something?"

"She has a boyfriend," Bill answered, thinking he could get off easy.

"Tsk, tsk, tsk. That shouldn't stop a Colton man. Really, you should go out there and break a few hearts."

"Mom, I'm going to marry Katarina! I don't care about anyone else!"

"I wish you'd give up that crazy idea!"

"Why?"

"We've been through this before, damn you. She's a Sagittarius."

"What's that, like, got to do with anything?"

"Won't you ever get it? Two people of the same sign shouldn't be together. They're too much alike. They'll squelch each other. It's that simple."

"Mom," Bill's voice cracked, "how can ya be so sure?"

"It's the law of the stars."

Bill looked away, not wanting to hear any more.

"What you had was a summer's romance, puppy love, nothing more. We've all been through it. Sooner or later you had to go through it, too. And, I'm glad you're getting it out of your system. But now it's time to grow up. You wait and see; someday you'll meet someone. Zap! You'll flip head over heels. You know, what you've felt is nothing compared to the real thing when the right one comes along."

Bill couldn't imagine what his mother was talking about. Every time he received one of Katarina's letters his insides went off like the Fourth of July. "What about you? Did you have a romance like me and Katarina?"

"Katarina and I! No, I was luckier. I never loved anyone until I met your father."

"What about Dad?"

"He had a sweetheart before he met me. Don't tell him I said this, but we saw her a couple of years ago in the supermarket. She was really fat and had six kids. I think your father was embarrassed."

Bill sensed a con.

"Billy, listen to your mama. I don't think it's a good idea for you to visit her anymore."

Bill turned, looking at his mother with a start. Did he say too much? Did she know his secret?

"You don't fool me for a second! I know what the stars say. When you go to sleep at night, you're out and about. You go visit her don't you?"

"Ah..."

"I know you do. You've got a wonderful gift, a gift that you've earned in past lives. But listen to me now and listen well. Don't ever tell a soul. They'll think you're crazy or something. People simply don't understand this sort of thing. Your father doesn't. He's been concerned about you for years. He thinks you have psychotic dreams. I know different. I've been studying your astrological chart. You're one of the few who are gifted enough to bring back knowledge from other worlds. This planet will someday be a better place because people like you have lived. I'm not going to let anyone keep you from your destiny, especially someone like her."

Suddenly, Bill was yanked from his vision by three raps on his hermitage door. He turned his body and faced the wall with his eyes closed while paying extreme attention to the sounds being made as his dinner was placed on a small desk. He sensed that it was Eileen who brought him food. His urge to turn and find out was almost overwhelming. However, an agreement was an agreement.

Hours later, Bill's introspection continued to tap memories around his senior year in high school...

One evening in early spring while Bill was studying in his bedroom, his father walked in and asked how school was going. Then he brought up the subject of career decision again.

"I really don't want to be an engineer," Bill complained. "I'm not good enough in math." Actually, electronics was interesting. Bill had his ham radio license and had built much of his own electronic equipment. He was even building a television from scratch. However, Katarina's father was an electronic engineer and she thought engineering was boring.

"But your grades are fine."

"It's too hard, really."

"A little work and sweat never hurt anyone, besides engineering will guarantee a good living and a few of the nicer things in life. You can always play music in a community symphony like you do now."

"Dad, L.A. State Symphony is not a community symphony. It's college. Don't you see? I'm already taking college courses and I'm still in high school."

"I'd hardly call playing in an orchestra going to college!"

"They, like, asked me. There aren't any other high school kids there."

"Well, tell you what," Chuck continued. "Your mother and I want you to know, whatever your decision, we will back you. We do want you to go to college. You've certainly got the grades for it. Therefore, I want you to know, we'll support you for four years of college no matter where that school might be and no matter what your major."

Bill sat at his desk, stunned. This was a first.

"But I will ask two things of you. Wherever you decide to go, I want you to try very hard to get a scholarship in order to help relieve the financial burden on me. Secondly, I want you to get a teaching credential if your major is music. That way if times get rough, you'll always have something to fall back on."

"Yes, sir! Thank you!" Bill jumped to his feet and vigorously shook his father's hand.

"Let's try it again from the top!" Bill commanded, making the fifth attempt at his audition tape for the University of Colorado.

Debbie turned the record knob on the school tape recorder.

"Bach, *Sonata Number One*, First Movement," Bill said in a mature voice. Then he played from an old worn out piece of music that had down-bows, up-bows, fingerings, shifts and tempo embellishments penciled all over it.

Debbie turned the record switch off.

"Well, I think we've got it. Finally! You've really been an angel helping me like this. Dinner is on me Friday night."

"Great!" Debbie glowed.

"Hope I don't have this much trouble with Viotti."

"I don't mind. Besides, it's fun helping you."

"Slow movements are always so hard," Bill continued. "You can hear everything. At least the first movement of Viotti goes fast. I can get away with more crap."

"Why don't you play Beethoven?"

"Don't play it well enough."

"Want to know something?" Debbie laughed.

Bill looked at her. He knew she was up to something.

"Always tell when you get a letter from Katarina."

Bill could feel himself begin to blush.

"It's the way you play Beethoven, especially the second movement."

"It shows?"

"You should submit that as an audition tape, you'll be in for sure."

The next Friday, after school, Bill was actually talking to Katarina through a forty-meter phone patch with a fellow ham radio operator in Fort Collins.

"…Billy, I don't think y'all should go to the University in Boulder just for me," the conversation continued. "I agree, there is a good school of music there. But there are other excellent schools, too. With your talent, y'all should go to Juilliard! Anyway, have ya received my letter yet? Go ahead."

Bill quickly toggled the transmit switch. "No, well I guess not. The last one was a little over two weeks ago. Over."

"Oh, I thought, maybe, that's why you called. I'm afraid." There was a strained silence, "I have a boyfriend," another pause, "go ahead."

Instantly, Bill was shattered. His finger began shaking on the transmit switch. He couldn't turn it on.

"Billy? Y'all there?" The far away voice in the speaker became tentative.

"Yeah." Bill had to force the switch, "Ya happy?" He knew this was really a dumb question, but could think of no other. "Over."

"Billy, you've always been my friend and you'll always be. But except by letters and a week together several years ago, I don't really know you. I need someone I can be with. Y'all know, I love to dance and go to movies. I want to enjoy life. Y'all can't really expect me to sit home doing nothing, waiting." Katarina paused. "Go ahead."

Bill's heart plunged deep into a compassionless abyss. He shook the transmit switch vigorously until the red light illuminated. "Guess I made some assumptions." He responded with an immature staccato. "Over."

"Billy, don't be disappointed in me. I know I'm not good enough. I'm just a country hick. Y'all deserve better." Katarina hesitated, "I'd better go now. Go ahead."

Bill signed off the air in a professional manner, even though his heart had all but stopped. Then he just sat listening to the airwave's hiss for a long, long time.

Seven weeks later Bill received acceptance papers from the University of Colorado at Boulder. "...and have been hereby awarded a 100% tuition scholarship for your freshman year."

Bill had applied with the understanding he could attend the college of his choice. But, when he proudly presented his accomplishment, his parents were unapproachable. Then, weeks turned to months as they avoided the issue. Toward summer's end, Bill knew there would be a row. Finally, in desperation, he approached his mother. She was easier to talk to than his dad was.

"Billy, don't you think you're a little young to be leaving home?" Virginia asked, sitting at the kitchen table, drinking her afternoon wine.

"Whadaya mean? Ya want me to go to college?"

"Of course! But your father and I think you should spend a couple of years here at State before you move out."

"What?" Bill questioned with astonishment. His mouth began moving, but nothing more came out.

Virginia looked at her half empty glass while lighting another cigarette. Then she blew her smoke directly into Bill's face. This was one thing Bill hated intensely.

"Ya, like, ya made a promise! Anywhere I want to go, as, as long as I go." Bill coughed out while fanning the smoke. "Please, mama, please don't do this to me!"

"Wait a minute, young man! We didn't make you any promise of the kind. Anyway, times are hard right now. We can't afford it even if we wanted to," Virginia said with a voice overly controlled.

Bill's surprise plunged deep into a pool of aged anger, anger as the result of other broken promises. His throat tightened, trying to hold back the anger, straining to get through. "This is not fair! You and Dad did make a promise!" Bill remembered the conversations very well. Also, he knew they could afford it. Just a few weeks earlier Virginia couldn't contain her excitement about how much money they had made in the stock market. Their holdings in Chuck's company had split twice in one quarter.

"Look, young man, we both know very well why you want to go to Colorado, right?"

"Mom!" Bill began to shout, "Katarina is only part of the reason I chose Boulder! They have a first class school of music there!"

"There are plenty of cute girls right here," Virginia retaliated.

"Mother!" Bill's voice exploded into rage, "Ya never let me do what I think is best for me. You always make me wrong! I, I just can't win!"

"I'm just trying to spare you pain, dear. You know what I've always said, 'experience is the best teacher but only fools use it!'"

Bill stared his mother square in the eyes. Then, out of control, he yelled, "Why don't you go FUCK yourself!" He turned and ran away, slamming the door to his bedroom.

Picking up Katarina's picture from his nightstand, he threw himself down on the bed, sending it crashing violently into the wall.

About an hour later Chuck walked into Bill's room without knocking.

"Little man!" Chuck was extremely upset. "You will never speak to your mother that way again! If you don't like it here, I suggest you get out!"

Bill was deathly afraid of his father. He said nothing, staring angrily at the floor.

"Your mother and I have decided you should go to State for a couple of years, then you can go to Colorado."

"That wasn't the agreement, sir." Bill tried to sound respectful.

"I don't really care! Sometimes things change, don't they. I'm afraid you'll just have to live with our decision! We can't afford Boulder, that's the end of it!"

"Yeah, and, like, in a couple of years you'll have another excuse!"

"Little man, I've had quite enough of you and your gawd-damn bullshit!" Chuck raised a trembling hand as if to strike Bill but stopped short. Instead he turned and left the room, slamming the door on the way out.

Bill walked over to the map of the United States hanging on his wall. As he looked at Colorado's Front Range, his rage reached its zenith. Bill picked up a marble paperweight sitting on the top of his desk, then he threw it, leaving it embedded in the stucco wall of his bedroom.

Twenty Seven

Unexpectedly, Bill was jolted to normal consciousness by three raps at the door. Earl entered and placed breakfast on the desk. However, this time Bill didn't look away.

"Fuck!" Bill screamed. "I don't know what you want me to do!"

Earl said nothing. He turned and left the room, not paying any attention to Bill's outburst.

Following his previous days' experience, Bill was certain he didn't want anymore to do with meditation. Every time he tried to quiet his mind, all sorts of shit boiled to consciousness. He seemed powerless to stop the memories.

Bill looked at the measly offering. "Guess they're trying to starve me, too! Cream of wheat, meager glass of orange juice. Shit!" He turned and walked away. Then he cracked the window shade and glared at the sun-parched earth rolling eastward toward formidable foothills. It looked like it hadn't rained in years.

After twenty or so minutes of staring, Bill walked back to the desk and began to eat his food. "Why?" He questioned aloud, thinking about the last several months living with the Watleys. Over the next several hours he began to panic. He'd heard rumors about college professors recruiting college students for covert government organizations. And in his paranoia, he remembered hearing a tape recording of an Army lecture about communist indoctrination, brain washing.

"I breathe in with tranquillity." Bill tried once again, hours later. There was nothing else to do.

"I breathe out with tranquillity." Bill exhaled.

"I breathe in with tranquillity, five, six, seven."

Following a short time or a long time, Bill wasn't certain, nothing seemed to happen. So he threw himself back into a reclining position on his bed and stared at the ceiling.

"This must be what it's like in the hospital. No one to see. No one to talk to. I can't imagine." Bill realized how much of a doer he was, never an idle moment, hands always busy. "I never take the time to look deeply inside, not really."

Magically, a voice appeared from the depths of his psyche. "That's because you never stop talking to yourself." Bill shuddered as he remembered Katarina saying one embarrassing afternoon, "The proof of insanity is when you find yourself doing the same things over and over while expecting different results."

Bill had to do something different. But what?

That night Bill had a dream. He saw himself as a little child in his grandfather's living room. Pappy was teaching him a Buddhist mantra.

"Let's see, how'd it go?" Bill asked himself, trying hard to remember the next morning, after breakfast. "'Gate, gate, paragate, parasamgate, bodhi, svaha.' Yeah, that's it." Bill closed his eyes and began chanting, desperate for something, anything to do.

"Gate, gate, paragate, parasamgate, bodhi, svaha. Gate, gate, paragate, parasamgate, bodhi, svaha." Over and over he repeated.

"But what's it mean?" Bill tried hard to remember. "I think, something about the true nature of consciousness being without ego, being void of form." In reality, Bill had no idea what it meant. To him, it sounded like one of his mentor's unanswerable riddles. But he felt good and he began to relax and enter a peaceful state of consciousness.

"Gate, gate, paragate, parasamgate, bodhi, svaha. Gate, gate, paragate, parasamgate, bodhi, svaha." Over and over Bill repeated the Heart Sutra.

Unexpectedly, Bill began to feel a pressure in the center of his forehead. It began as a very small point of blackness within the vision of his mind. Then it began to grow, and with it, a vision of a distant past came to life…

> Large piercing dark eyes shined with a life of their own as Fanny combed her jet-black hair with a tiny, cramped and stained mirror. Her mood was electric and she couldn't wait until the laughter of guests would warm the cold night air.
>
> "Fanny? Are you up there?" Fanny's mother called from the kitchen where the servants were preparing for the evening's pleasure. "We need your help! Please?"
>
> "I'm coming. Please don't fret." Fanny put down her comb and blew out the lamp. Then she trampled down the stairs, trying to remember to be lady-like. Her mother often referred to her as the family horse. At twenty, she was tall for a woman, perhaps one of the tallest in her village. But she liked it, because her hands were huge and she could easily reach tenths on the keyboard, something even her arrogant brother was unable to do.
>
> When Fanny entered the music conservatory, it was dark. So she caught a flame from the kitchen and lit the eighty-six lamps that would make the evening bright and cheerful. Soon, her father and brother clamored through the side door bringing in firewood.
>
> "Wow! You look ravishing. Your mother seen you?" Fanny's father stood in the doorway shaking the snow from his overcoat. He had that magical gleam in his eye. Evenings like this were special for him, too.

"She has! Mother is in the kitchen making certain that everything is just right."

"And, I suppose, you've been upstairs playing with your hair! Women!" Fanny's brother said mockingly.

"If I was your beau, you wouldn't mind a bit!" Fanny glared at her brother.

"Thank the Prophets, you're not!"

Fanny's mother entered the room with hot spiced apple cider and offered some to everyone. Fanny was glad for the interruption. She didn't want to argue with her brother, not on such a wonderful night.

Fanny took her mug and sat at the piano. She warmed up with a few scales while her brother picked up his violin and did likewise. Soon the room filled with laughter and music.

It wasn't long until the guests began arriving. They were musicians, artists, poets and philosophers, friends Fanny's family had known for many years. Their home quickly became a hot bed of discussion around local politics and the social repression of their Jewish community.

Later that evening, Fanny, her brother, and her beau performed a violin, cello and piano trio that she composed. Fanny was proud of her accomplishment, as was everyone else. However, when her brother began playing his most recent composition, a violin concerto, Fanny was obviously outdone. Yet she was happy for him. Even though he was several years younger, she recognized and honored his amazing talent.

That evening, Fanny and her brother played several duets of his compositions. Fanny played another composition of her own. Then her mother and two friends joined in for a resounding quintet. The eighteen guests listened, laughed and enjoyed the food.

The next afternoon Fanny was busy with a new composition. Her father entered their conservatory. Two weeks of overcast weather was finally gone and the room was bright from a welcome sun.

"Fanny, don't get your hopes up." Fanny's father said as he walked to her side and put his right hand on her left shoulder. "Composition is not the work of women. It belongs to us men."

"But Father," Fanny knew her overly expressive face showed disapproval.

"Now, now, hear me out! Even your brother confesses that you're the better pianist, as well as an equal composer. But the world is not ready for you. People naturally turn away from your work, because you're a woman. Your place is in the home, raising wonderful children, giving your gift of music to them. Won't you ever understand?"

"I'm sorry, my Father. What I do understand is, I have the right to follow my heart, even when you men don't agree."

"I'm a tulku, one who remembers. That's what Pappy once told me." Bill said under his breath as he pulled both his legs out from the lotus position. He slowly rose to his feet, then limped around the room, working out some stiffness.

"Gate, gate, paragate, parasamgate, bodhi, svaha. Gate, gate, paragate, parasamgate, bodhi, svaha," Bill began, following lunch…

The crowds roared and men screamed in horror as he unleashed their doom. "Christian dogs!" he shouted, laughing, watching his lions devour flesh and crack bone. It was a hideous sight, but he knew those Christians were the joke of the century. Except for the amusement of Nero and his patricians, they died for nothing!

Suddenly, Bill was himself once again. He was shaking. The past he'd seen was too horrible for his rational mind. Bill was once Luvickius, keeper of the lions, Captain of the Guard. He was honored among men and sought after by women. With the pull of a lever, he had delivered hundreds to the iron jaw of the beast.

The morning of the seventh day arrived slowly and painfully as Bill awoke from a nightmare. He saw himself as a young woman, almost sixteen years of age…

Anastasia Vonderheid lived in a small dirty village near Woburn, Massachusetts, late in the eighteenth century with her mother and two sisters. Her father, Herman, had recently died from an accidental knife wound that turned gangrenous. The family was devoutly Christian and active in their parish. But there were rumors, rumors about her mother. Some thought her poor father lost his life as a result of her mother's pact with the Devil. Of course, Anastasia knew better.

Anastasia was a happy child and she looked forward to her marriage to a young silversmith of good family. However, immediately following her father's demise another man, an old man whom her father knew well, spoke up. He claimed that Anastasia's father had betrothed her to him the day she turned sixteen, only two weeks away. Anastasia remembered the old man from her childhood. She despised him. He stank of hide and ale. His belly was so big that when he fell down it took two men to get him back to his feet. She didn't know what to do. As her birthday drew near, she became more and more terrified. Her young silversmith vowed to kill the old man if he ever laid a finger on her. Their village became divided as many friends turned to foes. In desperation, Anastasia told the old man that she was a witch and would give him a life of hell. That was too much for the town's people. That night they took Anastasia, her mother and her two sisters to a clearing near the town-square. They tried the four for Anastasia's blasphemies and burned the family at the stake.

"Who am I?" Bill cried aloud shaking with terror. "That was more than a dream!"

As Bill sat in contemplation, he began to question just how good a person he was, really? He thought about people he had been kind to, people he had been disrespectful to. Bill thought about his mother, his father, and his sister. He knew that in many ways he had been a rotten kid. Then for some reason Bill considered his obedience to religious law, since he thought himself a good Christian.

"You must have no other Gods before me." The first of the Commandments delivered by Moses. "That's an easy one. I worship no God except Yahweh. Well, maybe not so easy. In junior high I told some kids that I didn't believe in God just to piss them off. Years later I couldn't help questioning the rationality for a belief in a Supreme Being. After seeing a psychiatrist, I was certain it was all so much bullshit, that whatever spiritual experiences I'd had were pure fantasy. I found it easy to substitute Science for God. I'm guilty!

"You must not make any idols, any images resembling animals, birds or fish. You must not bow to an image or worship it in any way." Bill thought and thought. "Do I bow? Do I worship anything other than Yahweh?" That was a hard one. However, following careful consideration, Bill had to admit, in public school he was taught to worship a thing called The United States of America and its flag, as if it were a benevolent God. Guilty once more.

"You shall not use the name of Yahweh in vain. Again, guilty. When I thought I'd lost Katarina. I cursed God, my life, my parents. I even considered taking my life!

"Remember to observe the Sabbath as a Holy Day." Bill again had to confess guilt. Until Katarina gave him an excuse for going, he'd been in church only a handful of times during the past several years. Even then, he resisted attendance. He was not a joiner and had serious issues with church dogma. But neither did he set aside private time for relaxation, meditation or worship. Guilty!

"Honor your father and mother. That's a joke. It wasn't so many years ago that I told my mother to go fuck herself. Guilty!

"You must not commit murder. When? Only in this lifetime? Almost two thousand years ago I took pride in feeding arrogant Christians to the lions. But, but am I any better now? I go out of the way to kill insects. I've killed rodents. Once, I poisoned a neighbor's dog because I didn't like it. Also, there were times I'm sure I would have killed my sister if mom and dad had let me. I'm guilty by deed.

"You must not commit adultery. That one-night-stand with Debbie wasn't adultery, but I'm certainly promiscuous!

"You must not steal." Bill remembered taking a model train transformer from his grandfather's workshop when he was twelve. He finally threw it into the trash so as not to be found out. He cheated on an exam in his freshman year at college. "Obviously, I'm guilty.

"You must not lie." Bill knew that one goes without saying. "It's not possible to live in this modern world without lying from time to time. After all, who really wants to hear my truth? Who really wants to know how I feel, what my inner desires are, what my pain is. Who wants to know me outside those I have an intimate relationship with? Who?

"You must not be envious of your neighbor's house or anything else that he or she has. Envy? I envy people who can play the violin better than myself. I envy people who could stand up for themselves in confrontation. I envy Eileen and Earl for their possessions and having their lives so together. I even envy Katarina for her beauty and intelligence.

"It's painfully obvious. I'm not capable of keeping any of the Commandments, not a single one. My darkness is everywhere!"

Then Bill recollected something he'd read in one of the metaphysical books that Pappy gave him. "We would all be in prison if we were found out. None of us, not a single human, can go through life without committing crimes. Yet, in spite of this, we must have the courage to be the best we can possibly be. And we must have the compassion to forgive others for their transgressions. Because, we are all trying to live the best we can. Only the arrogance of a fool would have us believe that Heaven is the reward for only the pure and sinless. There are no pure and sinless!"

Bill thought about the Lord's prayer. "And to be forgiven as we forgive those who trespass against us." The word, "as," means in like manner. Bill realized the prayer says, quite literally, Lord, forgive me in the same way, the same manner, as I forgive.

"Shit! This means, if I'm unforgiving, I'm asking the Lord God to reciprocate!"

Hours later, after staring out his bedroom window at a rising moon, Bill had the sensation that he was flying. Then, suddenly, he was standing in front of Katarina's home in Fort Collins watching her drive into the driveway, shut off the engine of her father's bright red Dodge pickup. She quickly got out and walked toward the front door. As she approached the house she stopped briefly and looked right at Bill, who was now floating only three feet away. An expression of concern quickly crept over her face. Then she hurried through the front door and closed it forcefully.

Bill followed, passing through the front door in his astral body. Katarina was now heading for the bathroom next to her father's study while the monotonous drone of a vacuum cleaner echoed from the back of the house.

Bill entered Valdemar's study and noticed a duck call collection randomly placed on the top self of the bookcase. Several minutes later Katarina entered the study, walked hesitantly toward Bill as if sensing his presence. Then she picked up one of the duck calls and quickly returned to the hallway. Bill followed.

As Katarina approached the back of the house where the vacuum cleaner droned, she slowed her pace and became very quiet. Bill hurried past her only to find Rita cleaning the master bedroom, her back to the open door. Katarina began tiptoeing into the room making certain not to attract her mother's attention.

"Quack! Quack!"

If Bill had his body, he would have burst into hysterical laughter. Rita jumped and fell to her knees.

"Gawd!" Rita shrieked! "Can't you act like a normal person?"

"Mom, you know I'm not normal." Katarina laughed. "I'm from Rigel Kentaurus Seven. Take me to your leader, Earthling!"

"Go away!"

"I told you years ago, honey, ya shouldn't pull practical jokes on your children. Now you're paying the price!" Valdemar announced as he stepped from the master bathroom with a giant grin on his face. He turned and winked at Katarina.

Katarina's overly expressive face was filled with delight.

"So, did ya make up your mind? Are you going to the church picnic with Walt?" Valdemar asked his daughter.

Katarina's cheerfulness turned dreadfully serious. "Dad, y'all know I'm not ready to date again."

"Walt is a very fine young man. We've known his family for years. If not now, when?"

Katarina looked at her father but didn't answer.

"It's not like we're asking you to get serious." Valdemar continued. "Kitty! I fear for you. You've got to have a social life! The way you're headed you're going to be an old maid!"

"What do you want me to do? All guys want is sex! I want, I want more than that!" Katarina looked away from her father and stared at the wall.

Rita walked over to Katarina, extended her arms, then held her daughter tight. "It's okay, dear. We're not trying to be pushy. But, y'all gotta start trusting people again."

"I know. I know."

Bill was troubled by what he had just witnessed. He felt Katarina's emptiness, her despair.

Katarina opened her eyes and looked straight at Bill who was now standing off to her left side. Her face showed signs of recognition. Then she mumbled, "Damn you, Billy!"

Twenty Eight

Finally, four and a half weeks into his New Mexico isolation, Bill's was able to stop all the mind chatter and hold the quietness of meditation for long periods of time. Therefore, his forced silence was ended. Yet, there was little to say. Because, for the first time in his life, he felt an inner peace that was unprecedented and words seemed to get in the way of his experience. So instead of engaging the others in conversation, he spent the morning just hanging out and smiling.

"Magnificent piece of music, isn't it," Bill began as he walked up to Bruce, mid-afternoon. Bruce was sitting in the shade of the lath verandah connected to the east side of the summer residence. He was whittling a piece of wood while listening to an AM broadcast of the first movement of Elgar's *Cello Concerto in E minor.*

"Indeed." Bruce looked up at Bill and smiled.

"Think if I didn't play the violin, I'd play the cello. Tried it once in high school," Bill continued.

"What happened?"

"Caused my violin playing to become sharp. Ya know…" Bill held out his left hand and stretched his fingers as if uncoordinated, trying to demonstrate.

Bruce chuckled. "Understand you're quite the musician."

"Trying to be."

"Why don't you play something for me?"

"Well, I guess. Haven't played for weeks now."

"Can you still play? I mean a lot has happened, maybe you forgot!"

"Bruce, that's something I'll never forget!" Bill turned, walked back into house and retrieved his fiddle, waiting silently in the living room closet.

"Hello, old friend!" Bill took his partner from its case and rubbed his hands over it as if caressing a lover. Then he tuned up, hoping the desert heat and dryness hadn't deadened the strings. Instantly, he realized that he needed tuning, too. His hands were hopelessly sluggish. He put his instrument respectfully back in its case, then spent the next fifteen minutes stretching out and doing warm-up exercises as if he were an athlete readying for the big game.

"Let me start simply," Bill announced, returning to the verandah. "*Liebesleid*, by Fritz Kreisler."

Bill surprised himself. He played with the tone and confidence he had often dreamt about. Music simply rolled from his fingers.

"Let me try another!" Bill exclaimed excitedly. "Bach's, *Ciaccona*."

"Ravel's, *Tzigane*."

"Pretty damn impressive, kid! You've obviously got a very exciting career ahead of you."

"You think?"

"I know! You know, too."

"Yeah."

Bill put his violin back in its closet home, then returning to the verandah, he sat in a chair across from Bruce. Bruce had resumed his whittling.

"There are a lot of things I don't understand," Bill began following twenty minutes or so of pleasurable silence. Only a light breeze ruffling the trees, a distant woodpecker and Bruce's knife scraping oak disturbed the solitude. A slight smell of wet creosote wafted from a distant thundershower, miles to the south, somewhere over Santa Fe. The storm was heading northwest rapidly.

"What's happening to me?" Bill asked.

"I suspect that you know the answer already, but can't verbalize it."

"You give me too much credit!" Bill said as he pushed back into his chair.

"You've been experiencing other realities, other dimensions of time and space."

Whatever it was that Bill expected Bruce to say, it wasn't this.

"Like the masses of humankind, you assume that the reality you witness is the only reality possible."

"It isn't?"

"You already know the answer to that one."

"I'm afraid you have me at a loss, Sir."

"Earl told me that several times a year you have lucid sexual dreams about Katarina."

"Yeah."

"Is that reality?"

"I don't know? Most likely wishful thinking." Bill copped an answer.

"Really? Well, maybe you should think about it a little more. Because, either it is reality or you are crazy."

"My dad thinks I'm nuts."

"Forget him right now. Answer the question relating your own experience."

"I, I think I really do meet her in my dreams," Bill replied with a hint of uncertainty in his voice.

"And how is this possible?" Bruce got up from his lawn chair, walked to a nearby table and poured them each a glass of lemonade, then added half-melted ice cubes.

"You believe in astral projection?" Bill asked.

"Yes." Bruce said, turning and holding a glass of lemonade toward Bill.

Bill smiled as he accepted the drink. "Then, you don't think I'm crazy."

"No! You're anything but crazy. Your problem is you have little understanding, even less control." Bruce took several big gulps of his chilled drink. Then he returned to his chair and noisily sat down.

"Here's the problem," Bruce began. "We have the material world on the one hand. We have spirituality, things like astral projection, out of body experiences on the other. And to complicate things, there seems to be no common ground between them. Yet, we believe that both exist. How is this possible, Bill?"

"I'm afraid I haven't any idea."

"Nor do most people." Bruce put down his glass and pushed deep into his chair. "Complementary factors!"

"What do you mean?"

"Let me give you my explanation. Materialism and spiritualism are complementary factors of the same reality. It's not that one exists and the other is crazy making. They're both valid.

"Here's a scientific example of how this might be. You've had college physics. Remember when you did an experiment and proved that light was a wave function."

"Yeah."

"Then, only a few weeks later, you proved that light is a particle. You remember?"

"How could I forget. It's mind boggling. How could something be two different things at the same time?"

"Because they're complementary factors. We see light as either-or because of the way we observe it. That is, when we observe it as if it were a particle we see it only as a particle. Vice-versa, when we observe it as a wave we see only its waviness. These phenomena fall under what's known as the Heisenberg uncertainty principle."

"Huh?"

"According to Heisenberg's mathematical proofs, observation of a phenomena interferes with the nature of that phenomena. Therefore, we cannot simultaneously determine with certainty any aspect of a phenomenon other than what is being measured. Any effort to do so blurs our knowledge of any other aspect. The key, Bill, is the observer. It's the observation that forces an outcome to either this or that. This or that, being special cases of reality.

"Now, let me take you a step further. Our human bodies are observational machines. We have senses. And, moment to moment, these senses observe the universe, creating our personal and collective realities. The problem is, just like observing light, the act of an observation forces an outcome. That outcome is a special case of reality, not reality in its general or universal form.

"What I see is a special case of reality?"

"Of course! What's this?" Bruce asked, patting an old wooden table sitting next to him."

"A table." Bill reached out and felt the table. "It's hard, cool, smooth. It's dark reddish-brown."

"You don't see the energy fields that make up atoms or molecules."

"No."

"But you know these energy fields exist."

"Yeah."

"Bill, is it safe to say that when you observe physical table-ness you lose all the information about things like energy fields?"

"Of course."

"And, when you get sophisticated scientific equipment and observe the energies within the table, you lose all information about table-ness."

"Yeah."

"So, each observation is a special case, neither representing a universal picture. Tell me, Bill, what do your senses tell you when you're hanging out in astral projection?"

"I don't have physical senses, at least not the ones of my body."

"Still you have energy, movement. You have awareness, don't you."

"I think I understand." Bill grinned. "Neither materialism nor spiritualism are real solely unto themselves. Rather, they are each special cases of a more universal principle, therefore, complementary factors."

"You got it!"

Bill sat for several minutes in thought, then asked, "Are you saying Dreamtime to an Australian Aborigine is just as valid as Material Realism is to the Occidental?"

"Yes."

"But then, what are we, really, I mean at the primordial level? Do you know?"

"For now, I'm going to withhold my answer. It's necessary. You must witness the unknown directly for yourself. To put my views of reality in words will only bind you further in illusion. For you, my reality, my dream, anyone's reality, anyone's dream, are nothing more than ashes of some past event."

Twenty Nine

"Pay attention, damn you! Your life depends on it!" Worm commanded.

Bill shook his head again trying to stay awake. It was now Tuesday night, July 21st, 1964, close to eleven-thirty. Earl drove Bill and Worm north on a badly wash-boarded road east of Skull Valley, Arizona. Having been on a forced fast, as well as being on the road for over thirteen hours, Bill was exhausted. And, it didn't help that, for the last several hours, Worm tried to hold Bill's attention by explaining the subtleties of his up and coming "Vision Quest."

"Little Crow thinks he's hot shit. Boy, compared to what lies out there, ya ain't squat! Yesterday you were anger!" Worm said authoritatively, "Today you are fear!"

Bill recoiled from Worm's words as Earl pulled into a clearing off the side of the road, leaving the car's engine running. Worm immediately got out, commanding Bill to follow. Then, Worm went to the car's trunk and unloaded a large box along with Bill's backpack.

"Little Crow be okay if he keeps his wits! Remember! You have everything ya need! What ever ya do, don't run!"

Bill said nothing while Worm returned to the car, got in and slammed the door shut. Without hesitation, Earl turned the car around and drove slowly into the black of night.

Looking overhead, the stars were magnificent. Bill quickly found the Big Dipper, the North Star and then the Little Dipper. He'd never seen the stars so brilliant. The Milky Way was simply a blur of light. And as he stood watching the works of God in that awesome sky, he remembered himself as a small child. One night on the beach in Venice, California, a gruff old man asked him where he came from. Eagerly, Bill pointed to the sky. He pointed to the Horse Head Nebula in Orion and said, "There, there is my home!" Somehow he knew, even as a child, millions of years ago his home was on some distant planet orbiting some distant sun. Today that ancient home is dust floating amongst the stars.

"What now?" Bill asked, under his breath, trying to break the desolate stillness. Then he looked down and across an empty dark landscape. Fidgeting, he realized that he was becoming uncomfortably cold and returned to his backpack and opened it. He pulled out a flashlight and his jacket. He wished he'd brought gloves.

Bill considered Worm's words, "Now you are fear!" However, looking around as best he could, trying see between the silhouettes of plants and rocks painted gray by the distant starlight, there was nothing to fear. In fact, being out-of-doors and camping came second nature. The Boy Scout in him couldn't wait to pitch a tent. So it didn't take Bill long to unpacked his things and set up camp in a protected area near a small cliff. Then he unrolled his sleeping bag, climbed in and fell quickly into the warm embrace of sleep.

Around six-thirty the next morning, Bill was awakened by a pack of marauding coyotes scavenging their morning meal. Quickly, yet quietly, he peeked through the tent flap to get a view and to his wonderful surprise a beautiful young male stood looking at him from about thirty feet away. After several seconds the animal bounded away as if begging Bill to follow. Of course, Bill thought he had more important things to do and got up to meet the oncoming day.

Bill took care of his morning toilet, then walked over to the box that Worm had left. His belly ached with hunger and he considered breaking his fast. However, there was no food, only containers of water, extra blankets, sun block, a first aid kit and other odds and ends that one might need in the wild. Bill pulled out a straw hat and put it on. Then he noticed a gun.

Through the years Bill's dad made sure he and his sister knew their way around firearms. So he wasn't a novice. This gun was a .357 magnum with an eight-inch barrel, no toy, but nothing to get worked up about, either. He remembered getting checked out with a .44 magnum. That was a handgun! Taking aim at an unsuspecting prickly pear cactus some fifty feet away, he let her rip, leaving a good-sized hole in a cactus pad. The gun pulled about a half-inch to the right, not too bad.

As Bill placed the weapon back in the box, he noticed some rather odd things, things he thought one might use at a party, a bugle, a small hoop drum, and rattles. He found this confusing but didn't think much more about it.

Following tidying up his camp so that he could be comfortable for several days, Bill began to explore his surroundings. First he walked up the canyon in the southerly direction. It quickly narrowed into steep cliffs rising about a hundred feet or so, forming a small mesa. Along his haphazard trail he found many varieties of cacti and short scrubby palo verde trees. There were also several dry washes surrounded by tall cottonwoods, acacia and other trees he couldn't label. Noticing how dry and parched everything seemed, Bill thought it hadn't rained in at least a year. Yet the cottonwoods showed at least two inches of recent growth.

Bill found a spot and relieved himself. Then he walked back to his camp site, stopping only long enough to watch a tarantula hawk paralyze a spider almost twenty times his own size, then drag it off to some unknown fortress. He felt sorry for the spider.

Bill spent most of the afternoon hiking to the top of the western mesa. Once there, he looked back and forth across the canyon below. It occupied about ten square miles. "What am I doing here?" He finally asked aloud.

"Here I am, all alone in some God forsaken wilderness, clueless. I'm wandering around like a half-wit talking to myself."

"I don't want to be here," Bill confessed, realizing his melancholy feelings had deepened considerably over the last several hours. But there was nothing to do, no place to go. So, without further thought, he continued his hike toward some distant hills in a northerly direction.

Bill found himself tiring quickly. Perhaps it was the lack of nourishment, the altitude or the intense sun. Whatever, he stopped in a sandy wash to take a drink from his canteen. The coolness of the water felt good on his dry throat and for some reason he thought about the clear shady pools of fresh water in Oak Creek canyon, only sixty-five miles to the northeast. He remembered camping there while on his way to Philmont. He remembered floating listlessly in a big pool of water on his air mattress with several kids his own age one sunny afternoon.

Except for the road Earl drove in on, there was absolutely no evidence of human life, now or ever. Bill wondered about Indians. There must have been Indians at one time. Most of the Southwest United States shows evidence of aboriginal civilizations. Sitting down on the sandbank of a dry wash, some naggy feeling begged Bill to listen intently. However, except for a slight breeze brushing against the surrounding trees and the buzzing of distant cicadas, he heard nothing. Suddenly a shadow covered his body and the air temperature dropped several degrees. Bill shivered, as he looked up, relieved to see only a cloud passing overhead.

As Bill walked further into the unknown, the agonizing stench of death captured his attention. It turned out to be a half-rotted cow. Several buzzards were enjoying their feast but Bill didn't get close enough to annoy them away.

"What is my fear?" Bill questioned himself, aloud, quickly distancing himself from the miasma. "Is it death? Is it being injured? Is it being mugged or assaulted?"

Bill realized that the surrounding hills pulled on his solar plexus in some revolting way and he began turning back toward camp. But without warning, something out of place caught his eye in a large clearing to his left. He went to investigate. It was a human femur lying parched on the desert sand. As he picked it up, a shock wave rippled through his body. Spontaneously, Bill threw the bone back on the ground and ran from the rush of adrenaline.

"Weird! I don't think it's dying I fear. Maybe it's the emotional pain of watching someone else die brutally." Bill admitted after recollecting his composure.

Hiking on and praying there would be no more surprises, Bill ventured upon a small clearing resting at the base of a large tree-covered hill. A crescent shaped ledge was elevated slightly above the surrounding desert floor and loose sand held the faint outline of two skeletons buried beneath the surface. Two hands were stretching toward each other, but far from touching.

"Fu…" Instantly, Bill didn't want to see anymore. But something tugged him with more force than he could resist. As if in a trance, he walked slowly to the lower grave and stood at its perimeter. A knot tightened in his stomach and Bill's emotions ebbed and flowed as fast as he could breathe. For some uncontrollable reason he picked up a stick and began poking the remains. He'd heard stories about curses surrounding Indian burial sites. Common sense told him to leave at once. But his gut forced him to stay, even when his palms turned sweaty and his vision began to narrow.

Without warning the skull of this poor creature popped to the surface and gave Bill its frozen stare. Bill all but passed out with fright. Forcing himself to breathe deeply and get control, somehow, he knew. This poor creature was himself, from some other time. Instantly Bill was overtaken by a profound grief. He knew his end had been tragic.

Bill's lament continued for several hours while he tried to remember the events surrounding his demise. And as he did, he entered non-ordinary reality, experiencing his short life and the events surrounding the days his people came to this valley…

>Wolf's Tooth was born into a strong and healthy clan. His tribe did not want. There was enough for all. And except for child rearing, only four or five hours a day was spent at working the land, hunting and village maintenance. The remaining time was dedicated to socializing, dancing and play.
>
>As a child, Wolf's Tooth often demonstrated his intelligence. He was a born leader, had an inquisitive mind and asked many questions of the elders. He talked to the plants and the animals. He contemplated the sun, the moon and the stars. He listened to the old men tell their stories and sing their peyote songs. He liked rituals and was often found rehearsing in the privacy of a clearing down by the beaver dam, at least until the sun dried it up and the wind blew it away.
>
>After his manhood rights, Wolf's Tooth became a medicine man's apprentice. At seventeen he took Spotted Fawn as his wife. He loved her more than life itself, and she, him. Spotted Fawn knew that her husband would grow to be a powerful shaman like his father and his fathers, before them. Together, they had one son, Badger.
>
>Rooster's Crow, Wolf's Tooth's teacher, saw a disaster coming. But when times were good, many thought Rooster's Crow smoked too much pipe. Wolf's Tooth believed the prophecy, however. He knew his grandfather was never wrong about visions. Wolf's Tooth convinced

some to build food stores, others scoffed. But when drought came, what there was, was not enough.

Good times quickly turned bad as the tribe began to split into factions. The elders accused the youth, believing that the apathy in their hearts drove the Gods away. The elders believed that if the Gods could be appeased, the rains would return. So they danced their dances and sang their songs. However, the skies gave no reprieve. The youth, in turn, became angered at the old ones, blaming them for their incompetence. One afternoon several young braves tried to drive Rooster's Crow from their camp in a fit of rage. The next morning, Rooster's Crow left. No one ever saw him again.

After many moons of anger and rage, the hearts of the people turned to fear. They knew that without adequate food they could not survive the coming winter. Over time, they sent out scouts, most of whom never returned. They ate their remaining animals. Several old people sacrificed their lives so that the younger people might live. That helped, but it was only a short-term solution. One by one the clan buried its promise of future generations in the desert floor. Finally there was no doubt, if they were to survive, the tribe had to move northeast, despite the enemies who populated that land.

In non-ordinary reality, Bill remembered the day he entered this valley. It was parched and hot from a sinister sun. Two of his clan perished during the night. Suddenly and out of nowhere his enemies attacked. Badger was killed with many others as they tried to run for cover. It was just like his nightmares...

Bill was Wolf's Tooth as he lunged toward the Red-Faced adversary attempting to pull him from his war-horse. But before he could get a secure grip on the warrior's leg, he took two arrows in the back from passing renegades. Wolf's Tooth fell to the earth, writhing in agony. The stallion reared as the Red-Faced Indian screamed profanities. Then, slowly, as if he had all the time in the world, the warrior placed an arrow into his bow and shot Wolf's Tooth in the neck at the base of his skull.

Wolf's Tooth's pain quickly melted into nothingness. The only awareness left was his eyesight and the metallic taste of blood. The arrow at the base of his spine made certain that he would be forever a quadriplegic.

Screaming his war cry, the Red-Faced Indian dismounted his steed. He pulled his obsidian knife and ran toward Wolf's Tooth. However, seeing Wolf's Tooth utterly helpless, instead of slitting his throat, he repeatedly kicked Wolf's Tooth in the ribs and laughed. It was only when fresh blood began oozing from Wolf's Tooth's mouth and nose that his adversary stopped.

Lying flat on the desert sand under a huge acacia tree and next to her dead son, Spotted Fawn dared not move. However, her muffled sobs betrayed her. The Red-Faced Indian turned, ran and grabbed her by the right leg. Screaming with terror, she kicked and tried to escape. But he was a huge and powerful man. He pulled her from the ground and hit her on the side of her head. She fell and tumbled down a small incline, coming to rest only a few yards from Wolf's Tooth. Spotted Fawn panicked, trying to get to her feet. However, before she had the chance, the Indian hit her again and again. In agony, she reached towards her husband, begging him to save her. Then the Red-Faced Indian raped her and slit her throat.

Wolf's Tooth was left to die alone, beneath a scorching sun and ruthless biting ants.

As Bill returned to ordinary consciousness, he sat looking at the bones before him, feeling all the grief of those final days in hell. He cried and cried. Finally, picking up his skull and the skull of Spotted Fawn, Bill started back toward his base camp. As he walked, he remembered that his grandfather, Pappy, had described a Tibetan rite called Chöd in painstaking detail. Bill knew what he must do next.

Arriving back at his camp, Bill found himself more melancholy than he'd ever been in his entire life. He pulled the revolver from his belt and tossed it onto his bedroll. Nothing man-made would save his sweet ass, not in this canyon anyway. To survive the next sixteen or so hours would not be a matter of heroism, luck, or skill. Survival would only come from courage, intent and sheer will.

For reasons unknown, Bill emptied the contents of the box Worm had left him onto a blanket. He needed to find some way to make noise, lots of noise.

"Oh, yeah, the gun. That's a start," Bill said, picking it up, pushing it back into his belt. In the "party stuff" Bill pulled out a small drum, a bell, the bugle. "Of course! Earl and Worm knew what was coming! I've been set up."

Bill sorted and separated anything he thought might be useful for his coming journey. Then, just like the day of his death, tired and hungry, he packed his backpack and got underway.

Bill arrived at his barrow late afternoon. Wasting no time, he turned his blanket into a small tent and set up camp at the head of his grave next to a very large acacia tree. The tent's opening pointed East. Then with the fierceness and patience of his power animal, the puma, one by one, carefully and respectfully, he excavated both his and Spotted

Fawn's bones from the ground. He tried very hard to replace them on top of the sand in their correct position. During the excavation he found three nondescript arrowheads, one still embedded securely into the neck near the base of the skull.

Close to nightfall Bill was convinced that every bone was accounted for. He gathered some dried sage branches with their leaves still intact. Then he started a campfire and smudged the entire area and himself with thick choking smoke. Finally he waited, cross-legged, uncertain, dreading what lay ahead.

The canopy of night fell quickly across the desert floor. Bill was exhausted, depressed and wanted to sleep. But he knew that loss of consciousness would be extremely dangerous, maybe fatal. Worm had warned him. So he sat with forced intent, sounded his bell, watched the fire and waited. It wasn't long until a bizarre play began to unfold in the flames before him.

Again, Bill saw the drive his people made, two hundred and four starving souls. They were helpless as they entered this canyon. Without a hint of warning, their enemies stormed. Men were brutalized and killed. Women were raped, tortured and left to die. There were no survivors!

"This is my fear, helplessness and death! Now, according to the rite of Chöd, I must live my fear. I must carry it to completion!" Bill felt his body tremble. Then he began to weep. He wasn't sure he could go through with it.

Bill remembered Earl's riddle about standing on the tip of a needle, the abyss all around. Today, a solution was necessary.

Hesitantly, Bill picked up the gun and fired a round into the sky. The canyon exploded with reverberating echoes. He stood and bowing to the South, he began his spirit call:

"I call the spirits of the South, the Serpent path. Help me release the weight of my past, my anguishes and successes. Help me let go of my self-limiting beliefs. Be with me in this time of renewal."

Turning and bowing to the West, Bill continued, "I call the spirits of the West, the Jaguar path. Help me journey to my past. Help me face my fears and my death. Be with me in my rebirth."

Turning to the North, "I call the spirits of the North, the Dragon path. Help me journey and learn from my ancestors. Help me be open in life and integrity to those who would teach me. Help me gain knowledge of health."

Turning to the East, "I call the spirits of the East, the Eagle path. Help me go beyond my limiting self. Help me fly into the sun and become one with all things. Be with me on my path toward enlightenment."

Looking up and toward the infinite cosmos, Bill continued, "I call the spirits above, my personal guides and teachers. Teach me of love and of God. Guide me to enlightenment."

Looking down at the ground beneath his feet, "I call the spirits below, my power animals. Help me find the fearlessness in myself. Help me stand in strength and in truth. Help me do the work I came to do."

Finally Bill placed both his palms flat across his chest and looked straight ahead. "I call the spirit inside, the spirit of Bill Colton. I am open to my path. I am balance and light. I am love toward all beings, organic and inorganic. I give thanks to God, my creator."

Instinctively Bill began dancing the Spirit Dance he'd danced before losing his life in this canyon. Then he began blowing the bugle and beating the drum with a stick, louder and louder. His intention was singular. It was to awaken every ghost in the State of Arizona. Bill yelled profanities at his enemies. He yelled profanities at his enemy's ancestors.

Quite suddenly the wind picked up and turned icy. Bill threw more wood and sage into the fire. Sparks erupted and flew everywhere. The surrounding landscape became like a ghostly apparition engulfed in thick gray smoke. Bill heard sounds from all directions. Even the earth seemed to groan. Then there was a heavy thud. Pandora's box was now open.

Little by little Bill began to feel the presence of others, the ghostly remains of spirits still bound to this planet. He called them with his reacquired psychic knowledge. Soon spirits were all around. They danced their dance. They began to taunt Bill in turn. Some of them lunged. Some tried to grab. They tried to make Bill panic for his life. But Bill laughed. He laughed into their faces.

Suddenly Bill's laughter stopped. In front of him stood a giant of a man. He was the one, the man who had shot him in the neck, then brutally beaten, raped and killed his wife hundreds of years ago. Bill knew without doubt, he would do it again if he could.

The wraith screamed his war cry with a grotesque voice. His red face was disfigured and disproportioned. His aura was dark and foreboding. He was a man of enormous evil power. Bill's fear welled up as never before. He stood frozen at the sight. Then the apparition reached for him. Bill's head started to spin. He felt faint and could hardly breathe. But he knew this was no time to be weak or helpless. This was the time to gather all his wits and deal with the present, maybe like never before. In some place and in some time this scenario must end, forever.

Bill stood and faced his adversary. Compared to his human speed, the wraith's movements were slow and awkward. It was easy to step away from his advances. Together they danced around the fire while other apparitions flew between, around and over them. The sprits laughed. They taunted. These phantoms were friends of neither human nor ghost.

Bill began laughing, too. Then he beat his drum and blew his bugle. He blew the bugle into his tormentor's face. The wraith's anger erupted into full rage. But with the exception of Bill's emotional state, the spook couldn't touch him. He could touch nothing of Bill's reality unless Bill let him!

Knowing the game must end, Bill sat down at the head of his remains. His tormentor lunged. Bill imagined himself small, smaller than an atom. He passed through the phantom. The wraith turned and came again. Again Bill's smallness was untouched by the unearthly vapor. The process repeated and repeated, perhaps a thousand times. Finally the wraith began to tire. However, Bill still had his strength. In fact, he felt stronger than ever before.

Finally, Bill stood and put his left hand in front of the hideous red face. The phantom stopped his advance and stood before Bill like a hurt and confused school child. Then Bill said, "I have the right to be here. You have the right to be here, too."

The phantom looked baffled.

Bill said to his adversary, "To be free, you must understand, we are all God's perfect creatures working together through acts of reciprocity. Therefore, you must solve your problems with love, not retaliation. Because, to inflict violence on any sentient being is only to inflict violence on yourself. To be free, you must come to know that we all need each other. No sentient being is ever isolated. Now you must seek rebirth amongst the humans. Because, of all possible realms, the human form offers the easiest path to spiritual salvation."

The apparition began slowly backing away.

Bill said, "I forgive you. Now, forgive yourself. You must give up your ghost and return to the living."

The apparition looked as though he understood, but in a sorrowful way.

Then, from the depths of his own compassion, Bill said, "I love you."

Slowly the phantom evaporated and the taunting spirits returned to their self-imposed vaults.

Following a very long silence, Bill looked skyward. As the crest of dawn kissed the horizon, the stars had never shone so bright. Suddenly, Bill felt as though he had been released from his body and all the confusion in his life had now become clear. For several penetrating moments Bill was certain he was dead. Magically, his being was filled with love so profound that all he could do was swoon. Then the spirit of Spotted Fawn came to him. She embraced and kissed him. Together, they became as one.

Midmorning, Bill sat in his makeshift tent looking at the ashes before him. Several coals were still venting wisps of light gray smoke. The air still held the pungent fragrance of sage. Bill knew there was one more act needed in order to complete his adventure. Tired and hungry, he rose and stretched his aching muscles. Then, after adding additional fuel to keep his fire alive, he took a healthy drink of water from his canteen.

Walking approximately fifty yards northwest of his gravesite, Bill quickly found the small skeleton of his son, Badger. Beneath a lonely stand of huge acacia trees, it was just like in his nightmares, past. Slowly and respectfully, he dug the bones from the crusty soil with his pocketknife, scraping and cleaning caked earth where necessary.

Once Bill had every bone accounted for, he built three funeral pyre terraces out of dry wood, wood that he was able to scavenge easily from the desert floor. Onto the lowest terrace, he placed his own bones. Onto the middle terrace, he placed the bones of his wife, Spotted Fawn. Onto the upper terrace, he placed the bones of his son. Then he heaped additional wood and dried sage under, along the sides and on top of the pyre.

By early afternoon all the preparations were complete and he sat for the longest time remembering and offering silent prayers. He wondered if his little family would ever be together again. Or, was the past simply a stroke of chance?

Bill stood and bowed to the four cardinal directions. Then he caught several glowing embers from his campfire and lit the funeral piles.

In the hours it took to bring the cremation to its conclusion, Bill wept.

Thirty

Bill was extremely tired as he crawled into his tent and fell onto his bedroll. Within minutes he was deep into a nurturing and sound sleep.

The next morning, Bill was startled awake by a pack of coyotes. He exited his tent in short order. The young male who had watched him several days before and his mate stood looking at him as if surprised to see him. "Good morning," Bill said. But the dogs turned and scurried away.

After taking care of his morning toilet, Bill returned to his bedroll and simply enjoyed the solitude. Thinking about the day ahead, he had no idea what to do. He certainly wasn't anxious to leave his base camp and soon found himself praying that Worm and Earl would come for him. So, the morning hours passed quite slowly.

Around three o'clock Bill began an afternoon hike. He felt a strange call and was moved to hike to an eastern mesa. Once there, he was touched by the wind, sun and rain. It felt refreshing on his bare arms and chest and he danced a little dance of thanks while a thunderstorm echoed from a nearby canyon.

Once again Bill entered non-ordinary reality. There, he was greeted by his Grandfather. Smiling, Pappy said, "I'm proud of you."

"Thank you!" Bill shouted, looking up into a turbulent and cloudy sky. A chilling wind made it difficult to remain standing.

Pappy shouted back, "Find a cave and begin your meditations."

Bill didn't want to meditate and he turned in order to walk back towards his base camp. However, the Earth had different ideas. Within minutes a huge thunderstorm began throwing hail the size of golf balls forcing Bill to find refuge in a nearby cave. Bill waited, and waited—and waited. But the thunderstorm gave no reprieve.

"Okay! I get it!" Bill shouted, not beginning to match the racket outside his shelter. Then, as he sat down onto the sand-strewn floor, he entered a meditative state. As he did, once again, he found himself reliving another past life…

"Knock, knock, knock!" The hollow noise stabbed the evening's silence. Wang-Chuk turned toward the door and reached for his dagger.

"Knock, knock, knock!"

"Shit! Who comes to my door in the dark of night?" Wang-Chuk demanded!

"Tis I, Thöpaga. I come to see my old master, Lama Yungtun-Trogyal. I apologize for the late hour."

"Thöpaga?" Wang-Chuk opened the door of his little cottage and pushed a yak-butter candle into the darkness. "Thöpaga! I thought you were dead!"

Thöpaga laughed. "Many would like it to be so."

Wang-Chuk shook his head in disbelief. "Where have you been all these years?"

"Alas, I've been in a monastery, Dowo-Lung in Wheat Valley in Lhobrak. Maybe you've heard?"

Wang-Chuk shook his head once again. "Lhobrak is very far from here."

"I've been studying the Tantric Doctrines with Marpa the Translator. I've been trying to undo my evil karma."

"Karma indeed. You killed thirty-five people in one afternoon! If the people of Kyanga-Tsu knew you were still alive, they'd hunt you down!"

"I don't need to be reminded!"

"So, have you come to reclaim your estate at Worma Triangle?"

"No," returned Thöpaga. "I've come only to give my mother a proper burial. This is why I'm looking for my master, Lama Yungstun-Trogyal. I wish to give him all my spiritual books in exchange for him making Tsha-tsha bricks for my mother's stupa grave."

Wang-Chuk held up his hand, stopping Thöpaga. "Father has been dead many years."

"Oh! Guess I have been away a long time," Thöpaga answered with some pain. "Wang-Chuk? Could you help? Could you help me make Tsha-tsha bricks for my mother's burial? In exchange for my books?"

Wang-Chuk shook his head while looking at the ground. "I'm afraid!"

"Why?"

"Thöpaga, if I accept your books, your Tutelary Deities would haunt my house, my fields."

"Wang-Chuk, my Tutelary Deities would not haunt you, not when I give you my books freely. I no longer have need nor use of them."

"Really?"

"Trust me. Please!"

"So be it, then!" Wang-Chuk stepped away from the door to create an opening. "Come inside and sleep the night. In the morning I'll make Tsha-tsha bricks for you."

At morning's first light and following a quick breakfast of tsampa and chhang, Thöpaga emptied the backpack containing his mother's bones.

"Oh, she's been dead a long time." Wang-Chuk exclaimed.

"Eight years!" Thöpaga returned, with tears in his eyes. I had so wanted to see her again, alive. I stayed away too long!"

"And for good reason!"

Respectfully, Thöpaga began breaking his mother's bones into smaller pieces while reciting a prayer for honoring the dead. Wang-Chuk placed the bone fragments into his mortar and with a pestle he ground the bone fragments into dust. Once finished, without words, Wang-Chuk mixed the powder with fine quality clay and formed bricks. Then he fired the bricks in a kiln. The next day, the casting of the Tsha-tsha bricks complete, Thöpaga performed consecration rites and deposited his mother's remains into her final resting-place.

"Thöpaga? Please stay a couple of days so we might reminisce old times," Wang-Chuk asked once the ceremonies were completed and prayer flags erected.

"I'm sorry, I must hasten to practice meditation at once. I have little time for talk," Thöpaga returned.

"But I insist! We've been friends for years, at least spend the night. At least allow me time to furnish you with a small quantity of food and provisions."

"Your offer is good. So be it, then," Thöpaga replied, walking along side Wang-Chuk toward his house.

"Thöpaga? In your youth you destroyed your enemies with black magic. Now, in your maturity, I see you have become a religious devotee. This, indeed, is admirable. I'm sure you'll become a great saint some day. But, tell me, what Gurus have you sought? What spiritual text have you obtained?"

"I have obtained the doctrine of the Great Perfection through Marpa the Translator."

"Marpa? Who is he? How did you come to meet him?"

Thöpaga laughed and shut his eyes. "There is so much to tell!"

"At the beginning, please, for an old friend."

"It started in a dream. I saw that I'd created much evil. Many people died because of me. After much pain and suffering and with the help of your father, I sought Lama Rongtön-Lhaga. He initiated me with a doctrine called 'The Great Perfection' almost immediately. But I was so filled with pride and thought myself such a favored and gifted person that I wouldn't meditate. Instead, I would go to sleep over my task. As a result, I failed to put the doctrine to the test of practice.

"After many weeks, the Lama Rongtön-Lhaga came to me and said, 'Thou didst call thyself a great sinner, in that Thou were quite correct. For me, I have been too lavish in my praises of the doctrine. I cannot convert thee. However, in Lhobrak there is a great Indian saint, the worthiest among men. He has obtained supernormal knowledge in all worlds. He is called Marpa the Translator. Between thee and him there is a karmic connection from past lives. To him thou must go.'

"Upon hearing his name, I was filled with profound love and swooned. Soon, I set out to find this guru.

"One day, when I was walking along a road asking directions, for which no one could help me, I came upon a corpulent man plowing a field. The moment my eyes fell upon him, I was thrilled by ecstatic bliss and I lost all consciousness of my surroundings. When I recovered I asked him if he knew where Marpa the Translator lived. He didn't immediately answer my question. Rather, he followed with questions of his own."

"Whence comest thou? What dost thou do?"

"I'm a great sinner from the highlands of Tsang," I answered. "I seek Marpa the Translator to learn the True

Doctrine by means of which I might obtain deliverance from pain and suffering."

"Very good," the fat Lama replied, "I will procure thee an introduction to him if thou wilt finish this bit of plowing for me." Then he brought out chhang from under his hat and offered me a drink. Of course, I accepted.

"After a time, a lad whom I'd seen among the cowherds came to me and explained that the Lama was successful in procuring the introduction with Marpa. That very night I was shocked to find that the corpulent man was himself, Marpa the Translator.

"As was customary, I offered Marpa gifts and devotion. But, even though he promised to teach me, Marpa seemed to want nothing of what I had. I found that my spiritual books offended him. When I went into the village and begged alms so that I might offer him gifts of meat and chhang, that offended him, too. Nothing I could do was right.

"Finally a day came when Marpa asked me to build his son Darma-Doday a circular house. Marpa promised that, once completed, he would impart to me the spiritual truths I sought. But when I had finished only half of it, he came and said that when he'd given me orders he had not considered the matter very well and that it encroached upon joint property with other relatives. Therefore, I must stop construction immediately and return all the building materials to the places whence they came.

"Once I had carried out Marpa's order, he came to me and requested that I build a second house. But due to weird complications, it, too, was never completed. Then there was a third order for a masonry dwelling, then a fourth. Finally, I had enough! I had huge sores and was in much physical pain. I was certain Marpa would never give me the doctrine

I sought. I knew that without religion, life is not worth living. I was doomed and considered killing myself. However, for some unknown reason, I continued working on the residence anyway. In the meantime Marpa's wife, Damena, began instructing me in methods of meditation. One day she said that I should give it one last try and she gave me her personal turquoise to offer as a gift to Marpa for the instructions I sought. But, when I did, he became furious. He claimed that in marriage all Damena's possessions were automatically his. He took a stick and beat me. In my horror, I jumped out a window and ran for days.

"Finally, I made up my mind to seek another guru. I returned to Dowo-Lung monastery to say good-by to Damena since she had been so kind to me. However, she insisted that I speak with Marpa. When I did, he insisted that I finish what I had started and not vacillate in my aims and kicked me out of his chambers. I left the Lama's presence without uttering another word. I said to Damena, 'Reverend Mother, I have a great desire to see my mother once again and I feel sure that the Lama will not give me the Teachings. Task after task, excuse after excuse, nothing I do pleases him. Now I will return home. I wish health and long life to you both.' I bowed down to her and turned to leave when she said, 'Thou are quite right. But I have promised to find thee a guru. There is a pupil of Marpa's named Ngogdun-Chudor who hath the same teachings as the Lama. I will arrange passage and offerings for you.'

"Damena was true to her word. With her help I traveled to Riwo-Kyungding in Central Tibet and received the teachings from Ngogdun-Chudor. But the day came when my new guru asked me if I had a specific visionary experience. I had not. My guru was very surprised. For a moment I considered confessing my deception, but courage failed me. In my heart I knew I should have remained with Marpa.

"About this time, Lama Marpa, having completed his son's residence, wrote to Lama Ngogdun inviting him to the consecration of the house. The letter also said that Lama Marpa had heard about my being with Lama Ngogdun and requested that this 'wicked person' be brought back at the same time.

"The day came when Lama Ngogdun, together with his wife, myself and a very large retinue set out for Dowo-Lung. When we arrived at the foot of the hill on which Dowo-Lung stood, the Lama requested that I go in advance and announce his pending arrival. Luckily, I encountered Damena first. She consoled me. Then I entered Darma-Doday's new dwelling and found Marpa meditating on the top most story. I presented a silk scarf to him and bowed from the East. He turned away from me. I moved to the West and bowed once again. But Marpa burst into rage. I turned away, intending to commit suicide on the spot. But, then, Marpa said, 'Brave Grand Sorcerer, do not do so! Our Mystic Doctrine declareth that all our various bodily principles and facilities are divine. If we take our own life, we kill the divine within ourselves and must face due punishment for the same. There is no greater sin than suicide. Wishing that Grand Sorcerer might be absolved from his sins, I caused you to build the edifices single-handed. Had it been for my selfish purpose, you were right to leave. Had I had the chance of plunging you, my spiritual son, nine times into utter despair, you would have been cleansed thoroughly of all your sins. You would have born-again into the celestial realms, your physical body being forever dissolved. You would have attained Nirvana. But now, that will not be so. You will retain a small portion of your merits due to my wife's ill-timed pity and narrow understanding. However, you have been subjected to eight deep tribulations, which cleanse you of your heavier sins. Now I will give you those teachings and initiations that I hold so dear as mine own heart. Henceforth rejoice.'

"I was not sure if I was awake or dreaming. I wept with delight and made obeisance. That very night, offerings were laid on the altar and in the presence of the assembly my hair was cropped, I was ordained a priest, and my dress was changed for a priestly robe. Marpa said that in a dream-vision which he had had, his Guru Naropa had given me the name Milarepa. I was now required to observe the vow of a brother and enjoined to follow the path of those who aspire to be a teaching Buddha."

"Whew! So you made it after all!" Wang-Chuk declared. "You are a great saint."

Thöpaga smiled, bowing his head in reverence. "No, I am still learning. Though I easily touch Samadhi I have not reached Nirvana."

"Tell me, Thöpaga, what would you teach a poor sinner like me?" Wang-Chuk asked.

"Reach out—touch the cosmos—touch the earth. Know that you are one with all things. Separateness is an illusion, a game that ego chooses to play. Reality is an untamed wildness in the universe, beyond thought, reason and words. Reality is not the ego that society teaches. Your soul is a voice crying in the wilderness. It cries because social ego stops you from seeing the very essence of what you are, a being of divine and radiant energy."

"But, how, how do I stop ego?"

"Stop doing what you've always done. It'll only get you what you've always gotten. Meditate, meditate, meditate! Don't be arrogant like I once was, thinking you're some special being and above it all. Practice your meditation like learning a musical instrument, slowly and with patience. At first, all seems vain; you seem to go nowhere. But a day will come when your world suddenly stops and you enter the state of the uncreated. At that moment you are presented with the paradox of doubt. If you choose to react with the ego of objectivity, instantly you fall back into the world of determinism and spiritual dysfunction. However, if you choose to act in the wilderness of the uncreated, instantly you witness the creativity within your own being and your spirit fills with love so profound that you realize before that moment you were never really alive. Only now is the world different. Yet, it's the same world because it hasn't changed, you have. You've changed your energy and along with it the focal point of your awareness."

Years later Wang-Chuk was moved to make a pilgrimage to Drakar. He had no reason to go except for a tug in his heart. But when he arrived, along with many monks, nuns and religious devotees, he received the shock of his life. His old friend, Thöpaga, who was now well known by the name, Milarepa, lay gravely ill. Due to jealous rivalry, Milarepa had been poisoned by a wicked Lama from a local monastery.

"Thöpaga? Tis I, Wang-Chuk." Wang-Chuk bowed in reverence before his dying friend.

Milarepa smiled. "And we meet again. Please, rise." He held out his hand begging his friend to come nearer.

"They tell me you're a great saint. But I always knew that," Wang-Chuk announced, offering Milarepa a piece of valuable turquoise.

"I have no use for earthly treasures."

"I know. Still, my heart moves me. Karma?"

Milarepa turned and gave the turquoise to his sister, Peta. "Wang-Chuk, there are five poisons: lust, hatred, stupidity, egotism and jealousy, egotism being the worst. I know you've had a difficult life. But don't use your difficulties as an excuse to stop. You must use your trials and tribulations as aids on your spiritual path. Having adopted a religious career is not enough. Because, unless the teachings of the Buddha be blended with one's own nature, what gain is there to know by rote the Sacred-Text? Many lifetimes from now you'll be born again into mediocrity and curse the precious life you live. But you will be surrounded by angelic beings and you will finally realize the Buddha consciousness within your own being. When that day comes, I will be there, too."

Bill roused from his vision, stood up and stretched his arms and legs. For the first time in his life his mind was truly silent. He walked out of his cave and into the drizzling rain, holding his hands over his head and up to the cosmos. Then he brought his hands down into a prayer position in front of his heart. Turning his palms inward across his chest, his heart filled with love. Finally, he reached down and touched the Earth. In the west, bigger than life, the sun was beginning to set. Filaments of light shot towards infinity and in a cloud hung the image of his friend, Milarepa.

Thirty One

"Little Crow okay! Don't care what his momma says about him!" Worm announced with a gigantic voice for all the neighbors to hear while dancing up to Bill.

Bill was busy splitting wood for the evening's sweat lodge. He put down his maul, turned and smiled. "Little Crow don't care either! Mother's voice only one opinion."

Worm extended his right hand toward Bill. Bill stood straight and shook Worm's hand from the center of his own manliness. Then he looked silently into Worm's big friendly brown eyes for several magical moments. Finally, Bill turned to resume his task.

"Little Crow makes fire without matches?"

"You remember your point of reference?" Bruce asked Bill, following the sweat.

"You mean that thing where you and Worm pinned me to the floor six weeks ago?"

"Yeah! Want to try it again?"

"No!"

"Little Crow not same man." Worm announced, walking up behind Bill and pushing him firmly on his left shoulder.

"What's the point? Bill demanded, turning to face Worm, folding his arms across his chest.

"Humor an old Indian!" Worm laughed.

Bill knew what he must do and laid down on the floor, face up, even though he resisted being humiliated again. The expression on his face told that he didn't like what was about to happen a bit.

Earl walked over, pinning Bill's left foot. Bruce pinned his right foot. Worm pinned his shoulders while Kathleen pinned his right arm and Eileen, his left.

"How can I get away from y'all when I couldn't even begin to break two peoples' grasp last time?"

"Little Crow man now! Much stronger!" Look at muscles!" Worm announced, laughing.

Bill knew he was being conned. In the past month he'd done nothing to improve his physical strength, in fact, quite the opposite. He looked at his adversaries, each face, one at a time. He could feel the physical pressure of his opponents increase.

Bill closed his eyes and imagined himself a huge gorilla. He sucked in a deep breath of air and jumped to his feet, sending his opponents flying across the room in several directions.

"Oh my gawd!" Bill yelled, almost collapsing to the floor from the realization of his own strength. Then once he recovered from the shock, he ran over to Kathleen and helped her to her feet. She seemed to suffer the worst from his explosion.

"Little Crow learned lots!" Worm walked over to Bill and gave him a long manly hug. Then, one by one, each of Bill's friends embraced him.

"What now?" Bruce asked Bill after everyone had taken various seats around the tiny living room. "Where do ya go from here?"

Bill looked at Bruce. He knew he was different from the person he once was. But it was so difficult to put into words that he didn't know how to begin.

"Those who know, don't say. Those who say, don't know. Isn't that right Little Crow?"

Bill turned and looked at Worm. "Yeah."

"What we are is indefinable, beyond reason, beyond words," Bruce continued. "What you've seen these past several weeks is only a small part of who you are, Bill. You now know the answers to many things. But tell us, right now, at this very moment, what is the most profound?"

Bill remained quiet for several minutes. He thought about past lives and how they influenced the present. He thought about self-forgiveness. He thought about the complementary factors of the material world versus non-ordinary reality. He thought about his relationship to Katarina and began to smile.

"Creativity!" Bill exclaimed, looking around the room at his mentors. "Earl once gave me a riddle. 'Bill, you remind me of a man who stands precariously on the point of a needle. Below you in all directions is the abyss. Above you is nothing. If you jump from the needle you fall to your death. If you stay where you are, you fail. You might as well not have been born.' Of course, we were talking about my decaying love affair with Katarina. He asked me what I was going to do?

"I remember crying my eyes out for days. I had no idea what to do. One day, months later, thanks to Earl's and Eileen's assistance, I learned that whatever I had been doing in order to win Katarina's heart, I must, somehow, do things differently. You see, everything around me was telling me how to proceed, but in my own preconceived neurotic expectations, I wasn't listening. These past months have taught me how to listen. But more than this having heard, how to proceed with my life in creative ways.

"So," Bill looked directly into Earl's dark brown eyes, "the answer to your damn riddle is creativity! I can't jump, without dying. I can't stay where I am, without failing. But, I'm not so paralyzed. I can be creative. I can correlate new possibilities."

"So show me your creativity! Show it to me with your body!" Earl barked without warning.

Bill jumped with surprise, not expecting Earl's command. But he knew the answer. It was the final gift of Skull Valley.

The last morning of his Vision Quest, Bill had hiked to a northern mesa to meditate. That morning gentle winds and the rain greeted him. The sunlight seemed soft and the air was perfumed by the desert creosote bush. And as he sat to enjoy the solitude, Bill became aware of shiny filaments of energy, amber in color. They surrounded and connected everything. For the first time in his life Bill saw that he was connected to the both the earth and the cosmos in ways that could only be otherwise imagined. But more than that, he realized that these filaments of energy were capable of sending and receiving information. All it took was intent found within the egoless state of being. All he had to do was to stop the internal dialog and feel with his heart. In that state he was quintessentially creative.

Bill smiled, then he closed his eyes, turned off his internal dialog and felt the room's energy with his heart. Then, through intent, he filled the room with love.

Earl stood up and walked into the kitchen, returning several minutes later with a large bowl of warm water and a flask of scented oil.

"Bill, two thousand years ago a woman of bad name loved Christ so much that she washed his feet in precious oil despite of the scorn of others. She had the courage to be!" Earl picked up Bill's right foot took off his shoe and sock. Then he placed Bill's foot in the warm water, washed and massaged.

"Today I wash your feet in tribute to your success and my love for you." Earl placed Bill's right foot onto a towel, dried it then proceeded to wash and massage his left.

"You've earned a great gift, insight of self, insight into the world, insight into love itself." Earl respectfully lowered Bill's left foot onto the towel and dried it.

Bruce walked behind Bill and began massaging his shoulders. Eileen picked up Bill's left hand and began massaging, Kathleen, his right. While Worm began chanting, "Unga wa, a-unga wa…"

Earl picked up his flask of scented oil and sprinkled both Bill's feet liberally, then began massaging. Tears of happiness washed down Bill's cheeks.

"Christ spent forty days and nights in the wilderness dealing with and understanding his dark side. As a result, he found compassion, intimacy and love for himself and, in turn, for all of humankind.

"Bill, the road you've chosen to walk is the most magnificent of all. Congratulations!"

Thirty Two

"Checkmate!" Bill yelled, trapping Earl's King.

Earl leaned back into his chair, smiling. He interlaced the fingers of both hands behind his head.

"You let me win," Bill advised, looking back at Earl, trying to read his body language.

"On the contrary, you did that yourself."

"I did?"

"You're not helpless."

"Yeah." Bill smiled. Then he got up and walked through the back porch, out the screen door and into the back yard. A cool breeze played Eileen's wind chimes while the smell of the neighbors' Concord grape vines wafted across the back fence. For a moment Bill relived fond memories of his grandfather's house in South San Gabriel. Suddenly, several jays began scolding. However, Bill didn't pay any attention to their hysteria. Instead, he sat down on a lawn chair and appreciated the warmth of the sun and the blueness of the sky. Finally, the jays returned to their own business.

Bill, Earl and Eileen were finally back home in Boulder. It was a warm sunny Friday, mid-morning, the second week in August. The Watley home was always a gentle place to be and Bill had no plans for the day and seemed content to simply hang out.

As the hours drifted peaceably by, once again Bill began teasing himself with the question, "Who am I?" Now, he knew the answer. He was a whole bunch of people, ancestors, past lives, incarnations he could remember, those he couldn't or didn't really care about. The essence of himself extended back to the very creation of reality.

Earl walked around the corner of the house while watering a bed of rhododendrons along the southern fence while a sparrow landed in a tree, inches from his head. Bill watched.

"Earl?"

"Yeah?"

"How come birds and animals aren't afraid of you?" Bill asked.

"Because my mind is quiet."

"Oh."

Earl laughed. "Wild things see the color of noise in our energy bodies. When there is no ego, there is no noise. When there is no ego, there is love. Love is the altar of silence where truth resides. It is the only Temple in the Universe."

"Earl? How did you become interested in things like spiritual enlightenment?" Bill asked late in the afternoon, as he washed his hands from the garden hose. He and Earl had just finished fertilizing the back lawn.

"Like you, I found my life wasn't working."

"Really? Guess I assumed you always had it together."

"Not always. You see, I grew up as a very arrogant kid. My ego was bigger than my common sense. I grew up in a coal mining town in Eastern Pennsylvania. In high school I was the varsity quarterback for two years running. I was intelligent, all right, but not very smart. Didn't study. I hung out with the wrong kinds of kids, screwed most the cheerleaders. Three months before graduation I knocked up the principal's daughter. Luckily she had a miscarriage. But I didn't know that, see. Like an idiot, I panicked, ran away and joined the Army."

"Really? You didn't finish high school?"

"Nope. But that's not the worst of it, Bill. I wasn't as lucky as you. I killed a bunch of people before I woke up!"

"Shit!" Bill involuntarily placed the fingers of his left hand over his mouth.

"When I was your age," Earl continued, "I was in the Pacific fighting for God and Country. It was World War Two. That's when I came face to face with my shadow."

"You have a shadow?"

"Of course, all people do. It's part of being human. I met my Mister Hyde as an infantryman. I was trained in the use of a flame-thrower. I set stuff on fire."

"Oh, no!"

"Yes! One morning my platoon captured a very small and almost insignificant island off Palawan in the Philippines. The enemy was badly outnumbered and our assault was quick. During our raid, I torched twenty-two Japanese men. Arrogant as I was, I began rummaging through the personal possessions of those dead men. I saw pictures of families. I saw love letters from home. I saw their keepsakes, their mementos. Me and my comrades made jokes, mocking our enemy. We tossed their stuff around like we were kids in a candy store.

"The next day, during our final sweep of the island, we looked for survivors to take prisoner. In the jungle near a small cave on the north side of a huge escarpment, I came across an officer who was badly wounded. He had a hole in his back the size of my fist. Paralyzed, he couldn't move his arms or legs. In plain English he begged me to kill him so he wouldn't have to suffer any longer. He told me about a letter to his wife that he held in his shirt pocket and asked me mail it to her, if I possibly could. Without blinking an eye, I pulled my side arm and shot him in the head. Thought I was doing us both a favor, but when his body went into spasm and death rattled in his throat, I saw his soul rise and I fell to the ground in agony. Sometime later, seeming like an eternity, I reached down and removed the letter from his pocket. Next to that letter was his wife's picture. She was the most beautiful woman I'd ever seen. Without warning all the horrors of war were upon me. For the first time in my life I saw the darkness in my world. I ran. I threw my weapons into the sea. That was the day I vowed never to take another human life, ever.

"My commanding officer sent me to a psychiatrist. I was diagnosed as suffering from battle fatigue and reassigned to noncombatant duty. However, I knew, despite their diagnosis, for just one brief moment, I experienced another reality, though I didn't understand it at the time.

"Understanding came later. While at the base hospital, I met an orderly named Ken. Eventually, he became my spiritual mentor.

"At the conclusion of the war, Ken and I were both sent to Japan in the police action that followed. About six months after our arrival in Tokyo, Ken reached the end of his twenty-year enlistment and retired. He chose to stay instead of returning to the States right away, since he'd spent most of his childhood in Peking, China with his missionary parents. His desire was to return to Peking to visit his old haunts. However, the Communists had other ideas and he never did get to the mainland.

"I was discharged from active duty about a year after Ken and stayed with him in a small village outside Tokyo. He introduced me to the tenets of Buddhism and Zen in addition to helping me reinterpret my own Christianity. He believed the basic tenets of all religions originated from one source. It was through the misinterpretation of language over time that these basics became so diversified and misunderstood. As a result, I became passionate about studying Philosophy and Religion.

"We both returned to the U.S. in spring of 1947. I hung around San Francisco doing odd jobs until Ken got a position in a Southern Arizona hospital. I stayed in the Bay Area and returned to school. After passing my GED, to my surprise I was admitted to the University at Berkeley where I eventually finished my doctorate. During my summers off I went to Tucson to work and live with Ken. He loved the Sonoran Desert and the two of us spent many a night camping under the stars talking about the meaning of reality. I did my Vision Quest on Baboquivari Peak, southwest of Tucson.

"In my second year of graduate school, I met Eileen. She was an Anthropology student at the University of Arizona. It was love at first sight. We dated only three months before getting married.

"Following graduation from Berkley, I did my post doc in Australia."

"Bill?" Eileen called, stretching her head out the back door.

"Yeah?"

"Phone."

Bill turned and hurried to the wall phone, hanging in the kitchen. "Hello?"

"Billy?"

"Yeah?"

"Your dad."

"Good afternoon. I was…"

"Your mother, she's in the hospital."

"Huh?"

"An auto accident."

"Huh? How bad is it?"

"Bad, they're going to operate tomorrow morning. Can you come out?"

"What happened?"

"She was driving home from your Uncle Chet's, Thursday, late afternoon. Got hit by a semi some place on the freeway just south of Burbank. Totaled her car."

"I'll be out as soon as I can book a flight!"

Thirty Three

"I'm so very sorry, dad." Bill apologized as he walked up to his father in the Los Angeles International airport. Bill reached out, attempting to hug his father. However, Chuck immediately turned away.

"Why don't you shave and cut your damn hair!" Chuck blurted.

Bill was surprised by his father's rebuke, but let it pass. "Dad, I'm here for you and mom. I want you to know that."

Chuck said nothing. His hardened face still held years of anger. He turned sharply, nearly knocking over a young woman passing by. Without apologizing, he began marching toward baggage claim.

"I'm scared, too, dad," Bill offered, hoping to soften his father's shell.

Chuck stopped walking and gave Bill a hardened stare.

A sharp pain stabbed Bill's heart. Intuitively, he knew he was being set up for confrontation. Over the last several months he had begun to understand how his parents had used both himself and Susan to bind their anxiety.

"Susan? How's she takin' it?" Bill asked.

"Thought you knew."

"What?"

"She ran away from home, almost a month ago."

"That little shit!" Bill shook his head in disbelief. He wondered why Susan didn't try to call or write. "Damn!"

"We don't know where she is. Haven't a clue."

"Police?"

"Went through all that."

"I'm sorry, dad. Really, I am. She told me she wasn't happy last Christmas."

"What the gawd-damn hell is wrong with you kids anyway?" Chuck interrupted. "I busted my ass trying to give you two a good home, music lessons when we could least afford it, Boy Scouts, Girl Scouts. A lot of good that damned psychiatrist did ya. All Susan did was complain that we don't give her enough. Then what? Just like you, she runs away. Fuck! Ya know, you really hurt your mother bad. I'll never forgive you for that!"

Bill took a deep breath and closed his eyes momentarily. In his dad he saw the man he might have been.

"What the hell is so wrong with me that I deserve the likes of you kids?"

Bill pondered as he walked up to the belt and pulled off his suitcase. Could Chuck handle honesty? "All I can do is tell you about me, dad. I never feel listened to. I never feel worthy. I never feel welcome when I'm around you."

"That's a bunch of fuckin' bullshit and you know it!" Chuck voiced, rather loudly.

Several passersby overheard Chuck's outburst and quickly created space.

"Dad all any of us want is to be loved, to be accepted for what we are. I can't live up to your expectations, any, anymore than you could live up to your father's."

"And just what the hell is that supposed to mean?"

"Why did you quit playing the saxophone?"

Chuck's face turned red as a beet.

"Dad, music runs in our family. Your mother had it. You have it. I have it."

Chuck had to sit down on a near-by seat. He looked up and into Bill's face with great pain.

"Dad? What happened? Why did you quit?"

Chuck pursed his lips, looking for words. He didn't want to answer, but he couldn't stop himself. "Life as a musician was hard, impossible. Was the beginning of the Second World War. I was into the Big Band scene, riding high. Playing gigs for Hollywood nightclubs. I thought I had the world by the ass. I blew everything I had. One afternoon at rehearsal, Tommy Dorsey and I got into an argument over some stupid arrangement of *Pale Moon*. God, I remember it just like yesterday. The bastard fired me! Well, he was the big man around town and I wasn't. I couldn't get another job. There were no unions back then. My own dad threw me out on the street for not paying him rent. So, I enlisted in the Army, ya know, just to show 'em. When I got out, almost six years later, big bands were pretty much history. I hadn't played in years, now I had a wife and kid to support. You know the rest." Chuck had a far off look in his eyes, one that Bill had never seen before.

"We'd better go!" Chuck said while rising to his feet.

Bill reached for his dad, trying to give him another hug. Chuck recoiled, looking at Bill as if he were a faggot.

"I'm sorry, dad, really I am. Wish it could be different for you."

"She's still in a coma," Dr. Jenkins said while escorting Bill and Chuck to Virginia's semi-private room. "We need to do another operation. The bleeding in her chest, it's not stopping."

"She looks so white," Bill said as he walked up to his mother's bed.

Dr. Jenkins felt Virginia's pulse, then listened to her heart and took her blood pressure. "She's has a strong heart. That's the good news!"

"Any idea when she'll be out of danger?" Chuck asked.

"We can heal her body. She's not sick. But she is an alcoholic. Even as she lies there her body is going through withdrawal. That's taking its own heavy toll."

"The coma? How long?"

"Could wake up in the next minute. She may never wake up. That's out of my hands."

Bill looked closely at his mother's face. He knew that no one was home. Then he glanced around the room, seeing if he could get any sense of her astral body. He saw and felt nothing.

"Sir, I'll do my part," Dr. Jenkins said, addressing Chuck. "The rest is up to her."

"And God?" Chuck asked, the tone of his voice announcing he would mock any answer.

Dr. Jenkins didn't reply. Instead, he smiled, turned and left the room.

"Ya know, your mother and I had such hopes when we were your age." Chuck began, seating himself along side Virginia's bed.

"We had magic. We thought we'd live forever. Now look at us." Chuck's mouth quivered. But he wasn't about to show any real emotion. "I think there is no God. At least not a God that cares about the likes of me."

"Dad, there has to be a God. It's necessary." Bill took his father's hand and held it firmly. "It's necessary."

"And what would your God tell me, now, times like these? To have faith? Ha!"

"All things are transitory, creation, life and death, a cycle that always repeats. The universe is constantly changing, becoming. It's necessary."

"Nice words."

"More than nice words, dad. Look at your life. The story is alive even in the simplest things you do. You pour yourself a bowl of breakfast cereal. That's birth. You eat and enjoy your bowl of cereal. That's life. You wash and put your bowl away. That's death. Each task is enjoyed and carried to completion, else, someplace along the line there is a hell of a mess."

The day looked to be another scorcher, smog, abnormal humidity, the works. Bill couldn't wait to get back to Boulder. But it was the morning of his mother's second operation and he'd promised to stay in Los Angeles for several more days.

"Looks like the latest proposal for the Pomona Freeway might take your house." Bill announced to his father, looking up from the morning's paper.

"Sorry, I've nothing for breakfast. Perhaps we should go out," Chuck returned, purposefully not hearing Bill.

"Dad, I don't need to eat. If you don't mind, I like to spend some quiet time, meditating."

Chuck looked at Bill with concern. "Meditation? You into some kinda cult, now?"

"No. I've just learned a way to be in the world, a way that works for me."

"Sounds like some kinda pop fad."

"Ever tried it?"

"No."

"It's simple. I can teach you."

"I'm not into weird, little man. Next you'll be telling me you've smoked grass. Have you?"

Bill thought long and hard before answering. "Yeah, I have."

"Fuck you!" Chuck replied, shaking his head. He quickly turned and walked away.

Bill opened the door to his old bedroom and walked in. Except for a new bookcase his dad had recently built, several random boxes littering the floor and stacks of art supplies, it was pretty much as he'd left it. Virginia had taken over what was once his desk and there were several small unfinished oil paintings sitting on her easel. Surprisingly, the room seemed much darker and smaller than he remembered it. Also, there was a faint musty smell coming from stacks of old magazines sitting on the floor where his bed once stood. Bill opened the blinds and windows, letting in the morning's light and air.

Sitting on a chair next to his mother's easel and remembering what life was like in this confining space, Bill laughed and shook his head.

The two screws in the side of his old nightstand were still there. He'd placed them strategically to hold Katarina's picture. During high school, he must have jacked-off every night.

Bill noticed a blue photo album near the bottom of a stack of books. Curiosity made him pull it from the pile. It was his baby book and amongst the many nude baby pictures were several letters from various relatives. One letter stood out amongst the rest. It was a letter from his father's stepmother. Bill never knew her because she died only a year after his birth.

> Dear Baby-Colton-to-be:
> Someday when you're grown up, you might be interested in the thoughts of one who tried to help your father through a painful boyhood.
> Your father believed and stood for honesty, justice and fair play. He was always ready to defend a just cause. Even if you were a favorite, you received his constructive criticism if he considered your attitude wrong.
> He was a thinker, an analyst and a creator. His hands and mind were never idle—arts, crafts and music. He was serious and possessed a rare foresight—even in his early youth. However, it took quite a bit of urging to get him into a dance class in high school. He was shy and his interest in girls was from the sidelines. The Boy Scouts was his boyhood salvation and outlet. As you know, he attained tops in the organization, as he will in anything he undertakes. Your mother was his first and only romantic love. There was only one other relationship, aftermath to a correspondence friendship. It ended in disillusionment. Your father found her shallow and superficial.
> He was always clean in body, mind and soul. His character and life have been above stain or reproach.

Please God, may you have the loving care and understanding of your fine parents throughout your lifetime. Know the love and joy they have found together.

A lady named Snow

"What went wrong? What happened to their lives?"

Bill returned to Virginia's studio chair and sat down while reading a second letter, one written from his maternal grandmother, Theona. "Interesting. A real lack of literacy."

Bill could remember little of Grandma Theona. Whenever families would visit, she was always cooking something tasteless and greasy, or in the back bedroom sewing. She didn't seek out her grandchildren and neglected her matronly duties. In fact, neglect was something his own mother was always in judgment about, especially around her own childhood. Bill's main recollection of Grandma Theona, however, was her views on education. She was often heard to say, "Real education was gotten off the streets, not out o' some damn book." She passed away when Bill was sixteen.

Bill flipped more pages, finally coming to rest on a picture of his parents and himself standing alongside a black thirty-seven Chevy. Bill was holding a huge round container painted like a firecracker. It was filled with salt-water taffy and he had a big toothy grin. The picture was taken the second of July 1947, in the parking lot of the University of Southern California. His father was attending night school and getting ready to go to class. As often happened during the summer months, during Chuck's absence, Bill and his mother would play in a local playground or romp in the expansive rose gardens surrounding the Museum of Natural History. Bill remembered those days as happy times.

Unfortunately, Chuck never finished college and promotions at work went to younger educated men. As a result, Virginia resented college graduates and always found ways to put them down. Bill remembered his mother's best friend, Edith. As soon as she finished her degree in primary education, Virginia promptly broke off the friendship.

"I think my parents are threatened by educated people," Bill said aloud, looking out the bedroom window, watching two birds fight over a worm. "Interesting! Though they said they wanted me to go to college, I think they've subconsciously tried to sabotage me. Could it be that the bigger the ego, the less capacity we have for love?"

Bill closed the book, returned to the kitchen and called Debbie on the telephone.

"Was hopin' you'd be home this summer, Billy," Debbie began after giving Bill a long hug at her front door.

"Couldn't. Was off doing some anthropology stuff with a couple of my professors."

"Where?"

"New Mexico, Arizona."

"Really? Care for a beer?"

"Sure."

"Thought we had something pretty special," Debbie said shyly, returning from the kitchen.

Bill didn't say a word. He sat down on Debbie's davenport and opened his brew.

"Billy, you're breaking my heart! What do you want me to be? I'll be it!" Debbie remained standing, three feet away.

"My friend, that's what I want."

"Your friend? After all we've been through, after last Christmas? I want more!" Debbie demanded, her Latin temper beginning to show.

"What we had was wonderful, Deb."

"Wonderful, my ass! You promised to marry me. Then what do I get? Months of silence!"

"Deb, I wrote you several letters. I even tried calling you several times and left word at your parent's house. You never returned either my calls or my letters. Finally I gave up."

Debbie didn't say a word as she stood staring angrily at the floor, nervously tapping her right foot. She was so embarrassed about her writing skills that she never wrote letters to anyone. But more than that, in her heart, she knew Bill would never honor his promise.

"Deb, ya know, you're important to me. But I can't marry you. I'm really sorry I said what I did. It wasn't honest!"

"So now you are being honest?"

"I'll never lie to you again."

"Fuck you!" Debbie inhaled half her bottle while glaring at Bill. "Suppose you're balling that Katarina chick," she accused, while jutting her chin towards Bill, East Los Angeles style.

"No."

"Who, then?"

"Deb, please, don't do this. I can't make you happy. You know that."

"Ya didn't answer my question!"

"I do not have a girlfriend! The only one I've ever been to bed with is you. Happy, now?"

Debbie stepped across her coffee table, picked up her pack of cigarettes and slid next to Bill. "I can be anything you want," Debbie offered, lighting up, throwing the spent match onto a scarred hardwood floor.

"I want you to be my friend, like old times." Bill returned.

"We were good together, huh." Debbie said, softening a little.

"Best friends for years," Bill answered, looking into Debbie's eyes. They were alluring, cagey and deceitful. They turned him on as he remembered how it was to be with her. "Can I use your bathroom?"

"Of course." Debbie smiled.

Several minutes later Bill returned to the living room by way of the kitchen. Unwashed pots and pans were heaped in the sink; dirt and grime littered the floors, and the smell. Bill realized how far he'd come.

Without a doubt, Debbie could never make him a home. He wondered how he could have ever entertained the possibility.

Debbie offered Bill a half-smoked joint as he returned to the living room.

"I'll pass."

"Com' on. Sex is better when you're high."

"Think I should leave."

"Billy, I need you right now," Debbie pleaded, getting up from the davenport then walking over to Bill. She took him into her arms, held him close and began nibbling his neck.

Bill closed his eyes and touched his feelings, trying to justify his heart while Debbie pushed her right hand deep into his pants. He wanted her.

Once Debbie was certain she was going to get her way, she turned back to the coffee table, picked up her joint, re-lit it, took a long drag and handed it to Bill. He looked at her for what seemed an eternity.

"No! I can't do this. It's not right!" Bill turned and began walking toward the front door.

"You leave, don't even think about ever coming back!" Debbie yelled.

"Deb, I'm not going to play games."

"Fuck you!" Debbie picked up Bill's half-empty beer bottle and threw it at him. The bottle tumbled, spaying beer in all directions. Bill ducked, trying to avoid getting drenched. However, following a sweeping arc, the bottle smashed into the corner of a homemade book shelf sending large splinters of glass cutting the air, stabbing the stucco wall while the heavier glass bottom ricocheted back striking Bill in the left thigh, ripping both pants and flesh.

"Get out! Get the FUCK out of my house!"

Thirty Four

"She's out of the coma," Dr. Jenkins announced in the hospital waiting room. "But not out of danger."

Bill closed his book and rose to his feet. Then both he and his father followed Dr. Jenkins to Virginia's cubicle in critical care. She still lay unconscious with tubes and monitors hanging all over the stationary racks at the head of her bed.

"Technically the operation is successful. However, she still seems to be going downhill. It's as if she has lost the will to live," Dr. Jenkins said. Then he stood explaining the operation in layman's terms, outlining some of the internal injuries Virginia had sustained and the resulting complications.

Chuck looked at his wife. He felt an obligation, but the love of his youth was gone and he had no idea how to get it back.

Dr. Jenkins watched Chuck for several moments, then glanced at Virginia. He understood. "Well, not much more I can do here," he said while placing his hands behind his back and interlocking his fingers. He turned and left the room.

A great pity came over Bill. He walked to the chair alongside his mother's bed and sat down. He picked up his mother's right hand and stroked it gently. "When ya going to get out of this place and come home, ma?"

The only reply came by way of small eye movements beneath closed lids.

"Smokes too damn much Drinks too damn much. Ya know that!" Chuck publicized rather loudly as he and Bill exited the hospital, an hour later. "The Doc told me that her lungs are bad. Her liver's bad."

"I know."

"If she lives, this'll cost me a damn fortune."

"Sounds like you want her to die. Do you?" Bill asked, picking up his father's thoughts.

"No one wants anyone to die. But…"

"I understand, dad. Please, don't say another word." Bill opened the passenger door of his father's black Oldsmobile and got in.

"You think I'm a hard ass son-of-a-bitch, don't you?" Chuck shouted as he started the car's engine. "I should have left her, years ago, when I got out of the service. But I didn't, okay? I knew she couldn't make it on her own. Then, I stuck it out because of you kids."

"Dad, it's okay to hurt."

Chuck turned and stared at Bill for a few seconds. "Shit! What the hell kinda game you trying to play little man?" Then he turned back and slammed the transmission into reverse and squealed out of the parking stall lightly striking the bumper of the car next to him.

"Dad, I want to be your friend, okay? I hurt, too. I know she's going to die."

Chuck slammed on the brakes. As the car skidded to a stop, he turned and looked at Bill.

"I've known that the moment I saw her in the hospital, two days ago."

"How?"

"I can see, dad. Her spirit is already too far gone."

Chuck glared, not saying a word.

"All these years, you thought I was crazy. I'm not, ya know."

"You scare me. You scare me a lot." Chuck turned away. He could no longer look at his son.

"I know. Still, I give mom another day, two at the outside."

"The way she looks, you're probably right." Slowly, Chuck placed the transmission in drive and pulled out of the parking lot. Purposefully he did not look at the car he hit or to see if there were any witnesses.

"Dad? Could we go somewhere and talk? MacArther Park, maybe?"

"I want to tell you that I'm very happy with my life," Bill said as he walked toward the lake with his dad. Several rowboats floated in the calm water, glistening in the hot noonday sun. There were joggers and cyclists, accompanied by excited cries of children at play. Together, Bill and his father stopped and sat down on a park bench in the shade of a very old and robust maple tree.

"The past several years have been very difficult for me. I know I haven't been fully appreciative of you or mom. I've been naïve about a lot of things. For that, I apologize."

Chuck turned and looked at his son. His frown lines looked like they were cast in stone.

"I know you hold a lot of judgment about me and my choices. I know that I've brought you a lot of pain. But, after all is said and done, I must live my own life. I must learn, somehow, even if by the school of hard knocks."

Chuck's face showed no signs of softening.

"Dad, I must tell you that I don't entirely agree with your's and mom's belief, 'experience is the best teacher, but only fools use it.' Sometimes experience is the only teacher. Sometimes it's necessary to get the shit beat out you. At times I've really blown it, I know. Other times I've done it right. But, one thing I've learned, the pain of failure, the joy of success, they come to us as a package. What I've learned this past year is, when your life is not working, you've got to have the strength to get back on your feet and try something different.

"Ya know I play one hell of a violin, now. I'm learning the Paganini *Concerto*, the one I've always dreamt about. I got there through persistence. I practice hard, every day! What I know is true, practice and persistence, getting passed the mistakes, that's what makes for a successful life, whatever our endeavor."

Bill turned and watched several little boys, running, screaming, jumping into the lake.

"What I've also learned," Bill resumed, turning back to his father, "is when life throws its cabbages, its rotten eggs and tomatoes in your face, you've got to take a stand. Stand up for what you believe in. Else, you lose everything." Bill turned and looked at two filthy winos slouched on a park bench, twenty feet away. "Like them. Because, in spite of the insecurity, the uncertainty, the lack of perfection in our lives, we must have the courage to be. Without that courage, our lives are nothing but an ongoing existential crisis.

"Dad, take my hand and shake it." Bill extended his hand.

Chuck reciprocated, even though apprehensively.

"Dad, I'm here to tell you, I'm a man!"

The next morning Bill chose to spend some time with his mother while Chuck ran an errand. The bathroom sink needed new faucet washers. It was the excuse he needed to get away. Bill understood. When his father couldn't bind his anxiety by bullying people, withdrawal was his next coping strategy.

As Bill entered Virginia's cubicle in critical care, he realized his mother was semi-conscious and trying to say something. He took her hand. She returned a faint squeeze with all the energy she could muster. Her eyes were half-open and very dim. Bill sat down in the chair next to the bed and asked how she felt, did she need anything? However, Virginia offered no reply.

Bill watched his mother while several hours passed in silence. Hospital staff came and went, checking this and that, thanking Bill for his caring presence.

Virginia was only forty seven, but she looked sixty and beneath wrinkled skin and flesh there was a hideous strength pulling Bill's gut, even if now helpless. Bill finally understood that, as a child and later as an adolescent, he had sacrificed himself in order to be an emotional conduit, binding and grounding her psychic instability. He had been overwhelmed by the mood of her personality and had no choice. He also understood why his father was inaccessible. In his inability to set boundaries, she had sucked his soul dry.

"Yaaggg...danka..." Finally, Virginia tried to speak again. However, her words were garbled and incoherent. Still, Bill strained to piece the broken sentences together. It was something about an artist in the corner of the room painting her picture. When he was done, it'd be time for her to leave.

"Mother," Bill spoke quietly, slowly, and very deliberately, "I forgive you. I forgive myself." He repeated his words many times hoping she understood. "Mother, forgive me. But most of all, forgive yourself."

"I, I...ahhhh..." Virginia's eyes closed so very gently. The artist had finished the painting.

Thirty Five

Several weeks later, following Virginia's funeral service and in the quiet of his room in Boulder, Bill held a service of his own. After his summer's experience it was easy entering non-ordinary reality…

In his astral body, Bill found himself walking along a dirt road surrounded by green rolling hills, trying to get a sense of where he was. He thought it might be Tennessee. People were milling about. Several walked past him. As if in a trance, they were totally unaware of his presence. After some time Bill came to a tiny dirty village. It appeared to be from an age long past, no modern conveniences, people were unbathed and obviously didn't care about hygiene.

Bill walked up to Pappy, a brilliant being of light. He was standing next to Virginia. She was dirty and unkempt. Her over-weight body sagged and her face hung low, like a dog badly beaten. Her dissonant aura was dark gray with streaks of swirling orange and red. There were several blackened holes in her luminescence, holes made by possessing spirits, themselves eager for booze. Over the years they had used her as a human host in order to maintain their psychic drunkenness.

"I fear my daughter is in grave danger. Her light is going out. That's why I've called you," Pappy said.

"What can I do?"

"Talk to her. She can't hear me. She's still too earthbound."

Bill looked at his mother and knew she was filled with resentment and murderous rage. A great pity came over him.

"Mother?"

There was no response.

"Mother?" Bill moved closer to Virginia and nudged her.

"What the hell?" Virginia mumbled, moving away, obviously unaware of Bill's presence.

"Mother!" Bill shouted.

There was no further response.

Bill walked around Virginia several times trying to see where her attention was focused. Through her auric energy bands, Bill could see that her eyes were tightly closed. He nudged her several times and yelled her name.

Virginia looked up slowly and stared blankly into space.

"Mother, you're important to me!"

Virginia gave no further sign of recognition.

"Mother, look at me! Look at me! Look…At…Me!"

Slowly, Virginia turned her head. Finally, she looked at Bill. However, there were still no signs of recognition. "Wine…" She mumbled, as if intoxicated.

Bill despised his mother's alcoholism. He knew she used it as a tool to irresponsibly manipulate others. Like all alcoholics, she never realized that sinister spirits were manipulating her in return.

Bill looked to Pappy for assistance.

"Take all the time you need. You know what to do," Pappy said, quietly.

"Mother?"

"Who's that?" Virginia finally asked in a monotone.

"Bill. Mom, it's me, your son."

"Who?"

"Bill, your son!"

"Billy? My baby?'

"Yeah mom, it's me."

"Ya still seeing that slut?" Virginia said, pulling Bill's gut like an unresolved dissonance. "I'm the only one who ever loved you."

Instantly, all Bill's mother issues were in his face, just like old times.

"Be fierce! Remember your intent!" Pappy commanded.

"I forgive myself. The light of God flows through me," Bill began chanting.

"Men are all the same," Virginia crescendoed. "Treat me like shit. Your father, fuck him! Fuck you!"

Bill had to turn and back away to save his own sanity. He knew that, if left in her present condition, there were only two options open to his mother. Her soul would flicker into nothingness. Or, she'd return to the earth-plane and try to suck the life energy from some other poor alcoholic.

"Pappy, I don't need this. You better find someone else to help her!"

Pappy didn't answer. There was a very long silence.

Suddenly Bill's out-of-the-body experience changed completely. He found himself at the bottom of a very long stairway. Along the stairway were thousands of people. They were simply standing looking toward the top in hushed tranquillity.

In silence, Pappy began leading Bill up the long ascent. When they finally arrived at the upper platform, floating within a backdrop of infinite stars and space, Bill stood before a huge vortex of slow spinning light. Its colors were brilliant white with shimmering gold and violet on its perimeter. For some reason Bill was compelled to stick his finger into the light. When he did, violet eddies spiraled out in slow motion only to recombine in the whorl moments later. Bill withdrew his finger and looked at his grandfather, detecting a faint humor in his grandfather's eyes.

"Step through," Pappy commanded.

Bill did and in his amazement he found a multitude of hosts. Love quickly filled his entire being. Instinctively he knew what he must do next.

Through intent, Bill returned to the scene where he had left his mother.

"You bring me cigarettes?"

"No."

"You ungrateful son-o'-bitch."

"I know where cigarettes are, anything else you want."

"Where?"

"You'll have to come with me, mom."

Virginia appeared to be unmoved.

"Remember how you used to like to visit art galleries, how you used to oil paint?"

"Uh-huh."

"I know where the most beautiful art in the world is. It's more than a gallery. Mom, you can paint all you want, right alongside the masters."

"Where?"

"You'll have to come with me to find out," Bill said. Then he offered Virginia his hand and began slowly leading her toward a large green hill. He then closed his eyes and visualized the stairway leading up toward the vortex of light. Instantly, both he and Virginia were there.

"Where is this place?" Virginia asked. She looked around in astonishment.

"It's a passageway. See the light at the top?" Bill pointed with his right hand. "That light is a doorway."

"A doorway? To what?"

"To the gallery, mom."

Virginia pulled her hand from Bill's and began to back away. "I'm afraid."

"Afraid? Of what?"

"I need a cigarette!"

"Then climb the stairs. Go into the light."

Virginia stopped and looked at Bill, cold and hard. "You've betrayed me! You're unloving, ungrateful."

Bill looked at Pappy who was now standing next to Virginia. "What now? I fear she's right. I have betrayed her."

"Look within your heart, Bill."

"Who's that? Who are you talking to?" Virginia demanded.

"Your father, Pappy. He's right here."

"Bullshit!" Virginia looked left, to where Bill had been talking. Then, she scanned her immediate surroundings several times. "Bullshit!"

"Mother, everything you could ever want is on the other side of the spinning light—love, family, friends, peace, even God.

"Do you remember how much you loved your father?"

"Uh-huh."

"He awaits you in that light."

"But? But he's dead. He died five years ago."

"I know. And, he's here now."

"Am I? Is that?" Virginia pointed toward the vortex.

"Heaven? Yes, that's one explanation."

"Where is this?" Virginia demanded, panic working its way across her face and through her aura.

"Some call this purgatory, a place between heaven and earth."

"I'm dead?"

"Let's put it this way, you have no physical body. But, you're still very much alive."

"Then you're dead, too."

"No, mother, I still have a physical body. For me this place is Dreamtime, a journey of my soul."

"What?"

"Mom, remember how you used to tell me that when I go to sleep at night I'm out and about?"

"Uh-huh."

"Well, here I am, out and about."

Virginia looked more than a little confused.

"Please don't try to understand right now. Your destiny is at the top of these stairs. There, your happiness awaits."

Virginia looked at her son, then back up the stairs. "I fear I'm too weak and tired. Will you carry me?"

Bill looked at Pappy. Pappy shook his head.

"You must do this one yourself, mom. While others can show you the path, it is only you who can do the work. It has to be of your own free will and accord."

"But, but I'm so weak."

"Mother, all you need is intent."

"Intent? What's that?"

"It's your heartfelt passion. The thing you have to do, no matter what the odds, no matter what the obstacles. What is your passion, mother?"

"Don't know, least not anymore."

"What would it look like if you did know?"

"I, I…"

"Yeah…" Bill put both his hands in front of himself and coaxed Virginia with his fingers. "What would it look like, mom?"

Virginia looked into Bill's eyes and smiled. The hard lines in her face began to dissolve while the dissonant colors in her aura began to resolve. "I'd paint! I'd paint the most beautiful landscapes you ever saw."

"I know you would, Mom. That has always been your passion, huh. Well, tell ya what, in that spinning light at the top of these stairs is the doorway into that world of art. I think you should go check it out."

Virginia turned toward the stairs. "Will you come with me?"

Bill took his mother's hand and even though she struggled to keep her balance and could hardly move forward at times, Bill was patient. Together they climbed. Together they entered the light. On the other side they entered a large room filled with loved ancestors, art, music and laughter. Pappy's face was the first that Virginia recognized. He was standing next to an easel and a plethora of paints and brushes.

"Oh, Daddy!" Virginia reached out, her heart filling with love from the embrace.

After embracing Pappy, Bill walked with his mother and embraced Grandmother Theona, then many ancestors, both known and unknown. Finally, Bill turned so that he could return through the vortex, back to his meditating body.

"Who are you, Billy?" Virginia asked, holding her hand out and touching his arm.

"I'm awake."

Thirty Six

"I dreamt about her again last night." Bill turned away and looked out the kitchen window. It was a typical sunlit August morning, warm, the smell of Concord grapes wisping on a gentle breeze, butterflies floating, a mocking bird calling, several jays scolding the neighbor's cat, neighborhood kids playing street baseball. Bill saw the earth alive, reminding him that he lived in a magnificent world, a world he couldn't get enough of.

"And?"

"We had great sex!" Bill continued with a smile extending from ear to ear. He knew exactly what it meant.

Earl put his fork down and looked into Bill's eyes from across the table. "So when are you going to go to her?"

"This morning, as soon as I finish my chores."

"Bill?"

"Yeah?"

"Forget the chores!"

Just before noon Bill parked his '57 Chevy in front of Katarina's house and walked up to the front door and rang the bell as if he had the right. The sunlit porch was warm and the air heavy with the smell of latex paint.

"Yes?" Katarina's mother, inquired, walking up to and then peering out the screen door. "Billy! What a surprise! Come in, please!"

"Katarina?"

"She's in the back of the house, painting!" Rita said. She gave Bill a quick hug and then escorted him through the living room and to the back guestroom where Katarina was busy painting the ceiling.

"Billy!" Katarina screeched, throwing her paint roller into an empty bucket. Hurriedly, she climbed down from the ladder and began wiping her hands on an old brown bath towel. Then she removed her overalls, revealing Bermuda Shorts and a dirty paint stained tee shirt. "I like your beard!"

"Ya do?" Bill walked toward Katarina and extended his arms. "May I?"

Katarina's answer came by way of reciprocation as Cobweb immediately began twining around Bill's and Katarina's legs. Katarina looked down at her cat and chuckled. Then, she took off her multi-colored baseball hat. Her hair was wrapped in a tight bun. Bill had never seen it up before and prayed she hadn't cut another inch of it. However, he said not a word.

"It's good to see ya. I'm getting tired of all this painting, I'll tell ya what!"

"Can I help?"

"Naw, rather talk with you for a while. Been doin' this for days. Y'all notice the outside of the house."

"Yeah! It looks great!"

"Mom and I did it ourselves."

"Wow! You guys are industrious. Where's Erik?"

"National Guard." Katarina said, turning to leave the room. "Excuse me. I'm gonna wash up."

Bill wandered back into the living room, stopping to look at family pictures hanging in the hallway. There was one picture that caught him by surprise, a family photo, hardly a year old. In it, Katarina's smile pulled him like no force on earth. Hardly able to move, he stood enchanted.

"Billy, care to join us for some lunch?" Rita called from the kitchen.

"Mom?" Katarina interrupted, bouncing down the hallway and into the living room. "I want to make a picnic lunch. That okay?" She turned and gave Bill a wink.

Bill's face exploded with delight. Katarina's inner child shown through her eyes, just like in her picture.

"Okay, indeed." Rita answered with a matchmaker's grin.

Katarina walked over to her piano, pushed back the keyboard cover and sat down. She unclipped the gold barrette holding her hair. Then, shaking her head, her blond hair cascaded down her neck, just touching her shoulders. Bill stood watching in awe.

"Y'all bring your violin?"

"Oops."

"Let ya off the hook this time." Katarina began warming up with a few scales and arpeggios while Bill sat down on a chair immediately to Katarina's left. Cobweb wasted no time finding Bill's lap and swatting playfully at his right hand. Katarina played Schumann's, *Traumerei*, despite her aching hands.

An hour later, Bill and Katarina began their drive toward the Rocky Mountain National Park.

"Y'all do your Vision Quest?" Katarina asked as Bill turned west onto U.S. Highway 34.

"Uh-huh." Bill turned and glanced at Katarina. He had a broad smile on his face.

"Well, don't keep me in suspense!" Katarina turned in her seat slightly so she could give Bill her full attention.

"Guess I don't know where to begin, so much happened. I've learned so much."

"Oh?"

"Katarina? Let me start by asking you a question. Do you believe in past lives."

"Ya mean like, reincarnation?"

"Yeah."

Katarina got a strange look on her face. She took a huge gulp of air and replied, apprehensively, "Yeah, Billy, I do." Then she looked away and stared at the road speeding by.

"I sense that you're not anxious to talk about this kind of thing."

"Mom always warned me against it."

"Your mom?"

"She always said, with ideas like that, people would think I was a witch, or, or worse."

Bill began laughing.

"Billy, that's not funny!"

"I'm sorry. I know it's not funny." Bill took his eyes off the road and looked at Katarina. "I understand your concern. But, do you know how long I've wanted to have this kind of conversation with you?"

"Probably since Philmont."

"Yeah."

Katarina smiled while looking back at Bill. Bill slowed and pulled slightly to the right of the road while a white Porsche came racing up from the rear. Bill made certain that the Porsche could safely pass, despite the double yellow lines in the center of the roadway.

"I want you to trust me, Katarina. I don't think you're a witch, or anything of the kind. I think you're just like me, a person desperately trying to be the best they can possibly be."

"Thank you, Billy. Okay, here goes. I believe our soul reincarnates from human life to human life. I believe that friends, lovers, parents and children are often people we've shared our past lives with. I also believe that under the right conditions we get glimpses of our past lives."

"Your saying that helps me a lot, let me tell ya. Because, during my meditations and subsequent Vision Quest I saw a bunch of past life stuff."

"Really?"

"Some of it was pretty neat, some pretty horrible. I saw myself as a woman pianist and composer. I saw myself as a Roman Officer who did some terrible things. I saw myself get burnt at the stake for telling a lie. I saw myself as an American Indian. I also saw myself living in Tibet. I knew the Buddhist saint Milarepa. He was my friend."

"Wow!"

"But more important, I literally saw how a past life can effect my present life. Now, I understand some of the reasons I've been emotionally out of control all these years. As a result, I've begun to come to terms with my shadow."

"Shadow?" Katarina asked, looking at Bill out of the corner of her eye and cocking her head slightly. "I don't think I understand."

"Well, this summer I learned firsthand that people have two major energies that create their individual personality. One is ego, the stuff we consciously present to the world. The other is the shadow, the stuff we unconsciously repress. What I've learned is, while both ego and shadow are reactions to our social upbringing, they are strongly influenced by the experiences from past lives." Bill glanced at Katarina. She was obviously taking it all in.

"Consider, Katarina, every human on this planet is part ego, like Dr. Jekyll and part shadow, like Mr. Hyde. The problem is, until we break our trance state, like poor Dr. Jekyll, the Mr. Hyde part of us has its own agenda and we get stuck on a roller-coaster, unable to get off. I'm now convinced that the first step toward spiritual enlightenment is about self-forgiveness and coming to completions with our past.

"You did that?"

"Like to think so."

"How?"

"By facing my past, forgiving it and letting it go. By learning to be present in my life, right here, right now. By not forcing expectations on the future. By learning to be creative in each and every moment, without attachment to those creations."

"Whew!" Katarina heard what had Bill said. And, more than anything else, what stood out for her was not forcing expectations. "Bee?"

"Yeah?"

"I, I think I had a similar experience."

"Really!"

"Just last month." Katarina stopped talking and closed her eyes in deep thought. "I don't know if I should be telling you this," she finally said.

Instinctively, Bill pulled to the side of the road, stopped and turned off the Chevy's engine. He turned and gave Katarina his complete attention.

"I, too, took a good look at my life this summer, what you call shadow stuff," Katarina began. "Billy, I can't tell you how unhappy I've been these last few years. I've tried so hard to do the right things. Go to school. Play organ in church. Hold a job. Keep my studies up. But even with straight A's I can't please him. He always expects more."

"Your father?"

"Yeah." Katarina looked away. "I think the only way he knows how to love me is to manipulate and overpower me."

"Katarina, you don't have to do anything to be loved," Bill said softly.

Katarina looked back at Bill in disbelief. She placed her left hand over her mouth.

"Frustrating, huh."

"Yeah!" Instantly, Katarina knew Bill understood, that he cared, perhaps more than anyone else did. Her eyes moistened.

Bill placed his hand gently onto Katarina's forearm and said very softly, "It's okay to cry. I won't push you away."

The dam broke as Katarina burst into tears.

Bill didn't say another word. He opened the glove compartment and got out a box of facial tissue. Then he simply sat giving Katarina the time and the space to do what she had to do.

"Whew." Katarina blew her breath as she recomposed herself and dried her eyes. Then she looked at Bill in a way that she'd never looked at any man.

Bill knew he must maintain control. This was neither the proper place nor the time to do anything rash. "Shall we continue?" Bill resumed his driver's position and started the engine.

"About three miles ahead, on the left, is a forestry road. It's pretty bad, so you'll want to take it slow. But we won't have far to go," Katarina said quietly.

Bill turned where Katarina indicated. And, after being bounced considerably by the washboard, he parked his car in a public clearing. Together, they got out. Bill put on the daypack containing the lunch that Katarina had prepared.

"Follow me!" Katarina waved her arm forward as she began walking toward a trail heading east through old growth forest. She had a giant smile on her face. Her gait was light, almost childlike.

Together they walked, single file, along a narrow path. The afternoon sun made the air warm and the smell of pine was strong. Only the sounds of breaking twigs, along with Bill's and Katarina's heavy breathing, disturbed the forest's stillness. Finally they broke into a small clearing. Before them lay a pear-shaped crystal clear lake, about a quarter of a mile long and several hundred yards wide at its maximum perimeter. As they approached a rotting log planted firmly in the muck, several fish jumped at patrolling dragonflies. Water-spiders scurried in every direction, upsetting the sun-glistened surface.

"We want to go over there." Katarina pointed to a meadow along the far shore.

"This is absolutely magnificent, a dream!" Bill exclaimed, taking in a chest full of air, then slowly releasing it.

"My favorite place in the whole world, I'll tell ya what."

"Come here often?"

"Uh-huh."

Toward the end of the lake Bill was delightfully distracted by millions of tadpoles pushing the shoreline with frenzied vigor. Katarina laughed and stomped her right foot into the damp peat sending baby frogs leaping in all directions.

"Let me try that." Once the bog was still again, Bill stomped his right foot. A second time, frogs exploded into delirium. "Did you see that! Think I scared them for hundreds of feet. Look!"

Katarina laughed at Bill's enthusiasm. "We must have hit the peak. Haven't seen this many in years," she said as she turned and began walking toward a field of mountain daisies, shaded against the dense pine forest. She picked a dozen, or so, flowers and handed them to Bill. "Penny for your thoughts."

Bill thoughts were many, but he chose not to speak. Instead he smiled his mind.

Katarina blushed. Then shyly, she turned and walked to a huge boulder positioned near a small narrow stream that was feeding the lake. She kicked off her shoes, then sat down, letting her feet dangle in the crystal cool water.

Bill, impressed by Katarina's dainty feet and muscular calves, removed the daypack from his back. Then he set it next to Katarina.

"Looks like someone's camped here recently," Bill remarked as he walked over to some dirt covered charcoal remains in a small rocked circle.

"Mine."

"Yours?" Bill turned, looking at Katarina.

"Said I come here often."

"Alone?"

"You think it's odd, I mean to want to be alone?"

"Not at all. Much of my quality time is spent alone, perhaps too much," Bill said as he walked toward Katarina and then leaned against a pine stump, the remains from some woodcutter's axe. "I tend not to like people very much."

"Care for a sandwich?" Katarina asked, removing tuna sandwiches and cans of soft drinks from the daypack. A woodpecker landed on a nearby tree and immediately began jabbing for insects.

"Thank you." Bill reached out and accepted one of the sandwiches. Then, while looking up at the racket overhead, he peeled back the wax paper wrapping and took a healthy bite of his sandwich.

"Toward the end of July I camped here for several days," Katarina continued, bringing Bill's attention back to her. "Needed to take a good hard look at my life."

Bill said nothing. But he couldn't help smiling as his thoughts flashed across his own summer's events. He pulled his scout knife from his jeans' pocket and began to puncture the soda cans. The subsequent hissing sent the woodpecker flapping frantically for its life.

"What?" Katarina asked, trying to intuit Bill's thoughts.

"Nothing. Please, go on," Bill said while handing Katarina one of the opened sodas.

"Thanks. Well, that stuff about not being able to please my dad, that's part of it," Katarina resumed, looking directly into Bill's eyes. Bill had touched her with an intimacy that she'd never known. And if at all possible, now, she wanted more, whatever the risk. "Bee? May I speak openly?"

"I'd like that."

"I've made some very bad choices."

Bill said nothing, almost afraid to anticipate what she might mean.

"Yeah. Like, most of my life, I thought my dad was the greatest. I wanted someone in my life just like him, just as fierce, just as certain. I wanted a man who knew where he was going and how to get there, a man who could protect me. Who…"

"…wouldn't put up with any bullshit." Involuntarily, Bill finished Katarina's sentence. And as he did, he realized that he had violated her space, that it's not okay to put words in someone else's mouth. He realized that love is about letting someone have his or her own experience.

"Yeah?" Katarina looked questioningly at Bill. Then she changed her position, shifting her legs, trying to get more comfortable. "You remember Carl?"

"How can I forget."

"Thought Carl was such a man, ya know, like my dad, that is until he beat me senseless one night. He put me in the hospital with a broken collar bone."

Bill didn't say a word. Anger quickly touched his awareness.

"Almost two years ago. I've only been on a couple of dates since."

"And I scared the hell out of you."

"Yeah, Bee, you really did."

"I'm truly sorry." Bill reached out and took Katarina's right hand into both of his. Apology was written all over his face. "The last thing I ever wanted to do."

"I know." Katarina looked away momentarily, biting her lower lip. "Bee, I have to be honest. The thing I fear from you is perhaps your greatest gift."

Instantly, a surge of adrenaline warmed Bill's body. He didn't want to hear this. He closed his eyes and said several times in his mind, "I forgive myself, the light of God flows through me."

"It's your passion, the thing I need to learn, yet the thing I fear."

Bill opened his eyes, then he pulled very gently on both Katarina's hands, indicating that he wanted her to slide down from her stone chair. Once she did, he put his arms around her and held her completely. He held her with the inner strength of someone who truly understood.

"Bee," Katarina began, her head snuggled securely into Bill's neck. "Something very strange happened to me several weeks ago, right here, in this meadow. It was close to sunrise, a moment suspended between night and day. I felt the Earth tremble in the balance. Slowly the morning light began to finger through the darkness like some magical being dancing through the trees. Then the first rays of dawn pushed their way over the distant horizon. Suddenly I felt as though I'd been released from my body and that all the confusion in my life had been made clear. I felt as though I'd broken away from time and space. I saw myself as a being of light. Then there was love, feelings I've never known in this physical body. And for one sustained moment I knew. Bee, you and I are soul mates."

"I know, Spotted Fawn, I know."

Slowly, Katarina moved her head back away from Bill's shoulder so that she could look into his eyes. "Wow!"

Thirty Seven

"This morning I'll fix breakfast!" Eileen announced. "Bill, go sit. Today is your day!"

"I don't mind doing my chores!" Bill argued.

"Go sit!"

Bill walked over to the kitchen table, noisily pulled a chair and sat down while Eileen removed a carton of eggs from the refrigerator. Bill looked around the room, not knowing what to do with himself.

"Excited, huh," Earl offered, glancing up from the morning's paper.

"Hardly got any sleep, I'll tell ya what."

"Some coffee?" Eileen asked as she began pouring the black Columbian brew into Bill's cup. She was well aware of Bill's preference.

"Thanks."

As Eileen handed Bill his cup, he took a healthy drink of air. "I just love the aroma of this stuff!"

It was now a week following graduation. Finally, Bill had his coveted Bachelor of Arts degree in Music Performance and Education. Two major symphony orchestras were trying to recruit him and had made him job offers. However, he decided to remain in Boulder and begin Graduate School in the fall.

"Have you talked with Katarina?" Eileen asked as she lit a fire under her skillet and cracked two eggs.

"I agreed not to. Not until…"

"I'll bet you're ready to bust a gut!" Earl interrupted, laughing.

"Yeah, something like that." Bill turned and looked out the kitchen window. The morning was crystal blue. There were cirrocumulus clouds on the far eastern horizon. Mocking birds were already busy toying with their songs. A light breeze danced through Eileen's collection of wind chimes.

"The paper's weather report promises a spectacular weekend," Earl said, nonchalantly.

Bill offered a silent prayer of thanksgiving.

"Earl. Eileen." Bill said, speaking just above the pop and sizzle of frying eggs. "Want to thank you. You saved my life. I know that!"

Earl put down his paper in order to give Bill his full attention.

"I know I can never repay you guys."

"Yes, you can," Earl said, quietly. "In time you will pass your gift to someone else, just as it was passed to you, just as it was passed to Eileen and myself."

"The pearl without price?"

"Something like that."

Bill looked away, lost for words.

"Today you're a fully functioning human being," Earl continued. "Several people have taken the time to help open your eyes. But, consider this, Bill. If no one had been there for you, there's a good possibility you'd be spending the rest of your life in a mental institution. Worse, you might have ended up killing yourself."

"I know." Bill reached across the table, took Earl's right hand and gave it a firm squeeze.

Earl smiled. "Don't look back, Bill. Just continue to learn and grow. Enjoy your life to the fullest. Along the way, you'll find someone who will need your support and love. When that happens, you'll be there for them. That's the way it works!"

Bill and Katarina turned toward each other and joined hands.

"To love is the highest celebration of life. It is the realization of God within us. It is the binding force of the universe and under the canopy of love all things are possible.

"In love there is no past or future. There is only the immortal now. The wise men say, as it is above—so it is below. As it is below—so it is above. With this knowledge, we can work miracles.

"It is not surprising then that these two, who stand before you today, have chosen to celebrate their spirit in the rite of Holy Matrimony. They have gazed into each other's souls and recognized what has always been, what will always be.

"Yesterday we saw two individuals walking separate paths. Today we witness their convergence into one.

"Mutual love is a covenant that no man or woman has any right to question, nor any court has jurisdiction over. For God has already married them in their hearts.

"Let us pray:

"Almighty Architect of the Universe, hear the voices of our souls. Before you this day stand Bill and Katarina with the song of love singing in their hearts. Together they freely pledge themselves and unite themselves into one. Grant your blessings to these, their wedding vows.

"For, together they will feel no rain, each is a shelter to each other.

"Together they will feel no cold, each is warmth to the other.

"Together there is no loneliness, each is the companion of the other.

"And, though we see two bodies, there is only one life.

"Grant that their days be long and happy, together as one, upon this earth.

"Amen."

Following the singing of Rodgers and Hammerstein's *Some Enchanted Evening*, Reverend Cain turned toward Bill.

"Do you, John William Colton, take Katarina Marie Epperson, who you now hold in your hands, to be your lawfully wedded wife, to have and to hold, in sickness and in health, for richer or poorer, so long as you both shall live?"

"I do."

"Do you, Katarina Marie Epperson, take John William Colton, who you now hold in your hands, to be your lawfully wedded husband, to have and to hold, in sickness and in health, for richer or poorer, so long as you both shall live?"

"I do."

"In that love expect nothing more than what is freely given to you. Know that mutual love is God's covenant. Have you a ring to seal your wedding vows?"

"We do." Bill and Katarina spoke simultaneously.

Reverend Cain accepted two rings from Katarina's seven-year-old niece and held them aloft. "These rings, being a circle, are symbolic of eternal love. Being of precious metal, they are symbolic of the goodness and purity that already unite their hearts."

Bill accepted Katarina's ring from Reverend Cain, turned back to his beloved and said, "With this ring I thee wed and with my heart's affection I thee endow." Lovingly, he pushed the gold ring onto Katarina's finger while looking into her magical eyes.

Katarina, then, accepted Bill's ring from Reverend Cain, turned back to her beloved and said, "With this ring I thee wed and with my heart's affection I thee endow." Lovingly, she pushed her gold ring onto Bill's finger, reciprocating his thoughts and smile.

"And now, as Minister of the Boulder Community Methodist Church and by the authority invested in me by the State of Colorado, I proclaim Bill and Katarina as Husband and Wife.

"Bill, you may kiss your Bride."

Gently, Bill lifted Katarina's veil. The subtle fragrance of Shalimar wafted past his nose. He kissed her, almost bursting with happiness.

"Ladies and Gentlemen, may I present to you, Mister and Missus Colton."

"I love you!" Bill shouted as he took Katarina into his arms and kissed her again and again. Together, they didn't even hear the standing ovation of their fifty-two witnesses.

"What're y'all thinking?" Katarina was the first to break the silence following a torrid embrace. The newlyweds were now standing just inside the door of their honeymoon suite in Estes Park, Colorado, a wedding present from Katarina's father.

"How much I'm in love with you."

"Really? Y'all glad we did it?" Katarina knew the answer but she wanted to hear it anyway.

"You know I'm glad, as if we had any choice. You know what I mean."

"Just what do y'all mean, Mister Colton?"

"Well, ya see it's like this. Ah, Missus Colton…"

Unexpectedly, Bill's and Katarina's eyes met in a way neither of had ever experienced. It was as if their souls mirrored, reverberated and echoed off one another. There was a rushing sound in their ears, which seemed to change pitch with the intensity of their gaze. Katarina tried to speak but only babbled something totally incoherent.

Bill picked his bride off her feet, carried her to the bed and gently set her down. Then, on hands and knees he removed her shoes, then her silk hose, all the while looking deep into her sparkling blue eyes.

"You are so beautiful," Bill said as he pulled a bottle of massage oil from the nightstand and began rubbing Katarina's feet, feet that could be the envy of Cinderella.

Katarina closed her eyes and flowed with the feeling. She reached down and began massaging Bill's face and scalp.

Bill wanted Katarina, his excitement surging, his hands now shaking. But he knew he must take it slowly. There would be time enough for him. He unbuttoned Katarina's pastel blue dress, slowly, button by button, smiling into her magical eyes. Carefully he folded her dress and placed it neatly on the dresser, across the room their bed. Then he followed with her slip in like fashion.

A snap of Bill's fingers released Katarina's bra, surprising even himself how easily it could be done. Both Bill and Katarina laughed. Then, very gently he sucked and massaged each breast, one by one.

Katarina threw her head back, her long blond hair flowing free, and her breath became ragged. "Oh, Bee!"

Bill pushed gently on Katarina's shoulder, indicating that she lie down. An assisted tug and her panties became history. Respectfully, they, too, were folded and placed on the dresser.

Katarina watched her husband. She couldn't help noticing the bulge in his pants and, as he returned to the side of the bed, she reached out and began massaging him, unzipping simultaneously.

"Not yet," Bill whispered. Then he rolled Katarina over, face down. He climbed quietly onto the bed and with oil in hand, he began massaging her back, slowly, gently, yet strong. He loved the way she felt, soft, smooth, warm, sensual, human. He watched his hands moving her body, sometimes having no idea where they ended and her body began.

Slowly he worked his way down her back, to her tiny waist, to her rounded buttocks, then slowly back up to her shoulders again. Bill knew he had all the time in the world. Like a romantic sonata, each note demanded its due. Each phrase must be sustained within a wisp of parenthetical silence.

Bill began slowly massaging Katarina's legs, one at a time. They were muscular, strengthened from years of serious dancing.

Gently, Bill rolled Katarina on her back and began massaging the tops of her thighs. But she could wait no longer. She rose and gently pushed Bill onto his back, then helping remove his pants, she mounted him.

Twenty-two strokes and Bill was finished, screaming with delight. But his hardness didn't go away. He had energy he never knew existed.

Bill rolled Katarina on her back, re-inserted himself and began thrusting. He knew that he and Katarina were one being, separation was simply some sort of game that they'd chosen to play.

Gradually Katarina began experiencing muscle spasms of her own. "Oh, Bee, God! Don't stop! Yes! Yes! Ohhhh, fuck! Ohhhh…"

Bill thrust harder and harder. It was coming. All eternity lay before them. Lights scintillated across both Bill's and Katarina's consciousness' as their duet convulsed into one voice. "Ohhhh…"

Then, except for very heavy breathing, all was silent. All was still.

Bill looked seriously into the eyes of his beloved, while the sweat of his passion melded with hers. Katarina's deep blue eyes said it all.

Suddenly, Bill started laughing, Katarina joining in. Together they laughed so hard that Bill slid to the floor, massage oil and sweat providing the perfect lubricant.

Bill got up and looked at his wife, then he lay down beside her. He touched her face with his right index finger, lightly touching, lightly rubbing her mouth, her chin, her nose, her cheeks, her eyebrows, her forehead, her temples, her ears. All over he gently touched her.

"Bee, I want more," Katarina whispered into her husband's ear.

Hours later, embraced as one, Bill and Katarina shared a deep nurturing sleep.

Four days later, the Coltons found themselves sitting on the grass in San Francisco's Golden Gate Park listening to the U. S. Marine Band playing *Stars and Stripes Forever* along with other marches. They had previously stopped at a local grocery store, purchased fruit, bread and cheese. Then, with hundreds of other folks, they enjoyed their picnic lunch and the music. It was spectacular, exhilarating.

That evening, the newlyweds shared lobster and crab dinners on Fisherman's Wharf. Then, hand in hand, they walked through the local shops, watched the street people, enjoying their music, arts and crafts. Unfettered by duty, they were having the time of their lives.

Fort Bragg, California was last on the itinerary. The Coltons arrived a little after noon and stopped to visit an art fair. Bill was very interested in some silver work by a local artist and purchased a turquoise inlaid bracelet for his bright-eyed sweetie. Katarina was thrilled and promised him anything.

"You know what I want?" Bill knew his eyes gave him away.

"Can I have three guesses?"

"Sure, but the first two don't count."

"Right now? In front of all these people?"

Bill's eyes took on a mischievous glow as he grabbed Katarina's tiny waist in one arm and slid his other arm under the back of her knees. In an instant she was off the ground and being carried back to their car, her hair waving in the ocean breeze.

"Bee! People are looking!" Katarina's face quickly turned the color of a woodpecker's topknot.

"We just got married!" Bill shouted back to a gazing crowd.

Several people cheered, others clapped.

Bill drove south on State Highway One for a little over twenty miles. Pulling off to the side of the road, he got out and peered down from a ledge, atop a huge cliff. Then he walked back and opened the door for his bride. "Madam, would you kindly step out and follow me?"

"Mister Happy, just what are you up to?"

"Just follow me." Bill went to the trunk and got out their picnic basket, a small cooler and some beach towels.

Together, the Coltons hiked down the face of a steep cliff for almost a half an hour before reaching the sandy beach below. It was obvious, however, Bill had planned this all along. He opened the cooler and pulled out a chilled bottle of Almond Champagne, then opened it.

"To Mister and Missus Happy," Bill toasted.

Katarina's eyes sparkled as she downed the bubbly elixir. Then she took Bill into her arms and simply held him, letting the magical energy pulsate between them.

Following several hours of sunning themselves and romping through an enchanted surf, the wind began to blow. Katarina turned toward Bill, her long blond hair cascading horizontal from the ocean's bluster. She gazed into the depths of her husband's eyes. They were brilliantly lit from a luminescent sky. She had tears of rapture in her own. As the sun set over heaving white caps, there was a brilliant green flash. It lingered for a second in eternity, then it was gone.

Bill and Katarina turned toward each other and embraced. Then, simultaneously, they whispered, "I love you!"

Epilogue

"Bee? Whatcha writing?" Katarina asked one afternoon, late in August as she handed Bill a freshened cup of coffee.

Bill was sitting at Katarina's trestle table in deep thought. He was as quiet as the alfalfa growing in the nearby fields. Cobweb was curled up on a blank piece of paper next to his right hand and purring very softly, one eye barely open. A cooling breeze was wafting through the kitchen window and out the front of the house. Somewhere, off in the distance, the sound of a combine hummed its song of labor.

"My autobiography," Bill answered, looking up from his work and smiling at his beloved.

"Your autobiography?" Katarina walked behind Bill and looked over his left shoulder. She kissed him on the top of his head and then ruffled his hair with her right hand, a habit that Bill thoroughly enjoyed.

"Yeah. Here, let me show it to you…"

> Infocused and unaware, I walked a precarious road. There was a large rock in my path causing me to stumble and fall. Bruised beyond belief, I got up and wallowed in my self-pity. But it wasn't my fault. I was simply doing what I was taught.
>
> Infocused and unaware, I walked the same precarious road. There was a large rock in my path and I pretended not

to see it. Again, I stumbled and fell. Bruised beyond belief, I got up and screamed. Still, It wasn't my fault.

Aware of my chronic behavior, I walked the same precarious road. There was a large rock in my path. I acknowledged it. Yet, I still stumbled and fell. However, this time I laughed. I knew where I was. And, I knew it was my fault.

Outfocused, I walked the same precarious road. There was a large rock in my path. I found my inner creativity and walked around it.

Today, outfocused and aware, I walk a different road.

About the Author

John Worman was born in Central California, to his great surprise. Actually he wanted to come from Santa Fe, New Mexico, but his parents had other ideas. At the age of nine, East Los Angeles became his home. John was educated in the public school system, studied violin and was constantly chased by the local gangs. He tried his hand at college only to find his male hormones too overwhelming. John's salvation was a mentor who insisted that everything inside him was human. John began studying the world's great religions in his early twenties

John was fascinated by the Space Race and reasoned that through unique employment opportunities he might meet some exciting people. However, the closest he got to space was x-ray astronomy, gamma-ray moon-mapping, simulating the Martian atmosphere and getting a nose length away from Apollo moon-rocks. Finally he came to his senses and took the next freight out of town. He landed in the desert southwest of Tucson, Arizona, where he built his own house and finished his college degree.

Today, John still enjoys playing the violin. But his main occupation remains engineering. He has written many technical articles and a few fiction works. For recreation, he hits the ski slopes and has also been seen sailing a catamaran in the French Antilles. The closest he gets to Space is when he's flying a Cessna 182.

John is currently working on his next novel, *The Bottom Line*. It's a story about a Harvard MBA who loses everything and finds his soul.

John welcomes E-mail correspondence and can be reached at:
highest.mountain@anglefire.com